The girl
who changed
the world

MACHIEL HOEK

The girl who changed the world

For all children on Earth.
May you grow up in an increasingly beautiful world.
Your world.

PRAISE

I must admit that at the age of 66, I had never read a book from front to back. This book, "The Girl Who Changed the World," was the first one! Finishing it had nothing to do with my 6-hour train ride from Amsterdam to London through the channel and under the North Sea. I had plenty else to do. But from the moment I opened the book, Lisa (the main character), challenged me with her words, "Let's do this."

From page 1 to the end, Machiel's original and creative writing ability had me relating to and imagining I was Lisa. It seemed like her journey to find what life was all about reflected my own development and purpose in life. I was engaged by the insight and wisdom given and gained, despite or because of generational differences. I became invested in the outcome, which is why I can now say I read on to the last word and completed a book that truly makes a difference for its reader.

The secret of life that Machiel displays through Lisa reflects my journey to find the essence of my life which is to give back to others, to love others and to teach others to connect with one another. As Winston Churchill once said, "We make a living by what we get, but we make a life by what we give." As Lisa discovered true beauty within, I remind people that it's not about who you know that counts, but who knows you!

Thanks, Machiel (and Lisa), for sharing a remarkable story and reinforcing that the whole world is not against us, but besides, behind and in front of us to explore, throughout the walk of life.

Charles D.A. Ruffolo (Ruf) – MPA/MBA
President
The NetworKing BV

DEDICATION

Writing *The Girl Who Changed the World* has been an extraordinary 10-year journey, and this novel would not have been possible without the guidance, support, and inspiration from many incredible individuals.

First and foremost, I want to thank **Jennet**, my love, for your inspiration, your belief in me, and your never-ending perseverance in getting me to finish "The Girl." Your unwavering support has been the cornerstone of this project.

Lisa, my daughter whom I would never know in this life, thank you for coming to life in this enchanting story and for guiding us to **Miika**. Your presence in this novel is a tribute to your spirit and the love that transcends our earthly existence. And **Vera**, who feels like my own daughter, and who inspired me for Lisa's character.

To **Neale Donald Walsch**, your book changed my life, and your personal mentoring has been instrumental in bringing me to this point. Your wisdom and guidance have been invaluable.

James Redfield, thank you for the inspiration on how you went all the way to get your book out into the world. Your perseverance and dedication have been a model for my own journey.

I am deeply grateful to the worldwide **Burning Man** community for all the magic we have experienced together. Your creativity and sense of community have enriched my life and this story.

Sven Goedbloed and **Sara Hermanides**, thank you for initiating me into the world of invisible energy and teaching the art of surrendering through not-doing. Your teachings have profoundly shaped the spiritual aspects of this novel.

To **Baptist de Pape**, for showing me the power of my heart, your initiation into remote viewing, and for writing the beautiful foreword. Your contributions have added depth and insight to this work.

Charles Ruffolo, your enthusiasm, support, and laser-focused approach have been a driving force behind this project. Thank you for your unwavering belief in my vision.

Kristin Andress, my amazing editor, thank you for elevating this story to the highest level and for your continuous support in getting "The Girl" to all American readers. Your expertise and dedication have been instrumental in bringing this book to life.

In this story, Lisa is the girl who changes the world. To secure the future of humanity, we need many more women like her to rise and effect change. Numerous women in history stood up and made a positive impact and continue to inspire, as do so many of today's titans such as **Greta Gerwig, Brene Brown, Ellen DeGeneres, Shonda Rhimes, Marianne Williamson, Queen Rania, Michelle Obama, Sandra Bullock, Sheryl Sandberg, Lady Gaga, Reese Witherspoon** and **Oprah Winfrey**...the list is long. Additionally, there are **countless others** who may remain relatively unknown to the broader world, yet their championing and contributions are deeply felt within their communities. To **all of you**: thank you for your incredible efforts and unwavering dedication to making our world a better, brighter place.

To my readers. Your belief in the power of change and your trust in a better world keep me writing. This book is for you, and I hope it touches your heart as much as it did mine.

Lastly, I am eternally grateful for everyone who is and has been in my life; I hope you know how much you mean to me!

Thank you all for being a part of this journey.

With deepest gratitude and love to you all,

Machiel.

We can never obtain peace in the outer world
until we make peace with ourselves.
—THE DALAI LAMA

When there is a division between the observer and the
observed there is conflict but when the observer is the
observed there is no control, no suppression.
The self comes to an end.
Duality comes to an end.
Conflict comes to an end.
—JIDDU KRISHNAMURTI

The world has only as much power over you as you give it.
—SRI NISARGADATTA MAHARAJ

Life is based on choices
And nothing happens by chance.
—NEALE DONALD WALSCH
(*Conversations with God: An Uncommon Dialogue*)

Everything in our world makes sense
Literally and figuratively.
—MACHIEL

FOREWORD

By Baptist de Pape

Before you opened this book, your heart already knew what's in it. Your heart literally sees, knows, before your eyes even register it. That is one of many profound wisdoms I discovered when making the documentary and book *The Power of the Heart*.

After finishing my law study and about to start a career at a major international law firm, a strong inner voice told me to not become a lawyer, but to find my true life purpose. The question "What do I want from life?" changed to "What does life want from me?" That was the start of a never-ending journey of amazement, discovery, and fulfillment. It gave me the privilege to meet and learn from the world's greatest spiritual icons and gurus. Above all, it allowed me to share with the world what unlimited power lies within each of our hearts.

Machiel and I first met during a Remote Viewing training session that I lectured. Remote Viewing is an ancient technique, applied and fine-tuned by the CIA during the Cold War, through which one is able to obtain information about an object or situation that is not visible for the eyes. In short, this is done through achieving a state of heart-coherence and following a protocol. Machiel's amazement when he first drew an accurate picture of an object we focused upon was equal to my first experience. It is first-hand proof that we are, and all is, connected through a universal energy – unobservable to our five senses.

When I started reading *The Girl Who Changed the World*, I was enthralled by its resonance with the essence of the heart, a powerful source of wisdom and guidance. In my own exploration I found that the heart has its own language—a language of emotion, intuition, and interconnectedness. *The Girl* speaks to that same language.

Lisa, the heroine at the center of this story, is a beacon of light and feminine energy, showing us that even the smallest actions can have a ripple effect that spreads far beyond what we can imagine. Lisa's path to her final discovery mirrors the journey many of us take as we seek to create change within ourselves and in the world around us, no matter how seemingly daunting. It touches on universal themes while remaining deeply personal. The narrative is both intimate and expansive, inviting readers into a world that feels familiar yet fresh.

It's a story about finding your voice, connecting with your deepest self, and embracing the courage to step into the unknown. In *The Power of the Heart*, it becomes clear that when we follow our heart, we tap into a source of strength and universal wisdom that can guide us through even the most difficult times. *The Girl Who Changed the World* exemplifies that truth.

If you have ever felt the stirrings of something greater, if you have ever dreamed of making a difference, if you have ever dared or wanted to follow your heart, this story is for you. As you read, I encourage you to embrace its message of hope and possibility. Let it inspire you to believe and trust in yourself, and let it be your guide as you navigate challenges and receive the flow of opportunity. You are invited to step into your own unique journey.

As you're about to find out, it only takes one to change the world. And, of course, you're the one.

Baptist de Pape
Bestselling author of *The Power of the Heart* and *Learn to Manifest Like Oprah, JK Rowling and Anita Moorjani*
www.thepoweroftheheart.com

CHAPTER 1 | Falling To Rise

What would happen, if…?

In the silent embrace of this question that could change everything, Lisa's fingers clung to the weathered wooden beam with an independence that defied her control. They looked foreign, like sentient beings separated from her own flesh. The idea of release, of letting go, became more than a tempting thought—it became a siren's call.

Let's do this, a voice within her whispered, and as her fingers complied, a sense of imminent pain shadowed her resolve.

As time seemed to dilate, Lisa found herself sprawled on the barn floor, a chilling dampness of blood against her cheek, her beloved book lying discarded beside her outstretched hand. The ladder, her unintended companion in descent, lay toppled, echoing the finality of her fall. Her world turned hazy, possibly from shock, as the moments continued to stretch, elongating until time itself seemed to pause.

This wasn't the outcome she had envisioned. *Nothing? Seriously?* she mused. In the engulfing darkness and silence, she drifted into a state of serene emptiness, an experience that felt strangely familiar, as if it were a forgotten homecoming. Amidst this vast void, she felt an elemental bond, an unspoken recognition.

Who are you?... Was it her questioning the void, or was the void seeking her essence?

Two Lisas now seemed to exist simultaneously: one lying amidst the rustic remnants of hay and sawdust, the other, a detached observer, hovering over her physical form. It was clear to her—she wasn't dying.

Her fall was intentional, a calculated escape. She knew every inch of her grandfather's barn, every secret nook of the hayloft where she could lose herself in books and dreams. This was her sanctuary, where no one or nothing could hurt her—a reminder of simpler, joyous times, before everything changed.

The barn, once bustling with life and labor, now stood as a silent guardian; its stalls empty, and tools cloaked in dust, a quiet reprieve. If the walls could only talk. Lisa wasn't exactly alone.

Lying motionless, she felt no urgency to move, basking in a tranquil void that might be called peace.

Was she in pain?

What is pain anyway? As an only child, it wasn't uncommon to have a conversation with herself. *Reach. Fall. Rise again. Here I am.*

The rhythmic tapping of rain on the tin roof punctuated her thoughts, a staccato symphony offering its silent applause. They must have heard the crash, her cry. Yet, here she remained, contemplative in her fall. *I am odd. Or is it unique? Both.* Then aloud. "A teenager now, at the threshold of what exactly? Change?"

Not a bad feeling—to have time stand still.

And yet, it wasn't. She heard them coming...

Who are you?

What are you?

Why are you here?

Will you stay fallen...or...

Try to figure it out?

Whose voice was that?

Ω

Grandpa was first on the scene and knelt nimbly beside her. She felt his hands on her head and shoulder—watched as he calmly scanned her for injuries, his lined face soft under his worry.

Lisa placed her cheek on his knee, the denim rough from being clothesline dried. She breathed, comforted by her trust in him.

"Nothing is broken." Grandpa sat back on his heels and met her eyes. "So, what have we here?"

Did he know?

"Lisa! What did you do? What happened?" Her mom's voice was *that* voice. The one that knew how to whisk together fear, panic, and anger in one batch.

"Emily, she's okay. Took a tumble is all. You can relax." Grandpa picked up the book, a stray he hadn't missed from his personal library.

"What were you thinking! You literally just arrived and—"

"I'm okay, Mom." Lisa pushed herself up and moved a sticky strand of hair from her lip, wincing.

"You're hurt. Let me see." Mom moved in and after a quick look, she pulled Lisa close. "You scared me. You're injured, and here I go, leaving…"

"It hurts. A lot. Sorry."

Is this comfort? Get pain to get comfort? The hurt was a little deeper than the fall. Hmmm…

Time resumed its normal pace. The entry into and out of a blissful void was interrupted with the need to move on. In this case, out of the dim barn and into the bubble of the farmland vista.

They escorted her down the path to the yellow farmhouse, smoke rising from the chimney, the chill of autumn already in the air. Seraphina, the cat, watched from the porch.

Even Sera-cat is judging me. Figures.

———

A return to Grandma and Grandpa's house. Well, Grandpa's house now. And Lisa's residence when Mom traveled for work. Or this time—the first time—with a man friend.

Ω

Mom took the reins and grabbed the frozen peas from the freezer, placing them in a towel and then against Lisa's cheek. "It won't scar, Lisa. It's just a small cut and more of an abrasion, but it will swell and bruise."

Lisa believed her mom. Why not? She'd been a nurse for years and doctored Lisa more than once.

"That's good. Could be beauty pageants ahead for my princess." Grandpa smiled. "Or strike that, probably more like stages with the debate team. In any case, you know how to make a grand entrance."

"As always," Mom agreed. "Nothing subtle about this one. Thirteen going on thirty as they say."

Lisa ignored her. "Did you two get your talk completed?" *About me, no doubt.*

"Enough of it, anyway. And we brought in your things from the car." Grandpa nodded toward the suitcases and duffle bag by the stairs leading to the attic bedroom. "Though I thought you were only here for a week."

With nothing much to do, she thought but said, "Wardrobe changes for high tea, of course." *Which Grandpa and I have done since I could hold a teacup.* "No books packed." *Since I have access to a veritable Library of Congress right here.* "And some gear for fishing." She glanced toward Mom, "Oh, and I did bring a swimsuit if we dare to do the polar challenge again."

"No! Last thing I need while I'm away is to worry about pneumonia."

Ahh, but if only you knew. We are conspirators, Grandpa and me. And competitors too. He can still run circles around me.

"Speaking of away with you, Emily. We have this." Grandpa shooed her. "The rain's coming down and you better get along. Lisa, say 'bye' to Mom, and then take some of your stuff up and get into dry clothes."

Ω

When Lisa padded downstairs, Grandpa was emerging from the kitchen, carrying a jar of honey, the honeycomb visible through the glass.

"Did you forget the bees or the bread?" She perched at the dining room table.

"Funny girl. No, this is for your face. Did you know that some cultures view bees as messengers of the gods? It's true. Their honey has also been compared to the nectar of the gods, thus elevating bees to the status of royalty. And, since you are my princess, it is only fitting."

"Magical honey. One simple fall, and the lessons have already commenced."

"Yes! We are off and running."

Grandpa, in Lisa's heart and experience, was magical himself. His career as a psychologist and counselor led him to humanitarian missions and some complex life discoveries. He was a storyteller and she loved to listen and learn. Their ongoing two-person (Grandpa/ Lisa) book club had started when she was about nine, reading (and explaining) various 'tomes' not typically taught in school. 'Unordinary equals extraordinary,' he'd always say.

Grandpa began to apply the honey. "Every time you visit, I'm amazed how fast things change—how fast you change. One thing is sure though, you are not clumsy. What were you reaching for out there that caused that fall?"

Lisa tensed and took a deep breath. *How does he always know me?* It didn't surprise her because Grandpa always seemed to have an intuitive knack for understanding. *He knows my reaching was for something to hold on to, and not the ladder.*

"What happened, Lisa? Besides the obvious departure of your mom with her new friend, what's troubling you?"

Lisa tried to stop them, but the tears began to drip. "It all feels like too much, too fast."

Grandpa leaned in to hug her and whispered, "You can tell me anything. Sharing your feelings with me will make you feel better. You know that."

Grandpa was patient as she found her words. Since she was born, he knew her heart filled to overflow, as did her head. From the cradle, she saw more than she understood, and she saw him as he saw her. Their bond was immediate.

"All right, Grandpa. Here goes. I just feel so alone these days. It's like everyone is against me. Madison doesn't want to hang out with me anymore. I think she's embarrassed or ashamed of me. I may be a cheerleader now, and I know she didn't expect that, but I'm not popular. I'm still the 'good grades geek' who jumped ahead a grade—more like a grade and a half because stuff is still pretty easy. I'm the dork whose essays on Theia, the Greek goddess of light, or the symbolism of tulips and the meaning of love are read in front of the class. I mean, who picks those topics? Not normal teenagers, that's for sure." She furrowed her brow then rapidly continued, "Oh! And everyone is at least a year older than me in my class, and Madison is so tall, so pretty. Everyone adores her and listens to her, and now she's saying things about me that aren't true, and now the whole class is bullying me." Lisa stopped and looked pointedly at Grandpa for response.

Grandpa raised his eyebrows and sat back. "Quite a litany—a list—Lisa. Where to start. By the way, great essay topic selections, but let's get to the real point. If I recall last time you were here, Madison was your friend?"

"She used to be."

"Okay, so we have the Madison scenario. I might get it. Reminds me of my high school days. I know, eons ago. What else is happening?"

"Well, Mom. One minute she treats me like a little kid and the next she tells me to grow up. Then, I want to do things my way, by myself, but she won't let me. My friends and the other kids in my class are allowed to do so much more than me. They can go out at night, have a later curfew, take the subway alone—stuff like that. They see me as a helpless child, so they don't want to hang out with me. And, you already pointed out, 'the boyfriend.'"

"I called him a friend, but never mind. We may have to unpeel that one, but not yet. So far, Madison and Mom. What else? I know those shoulders of yours can handle that bit. So, there's more to you falling accidentally on purpose."

There's always more. "I miss Dad and wish we could live together again. And," she hesitated, "I miss Grandma."

Grandpa squeezed her hand. The farmhouse carried the essence of Grandma. Even her scent seemed to remain present.

Lisa's eyes brimmed and reluctantly she added, "If I am honest, there's even more. Grandpa, I love you so much, and I truly enjoy being with you, but I'm lonely now, and with no one to spend time with, just a garden and corn fields all around, I'm afraid I'll be bored for the next few days and feel even worse. I'm sorry."

"So this whole bundle of stuff ... that's why you let yourself fall out there?" Grandpa paused. "... You've instigated a reason to get back up."

Lisa looked down, mildly embarrassed. "You lost me. I don't know why, but I was reaching into what felt like thin air and just—had to let myself fall."

"Well done, my girl. I'm impressed."

"What? Impressed, why exactly, Grandpa?"

"Not impressed that you fell earlier or that you feel alone—or that you discounted that I am here and you've likely offended Serafina the cat who is also here," he kidded, "But that you articulated your deepest sadness and frustrations with me. You honestly expressed your concerns about what's happening in your world and our time together. And you knew I would understand why you let yourself fall, almost intentionally, and entrusted me. Thank you. That's impressive because it shows your honesty, purity, and sensitivity. It makes you a wise thirteen, beyond your age."

"Aren't you angry or disappointed?"

"No, quite the opposite. I assure you that you can never disappoint me or make me angry. Please always remember that. No, I'm simply glad you feel comfortable enough to share these emotions with me. And, of course, as your grandfather, I'll do my best to help you through it all."

Lisa avoided eye contact with Grandpa and stroked Sera who rolled over purring. "Sometimes I think Sera knows when I'm sad."

"Mmm … I named her Serafina for a reason. It means wise angel. Animals have intuition too. And you're stalling on your response to me."

"Grandpa, if history repeats, I know how you can figure out how to fix things, and it's really sweet of you. But you can't change Madison or the other kids bullying me. You definitely can't make me cool. You can't change Mom's behavior or make her let me be more independent. You can't un-divorce Mom and Dad and bring Grandma back, and you can't summon other kids to move here to hang out with me this week."

"You're absolutely right. And that, you know, that makes you wise."

"Or it makes me have common sense."

"Okay, I'll give you that, but you may come to see there is wisdom in it too. Let me ask you something. Does this issue with Madison feel like something that has changed beyond your control, even though you wish it hadn't?"

Lisa nodded.

"And with your mother, does it feel like nothing ever changes, no matter what you do, even though you desperately want things to change?"

Lisa nodded again.

"And does it feel like you have no friends here, and you miss your dad and grandma, and even though you know it won't change, you still wish it could?"

Lisa rolled her eyes.

"So, you want the things that change to stay the same, and at the same time, you want the things that stubbornly stay the same to change?"

"Say again?"

"I asked, 'You want the things that change to stay the same, and at the same time, you want the things that stubbornly stay the same to change?'"

"Yes. I suppose."

"That's a sign that you're growing up."

"If growing up means good things disappear, and the bad things stick around, I'd rather stay young. Don't tell me that's what getting older is all about!"

Grandpa sighed, "My dear, for most people, it's exactly that."

"But I'm not like most people!" Lisa smacked her hands on the table, causing Sera to split for cover.

"Lisa, most people don't feel like they are like most people. You'd be surprised by how much we all have in common. But you're right. It shouldn't be what growing up feels like, but most people haven't discovered the secret of life. Ah ha!" Grandpa stood and backed away from the table, placing a hand on his heart, "Perhaps I *can* help to make your stay with me and our time together enjoyable, maybe even challenging, and certainly worthwhile. You've given me an idea."

"And is—" Having watched the movie *Alice in Wonderland*, Lisa imagined Grandpa as the Mad Hatter. "—a rabbit hole forthcoming?" she grinned.

<hr>

He raised a finger in the air. "This requires a cup of tea. I need to give it a think. Let me get the pot boiling. Hold tight. Meet me in my study in fifteen."

Lisa took a deep breath. "Your *library*, it is."

CHAPTER 2

An Adventure: The Lisa Project—The Secret of Life

The project title was on a flipchart on an easel in Grandpa's study—aka library.

Just like Grandpa, there was nothing much ordinary about his 'home library.' The bookcases, designed and crafted by him, rose from floor to vaulted ceiling and were filled with spines organized in every genre. Lisa knew his vintage collection of Emerson, Shakespeare, Hemingway, and the old Bibles creaked when they opened to yellow and subtle musty smelling pages. The newer reads did not use the Dewey decimal system, but were logged by priority of what pick was next to arrive in hand, nightstand, backpack, car … always more than one reading in progress.

Their tea party had graduated from Lisa's Cinderella childhood table and plastic tea cups, to be served beside Grandpa's grand Italian desk, in either China cups and saucers or on this occasion, the blue-pattern porcelain. The tea steamed, already poured, and awaited Lisa's one sugar cube.

She added her cube and lifted the cup to her nose. A hint of chamomile, a reminder of Grandma's favorite in her equally favorite cups. A spreading warmth.

"What do you think? Like the project title?" Grandpa asked.

" *The Secret of Life*? Admittedly, doubtful. I mean, is there really a secret?"

After a beat, Grandpa raised his arms heavenward and smiled. "Ah, but there is!"

"Okay then, can that secret help me?"

Grandpa nodded. "Wanna find out?"

After a brief pause Lisa said, "I don't think you're going to tell me what the secret is, are you?"

"Why do you think it's a secret? Imagine watching a fun or exciting movie. Would you want to know how it ends halfway through? Would that make it as fun or exciting?"

"No, not really. It would take away the mystery, and I do enjoy a good mystery."

"Exactly. It's the same with the secret of life. If someone tells you what it is, you miss out on experiencing and discovering it. The secret loses its power because you haven't unraveled it yourself."

Lisa slumped, her head in her hands.

"What's the matter?"

"Well, you said I'm growing up and that life will happen just like it does with most people unless I discover the secret of life. But you won't tell me what it is."

"Oh, so you are shirking at the effort it might take. I see."

She sat up straight. "Hold on! You know I work—"

"Think about it." He lifted his hands, palms up, and then raised one higher. "Wanna stay fallen from a hayloft on a barn floor?" He raised the other. "Or wanna get up?" He paused, "Wanna discover some stuff that will help you through whatever it is that's eating at you? Or—do something about it?"

"Obviously, I want to do something about it. I can't stand feeling this weird."

"Then get up, literally. Pop up to the flipchart and let's revisit some rules. We've covered these together previously, and specifically on the last visit. Do you remember?"

Lisa nodded and jumped to her feet. "Think so." She wrote on the flipchart:

Rule One: If I want something, I have to take action to get it.

Rule Two: I should try to figure it out on my own first.

She turned to Grandpa, "Okay figuring out how to be confident in trying out for cheerleading when that was way out of my 'normal' was one thing, but we're talking about the secret of life. I don't know what to do or where to start."

Grandpa said, "Which brings us to *Rule Three: If I don't know what to do, I'll ask for help.*"

"But I just did that by asking you about the secret of life, and you won't tell me."

"Write it down anyway. Do you still remember the fourth rule?"

Lisa thought for a moment. "Yes. *If the answer I get doesn't help, I should try asking the question in a different way.*"

"And can you ask your question in a different way?" Grandpa asked.

Lisa hesitated. "Uh yeah, of course!" She put her hands on her hips and faced him, "Grandpa, would you be willing to *help* me discover the secret of life for myself?"

Grandpa nodded, satisfied. "Very well. I can help you experience things, so you can uncover the secret on your own. But I must warn you," he proceeded in a whisper, "this secret will profoundly change your perspective on the world and your life. Once you unravel it, nothing will ever be the same. Is that truly what you want?"

———

Without hesitation Lisa replied, "If it means choosing between nice things that disappear and bad things that bug me, or having my whole world turned upside down, then yes, I want that."

"I love the way you put it—*turning your world upside down*. In a way and in my experience, that's precisely what will happen. But you must understand that this will be a journey that requires significant time in the days ahead. I envision that we will embark on numerous adventures together. Are you up for this undertaking?"

"Yes, absolutely!"

"In that case, tomorrow let us begin *The Lisa Project: The Secret of Life!*"

Ω

Lisa lay in bed in the attic bedroom, surveying her surroundings. A beautiful mural of red tulips blooming canvased an entire wall. Knowing it was her favorite flower, Grandma and Grandpa had surprised her with it, explaining the red tulip field reflected perfect love, their love for her. Now, she also knew that the tulip meant rebirth, new life—and here she was, thinking about her own life and what will come next.

Memories flooded of when Grandma used to tuck her in and read her a story, and then tell another. Her lavender scent filled – the room? Lisa's skin prickled, sensing Grandma's undeniably real presence. She saw movement in her periphery.

Grandma?

No, a spider, massive in size, scaled the wall. She bolted upright. "Grandpa! Help!"

She heard his rapid ascension on the stairs, and he flung open the door. "What's wrong! What's wrong!?"

Lisa pointed. "There! Huge spider!"

Grandpa breathed. "So much for my evening yoga. I thought, well, never mind. Okay, you call that huge? I've seen bigger ones than that, young lady."

"Not here, I hope," Lisa said, and looked under her covers.

"No, not in here, but why are you so scared?"

"It's a spider. A *big* one! Look at it, of course it's *scary*! It's gross!"

"Scary?" Grandpa raised an eyebrow. "Did it hurt you?"

"No, but it might. Look at how it's moving. With its dirty, hairy legs!"

"And why did you call me?"

"To get rid of it! … Oh no, it's moving! It's going to hide somewhere. Hurry, Grandpa! Kill it before it escapes."

"But once it's gone, you won't see it anymore. Problem solved, right?"

"You're teasing me now, and no!" Lisa said. "It could be anywhere, and it might end up in my bed. Catch it, Grandpa, and kill it!"

"So, you think *I'm* not afraid of spiders?"

"Grandpa, please, catch the spider now, or I won't talk to you for the entire week!"

With a swift motion of his right hand, he snatched the spider off the wall and walked toward the window, opened it, and extended his hand to let the spider fall out. He closed the window.

"Why didn't you kill it?"

He sat on the edge of her bed. "There's no need. It didn't threaten me, so why should I harm it?"

"But it threatened *me*. Now it's alive, and it might come back."

"That won't likely happen," Grandpa reassured her, waving a hand toward the window. "By the way, has a spider ever hurt or bitten you?"

"No, and it will never happen because I kill them if I can—if they're small."

"So, when they're small, they're not as scary and you can kill them?"

"Yes, and it prevents them from growing bigger!"

"And what do you do when they're too big?"

"I call you or Mom."

"And does your mom take them away, just like me?"

"No. She grabs the vacuum cleaner and sucks up the spider, then seals it so the spider can't escape."

"Well, that's a clever approach. Why is your mom afraid of spiders?"

"Because," Lisa sighed dramatically, "they're scary and disgusting."

"Some are actually pretty. Nonetheless, I have an interesting tidbit for you. Did you know that babies aren't initially afraid of anything except maybe snakes and spiders? No? Well, fear has evolved to help people survive. But as you grow up, that fear can fade away. I remember vividly how, as a toddler, you used to explore our garden and play with all sorts of creatures. Your grandma and I would show you a beetle, a worm, or a spider."

"Ick. Disgusting."

"Evidently since then, you became scared of spiders, or scared again. And that's quite interesting."

"Why?"

"Because *the greatest gift of your life often comes wrapped in your greatest fear.*"

"Forget about that gift," Lisa firmly stated. "You'll need a better example than a spider to make a point."

"Maybe so. I was going to come up and bid you goodnight, but it seems now you're wide awake."

"I'm guessing this spider-lesson—*greatest gift often comes wrapped in greatest fear*—sort of started our project?"

"Oh, yes. Remember, I mentioned that this project would transform your view of the world and your life. What were your thoughts and feelings when I said that?"

"I don't know. I think I felt intrigued and thought it sounded exciting. I love new things, well, at least if they are good things."

"Intrigued? Good word. You've been reading." Grandpa grinned. "And so, if you love new 'good' things, what are your feelings toward old things, like me?"

"It depends. If old things are wonderful, I adore them. But if they're not, I don't. You needn't worry as you fall into the prior category."

"Why thank you," he smiled. "However, to be clear, you want to keep everything nice and discard the bad?"

"Well, duh, obviously. Who wouldn't?"

"What do you want to get rid of? Besides a spider, of course."

"I already told you. Mom treats me like a child. She's overly protective, even taking me to school. No one in my class gets dropped off by their parents."

"Okay, but was there a time when you enjoyed it?"

Lisa gazed toward the sky and the few stars visible from the attic window. She remembered the rainy days in the warm car beside her mother who leaned in for a hug before letting her step out the door. She knew her mom watched her until she entered the school, and she knew she would reliably pick her up later, ask her about her day, and often have hot chocolate waiting at home.

"Enjoyed it? Well, yes. But now, I can handle it on my own."

"No doubt, but can you recognize that there are things you used to enjoy but now find bothersome? That, at different stages in life, something enjoyable can become the opposite."

"Yes, because I've changed," Lisa declared. "I'm growing up, becoming more independent."

"Perhaps your mother needs to realize and accept your transformation before she can change herself. Now, let's talk about Madison. Something has changed with her too. She no longer wants to be your best friend."

Lisa looked down, feeling a pang of sadness. "So, she doesn't want to be my friend because *she* has changed? It has nothing to do with *me?*"

Grandpa nodded.

"But that's not entirely true. It does involve me because she says hurtful things about me."

"It's a reflection of her own insecurities," Grandpa explained. "When someone belittles another person, it's often due to their own lack of confidence. Maybe she is jealous of your grades or that you are now a cheerleader. Madison has grown too and suddenly become popular in your class. All that attention has changed her, affected her, and made her insecure because what if she loses that popularity, or what if you get more popular? What if she is trying to maintain her status by directing negativity toward someone else? And you, as her former best friend, are an easy target."

"So," Lisa mused after a moment, "if Mom doesn't change alongside me, I won't like it. And I don't like that Madison has changed either because I've lost my best friend. It hurts that she bullies me, but I should actually feel sorry for her. I should see her as pitiful because of her insecurities?"

"Don't pity her, have empathy for her. Put yourself in her shoes, so to speak."

Lisa's words spilled, "Maybe Mom is afraid of my growth because she feels like she's losing her little girl. But I'll always be her daughter. As I said before, I'm simply growing up and becoming more independent."

"Good, Lisa. Now that you understand what might be bothering her, you'll have empathy for where she's coming from, and shedding light on that may help alleviate some of her worry. And perhaps she can accept that you're changing and will continue to change herself."

"I get it. It helps to understand where the other person is coming from, and then I'll either understand why I feel the way I do or I can better explain what I need."

"Yes!" Grandpa said, a smile lighting up his face as he stood up. "I see we've already gotten the project underway, and we'll continue the adventure tomorrow. You need to get a good night's rest because it's going to be an intense day. So, I bid you goodnight."

Lisa lay back and her gaze returned to the field of red tulips, the soft brushstrokes of her grandparents opening a horizon.

Tomorrow awaits.

THE LISA PROJECT:
The Secret of Life

Day 1

CHAPTER 3 | Vibrations

Making Sense of the World

Grandpa treated Lisa to a personally prepared bacon and waffle breakfast, followed by applying his 'divine honey' to her abrasions. Lisa scooted her chair back from the dining table and rubbed her hands together looking at Grandpa expectantly.

"Ahh, ready to get started on our project, I see. Okay, then. I have something for you." He handed her a weathered leather-bound book.

She opened it to empty pages. "It's a journal." On the first page in his handwriting she read:

The Lisa Project: The Secret of Life

Day 1

"I've had this one around for a while, waiting for the right occasion to use it. It looks old, but it's new. Kinda like us. Or in your case, you look 'new,' but have—"

"—an old soul. So, I'm told," said Lisa. She smiled. "Thank you, Grandpa." She removed a pen from its placeholder. "I'll put this to good use."

"We can't exactly haul the flipchart around as we go about our project, so you can use this to capture thoughts and notes. So, while I schlep the dishes, why don't you write what you recall from yesterday, like the purpose and why you want to do this."

Lisa nodded and began:

The Lisa Project: The Secret of Life
Journal-Day 1

PURPOSE: Discover the secret of life.
WHY: I'm not enjoying my life. I want to be happier.
CHANGE

- Mom doesn't appreciate me changing.
- I don't like that Madison is changing either. but I should try to put myself in her shoes–it will help to understand her. Grandpa called it empathy.
- But if I don't mind Madison's changes because they have nothing to do with me. then Mom shouldn't mind my changes either since they have nothing to do with her.

If I don't change. things around me will still continue to change. So. I must change. Is it because I change without realizing it? Does everything always change or are there things that never change? I don't quite understand this yet.

Grandpa said to achieve discovering the secret of life, my life could or would "turn upside down." I don't know what that means yet either. I need Grandpa's help.

HOW to discover the secret of life:

- Turn my life upside down, with Grandpa's guidance.
- If someone tells you what it is, you miss out on experiencing and discovering it. The secret loses its power because you haven't unraveled it yourself.

Greatest fear = Greatest gift (maybe not always?)

Ω

Lisa presented her journal entries to Grandpa who read them quickly.

"Good start. I'm impressed with how you articulated your own thoughts. I'll encourage you to write in your own words as much as possible, but what you just wrote needs an addition because it fits so well and serves as a good starting point for this project. It's your journal and it's personal. Do I have your permission to add something?"

"Permission granted."

Grandpa wrote:

I accept that others change.

I accept that I change.

"I don't understand the second sentence," Lisa said. "I understand the first sentence. I accept that Madison is changing because I now realize her behavior toward me has nothing to do with me. But I accept that *I* change anyway, right? So shouldn't that second sentence be, 'Others have to accept that I'm changing'?"

Grandpa smiled. "It might seem that way, and you're right—most people in the world think like that. However, it often leads to misunderstandings and irritation. Hold on to this important question. You'll find an answer during the project."

Lisa added her question and a big question mark:

Do others have to accept that I'm changing?

"First, let's get tuned in. Follow me. Bring your journal. I've got the flashlight." He patted his back pocket. "Time for a sensory experience. You like all kinds of music, right?"

Ω *Senses* Ω

They entered the living room where Grandma and Grandpa sometimes entertained. Grandma's touches were everywhere. Nothing fancy, a reflection of them, welcoming. The light coat of dust was evidence that Grandpa didn't spend much time there. The piano lid was closed, and the lamps were off.

Lisa went to open the curtains to allow in light and Grandpa stopped her. "Not just yet. This exercise is one to tune in—in more ways than one, starting with your senses." He flipped on a table lamp.

"I can sense Grandma in here. I remember that old stereo and playing a record album—when they existed—and you two dancing. Mom and Dad would pull me up to join."

"Good memories. They definitely charge the senses. That's partly why we are in here, but let's set the stage: *The Lisa Project: The Secret of Life*. Lisa, what senses do you possess?"

"You're asking me? Sort of a basic question, isn't it? Did you stay up all night planning this one?"

Grandpa cocked his head.

"Well, sight, sound…" began Lisa.

"Tell me what you use to have these senses?"

"Okay, senses. Eyes, ears, nose, tongue, and, um—skin? We see with our eyes, hear with our ears, smell with our nose, taste with our tongue, and feel with our skin."

"Well done. What are our five senses collectively?"

"Uh—I'm not sure what you mean."

"Imagine this, what would happen if none of your five senses worked?"

Lisa tried to imagine it. "Well, if I couldn't see anything, hear anything, smell anything, taste anything, or feel anything, I wouldn't be aware of anything?"

"That's correct. Without your senses, you wouldn't be able to perceive the world. So, your five senses are like doors that allow the world to enter and be experienced by you. Now, try to imagine not having any senses."

Lisa closed her eyes. "Okay, I'll give it a try," she said, taking a deep breath and falling silent. After only a minute, she opened one eye.

"You didn't give it much time, but did you notice anything?"

Lisa remained silent.

"Lisa?"

Still, Lisa said nothing.

Grandpa leaned forward. "Lisa?"

"Quiet. I am trying not to hear or notice you."

"Cheeky girl. Give it another go—for more than sixty seconds. See if you can make it five minutes without fidgeting. Tune in."

Lisa stilled and sat motionless as Grandpa observed.

After five minutes, he finally asked, "Now, what did you actually experience?"

Lisa opened her eyes and blinked. "First, it's hard to sit still and quiet for that long. In fact, it's difficult not to notice anything at all. I could still hear the birds outside and feel you beside me. And then—it sort of felt like I couldn't hear or feel anything for a while. I started thinking it was strange, so I wanted to open my eyes and stop before you told me to."

"That's fantastic!" Grandpa exclaimed.

Lisa was surprised. "What do you mean, fantastic?"

"Because now you've experienced how challenging it is. This is what people try to achieve through meditation—stopping the monkey mind, the noise in there." He tapped her forehead. "It's what I do every morning—practice on my yoga mat—reaching a state of relaxation where there are no thoughts or feelings."

"That seems impossible to me."

"It can be difficult, and some people spend years trying to attain it. It's much easier if you start when you're young."

"Like me."

"Yes. Let's return to a previous question," Grandpa said. "What happens when your senses don't work? Who or what are you then?"

"You're getting deep, Grandpa. If I can't see or hear anything anymore and I can't feel anything either, then it's as if I don't have a body. So, what am I then?" She shrugged.

Grandpa prompted, "What do you think?"

Lisa paused. *What do I think? I think I am still here. I am still me.* Aloud, Lisa said, "Ah, I am my thoughts!"

"On track. Close your eyes. Give it another whirl. Continue."

She closed her eyes again, took a deep breath, and another. After a while, she said, "Okay, I am my thoughts, and regardless of having a body or not, it feels like I am nothing. But where are my thoughts? And where are you, Mom, and Dad? Where is everyone? I'm all alone! There's nothing else."

Grandpa took her hand, prompting Lisa to open her eyes once again. "Very insightful," he said softly. "You've encountered an age-old existential struggle of humanity—what defines you as an individual, and what remains when the world and people around you disappear? You've also experienced that *you are always, at the very least, your thoughts and your feelings.* That's deep.

"Let's set that aside for today. Tomorrow, I'll help you explore what it means to be in nothingness in a different way."

"I'm not sure I'll enjoy that."

"Tomorrow is a new day," Grandpa replied. "Today is today."

Lisa bowed, teasing. "Whatever you say, *Sensei.*"

"Okay, okay. For now, let me show you something else."

Ω Sound Ω

Grandpa walked over to the old turntable and turned it on. "Come sit on the floor in front of the speaker.

"Old school." Lisa sat in front of the speaker.

"I do have a CD player too."

"As I said, old school."

"Functional." Grandpa inserted a CD into the player and turned it on. "In a moment, I'll play some sound and I want you to observe the bottom circle closely—it's called the woofer. Listen, watch, and pay attention to what you feel."

Lisa heard a deep, low humming sound. In fact, she could feel it in her stomach. She watched as the woofer pulsed back and forth.

"This is twenty hertz," Grandpa explained, pressing a button on the CD-player, skipping to the next track. The woofer oscillated faster. "This is fifty hertz. Hertz represents the number of vibrations per second. Place your hand right in front of the woofer."

Lisa felt air brush her hand.

Grandpa pressed another button, and the pitch became higher and with another increase, even higher.

"This is five hundred hertz. Can you still observe the woofer's vibrations? Do you feel anything?" Grandpa asked.

Lisa shook her head. There was no more movement, and the air ceased to vibrate.

"Now I'll turn up the volume," Grandpa said, adjusting a knob.

The sound blasted, causing Lisa to cover her ears.

"Observe what happens now," Grandpa shouted.

The sound increased in intensity, like a siren. But then it started becoming quieter and quieter, until Lisa could uncover her ears.

Grandpa said, "I can't hear anything anymore. Can you?"

Lisa nodded, "I can." She was perceiving an extremely high tone. It continued to rise until the sound also vanished for her.

At that moment, Sera-cat rushed into the living room as if she were chasing something that turned into nothing? She looked confused.

Grandpa turned off the CD player, and Sera abruptly stopped and rolled onto her back in front of Lisa.

Grandpa sat on the sofa beside them. "Can I have your journal again for a moment?"

Lisa handed it over and watched as he turned a page and drew a wavy line across the paper.

"You saw how the woofer moved back and forth when we started with that very low-pitched sound?"

Lisa nodded.

"This represents the movement of the woofer: out, in, out, and so on. We call it a *sound wave*. When we increased the frequency from twenty to fifty hertz, you witnessed the acceleration of the woofer's movements. The actual sound waves looked like this," Grandpa said, drawing a new wavy line that went up and down multiple times. "We refer to this as *frequency*—the number of times the woofer moves back and forth per second. The higher the frequency, the higher the *pitch* of the sound. Do you follow?"

Lisa nodded and said, "I could hear it, and I could see it too."

"And you could also feel it when you placed your hand in front of it. Then, after that, I raised the volume, and the sound became louder, causing the sound wave to look like this," Grandpa said, drawing a wavy line which extended much higher and lower. "We call it the *amplitude*. Sound consists of these two elements: frequency, which determines the pitch, and amplitude, which determines the loudness. Together, we refer to them as vibrations. Do you still understand?"

Lisa nodded. "I think so, yes."

"As you noticed, you could *see* the vibrations, *feel* them, and *hear* them. As the sound became a bit higher, it became invisible, then inaudible, and finally imperceptible—to me first, then to you—and that's when Sera reacted to it." Grandpa paused for a moment. "The key takeaway is that everything in the world is vibration."

"Huh?" Lisa said, bewildered.

"*Everything in the world is vibration,*" Grandpa reiterated calmly.

"Grandpa, I don't get it," Lisa replied.

He repeated himself, pausing for emphasis, *"Everything. In the world. Is vibration."*

"Grandpa! Repeating something I don't understand won't suddenly make me understand."

"No, not unless you choose to engage in some thoughtful contemplation. Think."

She sighed and peered at Grandpa's notes. "Fine. You mentioned that everything in the world reaches me through my senses, and you also said everything in the world is vibration. So," she took a breath, "if everything in the world is vibration and my senses transmit those vibrations to me, then my senses simply transmit vibrations?"

Grandpa stared at her, unspeaking.

"You look perplexed. Did I say something funny?" *Or am I a savant—ha!*

"Not at all," Grandpa replied. "You said something brilliant. You've encapsulated a fundamental piece of ancient wisdom[1] that scientists have been trying to comprehend for centuries."

"Well, I honestly still don't fully grasp it. I simply connected the dots based on what you said. I get the concept, sort of."

"But at least you understand the principle of sound now, right?"

"Yes, sound is basically vibrations in the air, and I've personally experienced, felt, and of course, heard these vibrations."

"Good." Grandpa continued, "Now, extend your arms. Between your hands, you have what we call the full frequency range of sound.

Here, on your left, it starts at zero, representing silence. As you move to the right, the frequency increases, and the pitch gets higher and higher. Where does it end?"

"How would I know?" Lisa shrugged. "Maybe it never ends?"

"That's a potential philosophical response," Grandpa said, "but in practice, it does end because sound relies on a medium for its existence. In this room, the medium is air. At a certain point, air can no longer transmit sound, but that occurs at a very high frequency. Now, if you were to indicate with your arms the range of frequencies audible to humans, how large do you think it would be?"

Lisa brought her hands together, forming a halfway mark.

"Not bad," Grandpa remarked. He took her hands and almost placed them together. "This is the actual range."

Lisa blinked. "Are you saying that we can only hear this teeny-weeny portion of all the sounds that exist?"

Grandpa nodded. "The sounds we can't hear are high frequencies, like radio waves and delta waves, as well as sounds produced by certain animals, such as mice, dolphins, and bats. Cats can hear these sounds, but can't produce them. Their hearing aids them when they're chasing mice."

"Does the same principle apply to what we can and can't see?"

"Yes. Well-deduced. It's the same principle."

"So, this could also apply to what we smell, taste, and perhaps even what we touch. Take air, for example. Air is present, but I can't physically feel it unless I move my hand through it," Lisa said.

"Bravo. Now, let's assess how your senses work for things you can see—or smell. Take a seat on the sofa."

Ω Sight Ω

They settled in.

"All right. Can you see the painting hanging on the wall at the end of the hall?"

"Maybe the outline. Pretty dark," said Lisa.

"Remember that for later," Grandpa said. "Now, let's start by turning on another table lamp. Think of the two lamps lit as the speakers we used earlier. But instead of sound, these lamps emit light."

He switched on the second lamp. The light from under the shade was a dim red.

"Compare this to the low-pitched sound you heard from the speaker earlier, okay? This light has a low frequency, a low vibration. Now, let me turn up the other lamp with the white light. This," he continued, "represents a very high-pitched tone from the speaker. Can you imagine it?"

Lisa nodded.

"Now observe." Grandpa adjusted the brightness of both lamps.

"It's like you're turning up the volume. I see."

"Very good." He continued, "The power or strength of the light corresponds to the volume—the loudness, the intensity or the amplitude of the wave. But what about the frequency?"

He paused.

"No remark on that one? Well, let me tell you then. This light is warm and red, whereas this lamp appears whiter and colder. *Color* is the frequency—"

Lisa stopped him. "Okay, but with sound, there was a point where you and I couldn't hear it anymore, but Sera could. How does that work with light? I can still see both colors, both lights."

"In the same way," Grandpa replied.

"Take a look." He picked up the television remote control and turned on the TV. "Did you see a beam of light?"

Lisa looked perplexed. "What beam of light?"

"Aha! You didn't see it! But the TV did, and that's why it came on."

"Are you saying there's a lamp inside the remote control?"

Grandpa nodded. "It's called infrared light. We can't see it, but it does exist, as you just witnessed."

"So, what you are teaching me is that just because I can't see something doesn't mean it doesn't exist. Just like when we couldn't hear the vibration, yet it did exist."

"Sera's reaction was timely evidence. Yes. Let me show you something else that's cool."

"My hip Grandpa … cool."

He smiled and walked to the curio cabinet and returned with a glass triangle-shaped figure. He picked up the TV remote again, turned off the lamps, and switched off the TV. "Okay, Lisa, what did you see?"

"An episode of—"

"No. No. What did you see before the TV went black?"

"Nada. Nothing."

"And now?"

"We're in the dark, Grandpa. I can't see much of anything, but I know it doesn't mean nothing's there."

"Give it a couple minutes."

They waited.

"Now, can you see the painting at the end of the hall?"

Lisa stared down the hall. "Yeah, I can see it, still barely, but better than before."

"That's because your eyes have adjusted to the darkness. They've become more accustomed. What do you see now?" Grandpa switched on the flashlight he had in his hand and directed it toward the painting.

"Now I can see it clearly, with all the colors."

"Let there be light! I know, goofball. But what color is the light coming from this flashlight?"

"Obviously, it's white," Lisa replied.

"Look," Grandpa said as he then beamed the flashlight at the glass triangle. A range of bright colors appeared on the other side, each shining in a slightly different direction.

"Wow! It looks like a rainbow."

"It *is* a rainbow," Grandpa confirmed. "A rainbow consists of these exact colors. Notice how it starts with red at the top, the warmest color with the lowest frequency that we can see. Then it progresses through blue, indigo, and violet at the bottom, which are the highest frequency colors we can see. Additionally, there is infrared on the low side and ultraviolet on the high side, which we can't see. You're familiar with UV rays, right?"

Lisa patted her arm. "They come from the sun and can give you a tan or even a sunburn." She examined the glass triangle. "But—how does this triangle create those colors? It's just glass, isn't it?"

"It's called a prism," Grandpa explained, "and it reveals the composition of the light from the flashlight."

"But that light is white. It doesn't have any color to reveal," Lisa stated.

"Ah, but it does. White light is actually a combination of all colors. This prism separates each color's frequency and presents it in its original form. Get it?"

"Not so much. I'm having trouble following." Lisa sighed.

Grandpa turned off the flashlight, stood up from the table, opened the curtains on both sides of the room, and positioned himself behind the piano. He played a chord with both hands. "How does that sound?" he asked.

"Beautiful."

"Come on over."

Lisa approached the piano where Grandpa continued to press keys.

"How many individual notes are in this chord?"

"Seven keys in a chord," Lisa answered.

"Correct." He proceeded to press each of the seven keys individually, then pressed all at once. "One at a time, they have an independent sound. Together, the combined sound of a chord. With light, the Roy G. Biv colors of the rainbow collectively create white light."

"Now I get it, Grandpa. Wait, where are you going? What are you up to next?"

Ω Smell Ω

Grandpa had risen from the piano bench and darted toward the kitchen. Lisa stayed put, idly pressing keys, remembering a recital from the past. Serafina jumped onto the bench beside her and snuggled against her. Lisa just about made it to the song's chorus, when—

"Do you know what I did in the kitchen?" Grandpa had returned.

Lisa's expression silently inquired, *How would I know?*

"You don't know," Grandpa responded, "but she does."

Lisa looked down at Sera whose whiskers were twitching, sniffing. She promptly jumped down and sauntered toward the kitchen.

"What can you smell?" Grandpa asked Lisa.

Lisa imitated Sera by raising her nose in the air and making sniffing noises. "Cat litter? Kidding. Nothing."

"Shall we follow her?" Grandpa suggested, and they proceeded to the kitchen where Sera was scarfing new food in her bowl.

"Now I can smell it. Tuna fish."

"You've just witnessed vibrations in action," Grandpa explained. "A cat possesses a much more sensitive nose than a human, so she smelled the fish long before you did. The smell traveled through the air as an invisible vibration. Although the scent's volume was too low for you to detect from the living room, it wasn't for Sera. It helps that I'd forgotten her breakfast."

"Okay, got it. Sound is a vibration, light is a vibration, and even smell. But how does this apply to everything that I can see and touch? When I touch this counter, it doesn't seem to vibrate."

"Close your eyes."

Ω Touch Ω

Grandpa took Lisa's hand and led her back to the living room. "Keep them closed." He guided her hand to an object. "What kind of material are you touching?"

"It's wood," Lisa replied.

"Correct. And what about this?"

Lisa felt a smooth, cold surface. "Um … it's either stone—or glass."

"Correct again. Grandma's vase." He led her to sit on the couch and placed her hand again. "And this?"

Lisa smiled—soft, smooth, linear—fur. "Sera eats fast."

"Well done. Now you can open your eyes. Can you imagine that everything you just felt was a variation in vibration? Your sense of touch detected the different vibrations of the materials. They felt different, and you recognized each."

"I believe so," Lisa replied. "I have to remind myself that vibration doesn't just have to be something I actually feel moving. It means everything has a certain form and that's the vibration, and I can recognize it with my senses."

"That's right," Grandpa commended. "You could say that each object, material, sound, light, and even smell manifests—or reveals— itself in the world through its unique vibration, like a fingerprint. You know that every person has unique fingerprints, don't you?"

"I do. I've seen cop shows." Lisa gripped Grandpa's hand and rose from the couch, tugging at him. "Sera got brunch, but I'm ready for lunch. And … I need a break."

"Tuna fish?"

"I think not."

"PBJ it is."

Journal: The Lisa Project:
The Secret of Life-Day 1-Continued.

If my senses are constantly detecting vibrations and everything I see, hear, and so on is conveyed through my senses, does that mean I'm constantly aware of vibrations?

"Everything. In the world. Is vibration."

Just because I can't see something doesn't mean it doesn't exist. And at some point, we couldn't hear the vibration anymore, yet it still existed.

Everything has a unique vibration-like a fingerprint.

But I've also experienced instances where Grandpa and I failed to perceive certain vibrations. Sera smelled the fish, but the scent's volume was too low for me to detect. The TV received the infrared signal, but our eyes couldn't perceive that specific vibration. The same goes for the sound from the speakers.

Could this concept apply to emotions too?

Ω A Taste of Perspective Ω

Lisa sat at the kitchen table, finished with her journal notes for the time being and began sketching a pair of eyes.

"That looks nice," Grandpa remarked and placed her sandwich beside her.

"Yes, I thought what you said about eyes was fascinating, so I tried to draw my own eyes. But it's not that easy."

"But it's given me an idea."

"What?"

"Come on, let's conduct another experiment. I'll sit next to you, right here, and we'll each draw the living room as we see it."

"Do we have to?" Lisa sighed.

"Yes, and you'll understand in a minute. Let's just draw and eat."

Lisa and Grandpa started sketching the living room with pencils on blank sheets of paper. Lisa reluctantly began. She captured Sera-cat in her basket, the ever-present tulip vase on the fireplace mantel beside the framed photograph of Grandma, a special plant by the window, the TV, the 'newly discovered' turntable, and a crocheted blanket of Grandma's. Just as she was starting to have fun, Grandpa told her to stop.

"Already?"

Grandpa nodded, and they placed their drawings side by side.

Lisa examined Grandpa's drawing. "We were supposed to draw the living room, right?" she asked, perplexed. Grandpa's drawing didn't resemble the living room at all. It looked more like a furniture store with only sofas, chairs, and a dresser. "Were you in the same room as me?" she inquired.

"I was about to ask you the same question. Do you now see that we both have different ways of looking at things and as a result, perceive tangible objects differently? You drew things that are significant to you, tied to memories. I tried to depict the living room as accurately as possible from a functional standpoint. Now you see that we have distinct views of the room and experience it differently."

Lisa felt confused. "But that's not because our eyes are different, is it?"

"Well, that might play a part too. It's mainly because the images we perceive are filtered before we see them."

"What do you mean?"

"Our senses vary from person to person. It's influenced by our parents, our DNA, and how our bodies have developed. I'm slightly color-blind, but you're not. Moreover, it's also influenced by our age. My hearing isn't as sharp as yours. Our senses transmit signals to our brains, and our brains translate those signals into what we perceive as images, sounds, or tastes. And this translation is based on the sum of all our unique experiences up until that point."

"Grandpa, I'm having trouble understanding."

"Sorry, maybe I should explain it more clearly. Let me teach you four things. May I have your journal again?" He spoke as he wrote:

1.   *Our senses detect vibrations.*
2.   *Each person's senses differ. we pick up different vibrations.*
3.   *Our senses register these vibrations, but our brain then converts them into an experience, such as an image or a taste. This conversion is based on each person's individual experiences.*
4.   *Your position, where you are at a particular moment, is crucial in what your senses can perceive.*

Lisa took the journal and reread his notes. "I understand the first part. You demonstrated it, and I could hear and feel it easily. The second part makes sense to me now. Your eyes are different from mine. As you age, your hearing and other senses become less sharp."

Grandpa nodded.

"But I'm struggling with the third part. I'm using my own eyes, right? I'm tasting with my own tongue, right?"

"It may seem that way, but everything happens in your brain. Your eyes don't actually see anything. Your tongue doesn't taste anything. The images and tastes are created solely in your brain."

Lisa looked bewildered.

Grandpa stood up and picked up an old radio from the kitchen countertop. "You know what this is, right?"

Lisa rolled her eyes. "Yes, I know what a radio is, Grandpa."

"When I was growing up, this device was just as exciting to me as your phone is to you now. But I want to show you something." Grandpa switched on the radio, and static noise emanated from the small speaker. He extended the radio's antenna, and they immediately heard music. Then, Grandpa adjusted the tuning knob, alternating between interference and different radio stations. "You see? The antenna is like the sense of this radio. It detects vibrations, but it doesn't produce the sound. The radio converts the vibrations into sound."

Lisa was slightly unsure and shrugged.

Grandpa unscrewed the antenna from the radio and placed it in Lisa's hand. "Now you have an extra sense. Do you hear music now?"

Lisa laughed. "Yes, now I understand what you mean, Grandpa! This antenna still detects vibrations, but my body and brain can't do anything with them, so nothing happens."

"Well done." Grandpa nodded, took the antenna back from her, and screwed it back into the radio. He switched on the radio and tuned it to a station playing music. Then he walked around the room with the radio. Sometimes the music became distorted or when Grandpa moved to a corner, there was only interference. "You've probably noticed this with your phone," he said as he returned to the table.

"Oh, yeah," Lisa realized, "that's true. In certain places, the connection isn't as good, and in some buildings, there's only one spot where you can hear clearly. Why is that?"

Grandpa grabbed a pen from the table and threw it forcefully against the wall. Lisa was taken aback by the sudden action. "What are you doing?"

"What did you see?"

"Well, you angrily threw a pen against the wall."

"Interesting. Seeing anger was from your perspective, but we'll come back to that later. But I did throw a pen against the wall, and it bounced back. It didn't pass through the wall. You've just learned that everything has a vibration. However, the vibration of the pen couldn't penetrate the vibration of the wall. It's the same with radio waves or the vibrations emitted and received by your phone. They can't pass through everything or, at least, not equally well. So, there are places where reception is poor or non-existent."

Lisa tried to grasp the significance of this.

Grandpa helped her. "Okay, *you now realize that your position determines what your senses can perceive.* I have another way to make the point. Let's take a walk. Put on your coat."

"It's not that cold outside, and I'm not cold. In fact, I'm quite hot," Lisa remarked.

"That's up to you. I'm going to put on my heavy coat because I don't think it's warm. My perspective, you see."

Lisa grinned, "Your experience. I see."

Ω Color (Colour) of Perspective Ω

In the crisp outdoors, Lisa and Grandpa took a stroll down the lane. The farm sprawled on either side, an ecosystem of corn and wheat fields, and a meadow and pond. The maple trees rose high, their trunks thick with the years, the leaves changing to burnt orange with the onset of fall weather. And the memories most certainly bloomed.

Grandpa was gazing across the land and said, "This is an ideal place to experience the senses, Lisa. We employ all of them here—so much to see, hear, smell and touch."

"And feel."

Grandpa smiled. "Yes. And feel. These senses allow us to exist, survive, and express ourselves. They work perfectly for these purposes. What we see, we can usually touch, so we can feel it. When we tap on something it creates a sound allowing us to hear it. Everything we see and touch, we can taste by putting our tongue on it. And in most cases, we can also smell it too. So, our senses work together to perceive the tangible aspects of our surroundings.

"I have a lot of feelings while I am here. Both happy and sad."

"I know you do. Me too. According to ancient wisdom, feelings and emotions have their own vibrations, and we perceive them through a sixth sense."

"A sixth sense?"

"Yes, many people dismiss it as nonsense," Grandpa said. "You can imagine it to be true. I know it's true. But let's save that discussion for later. For now, let's stick to the five well-known senses that deal with the tangible and visible world around us."

"But Grandpa, some people are blind or deaf. Some can't taste or smell, or they are paralyzed. So, some people are missing one or maybe two senses."

"That's true. There are many stories about how people learn to compensate. Do you think all five senses work perfectly for the majority of people?"

"Well, no, not perfectly. Like, you wear glasses, so your eyesight isn't as good as mine."

"My eyeglasses are a much different form of compensation than for someone who cannot see at all. Let's use them as an example though. When I'm wearing my glasses, I can see just as well as you, or at least I think so. The eye doc says I have 20/20 vision when I wear these. But

I'm pretty sure that I don't see as well as you, and you don't see as bad as I do. That is to say, we don't see the same."

"How do you know that?"

They paused beside a thick tree trunk with a low hanging limb. "Can you see the fall pansies in Grandma's flower garden by the house?"

"Yes, of course, they're clearly visible. She loved purple."

"Great. I can see them, but not necessarily in purple."

"She planted pink ones too. Can you see those?" Lisa asked.

Grandpa shook his head. "Nope, because I'm slightly color-blind. Other colors like red and green often appear the same to me. That's because they have almost the same vibrational frequency. And can you see my black jacket hanging from the clothesline, drying from yesterday's rain?"

Lisa peered back toward the house trying to spot what Grandpa was referring to. She scanned a— "Oh, there it is."

"Well, it's effortless for me, being semi-color blind. And I also see better at night than you do because color-blind people perceive more light."

"So, each of us sees certain things better than another person might. I get it. Sad, you can't see all colors though."

"Ah, but I'm accustomed to it. I've compensated. And besides, you can help me see things through your eyes. Now, what if we had exactly the same eyes? Would we then perceive everything in the same way?"

"Seems like it." She pulled a piece of bark from the tree. "Look, this is tree bark. You see it just as well as I do. One thing is one thing, and it can't be any different for you than it is for me. Black is black, and white is white. Everyone knows that, even if you're color-blind."

"Let's take a look." Grandpa picked up a fallen leaf. He held it out. "What color is this leaf?"

"Still green."

"Are you sure?"

"Of course, I'm sure. Aren't you?"

Grandpa reached into his back pocket and extracted his wallet. From it, he withdrew a card and held it in the palm of his hand for Lisa to see. "Let's try another. What color is this card?"

"Black, Grandpa." She rolled her eyes in fake exasperation.

"Can't it also be white?"

"No, no way. My eyes are perfect, and that's pitch black."

"Alright," Grandpa said as he turned the card around. The other side was white. "And now what color is it?"

"Ah, but I couldn't see that side!"

"That's right, you couldn't see it. From where you were standing, you could only see one side. If you had been on the other side, you would have seen only the white side."

Lisa pointed at the green leaf. "So now I'm guessing that's a two-colored leaf."

"Very astute." Grandpa turned the leaf around to show an orange back. "Okay so you get it. If we could not see both sides of the leaf or the card—or any situation—we wouldn't agree with each other or even understand each other enough to agree to disagree. I keep this card in my wallet as a touchstone to remind me when I'm unsure how to see something or even someone. Life sometimes has its little tricks to surprise you in a nasty way and make you forget to check the other one's point of view. I have another card I will give to you to keep."

Grandpa replaced the card and continued, "So, as the old adage goes, not all things are black and white or in the case of the leaf, green and orange. The point is if each of us sees something from only our own position—our own perception or viewpoint—we don't understand each other. We will then only talk about what we see because that's all we know."

"We might disagree on who is right or wrong," said Lisa.

"Like beauty, that's in the eye of the beholder. And now, let's make it even more interesting," Grandpa said. "Come with me."

———

They walked into the grass several yards.

"Now, look back toward the barn. Do you see the bicycle?"

Lisa looked at the big doors of the red barn. "A bike? No."

"You can't?"

"No, I can't."

"Are you sure?"

"I'm absolutely sure. I don't see one."

"But I do. So, who's right?"

"I am. There's obviously no bike there to see."

"Yet there really is a bicycle there. Isn't it strange that you can't see it?"

Lisa didn't respond.

"Okay, let's say you are right. Could I be right too? What if you opened the barn door? Might you see the bike I parked just to the side of the entry?"

"That's not fair."

"It is. The bike is there. Just not visible to you because you didn't see it previously."

"How could I have known?"

"You could have asked why I think—or know—there is a bike there and then you'd get my side of the story. Then if you 'saw' it for yourself, you could agree I am right. If you put yourself in my shoes— or my mind's eye in this case—you would also 'see' the bike."

"So sometimes things are present even if unseen—at least from someone else's viewpoint. And you won't understand them or respect their viewpoint until you find out what it is."

"But you were also right, from your viewpoint," said Grandpa.

Lisa continued, "I was right when I said I didn't *see* the bike, but not when I said there *was* no bike."

"That's how it appeared to you. And I didn't put myself in your position. You didn't know what I know. But you were just as right as I was."

"Let's summarize:

"You reason from where you stand—your position—and your reasoning is based on what you see from there.

"As long as you don't see that bicycle, it isn't there.

"So, you are right based on your observation.

"At the same time, of course, I am also right.

"The bicycle isn't there for you, but it is for me, which means it is both there and not there simultaneously.

"We're both right.

"Then you decided to put yourself in my shoes and saw what I saw.

"I could have come up to you and said I understood that you didn't see the bicycle.

"We reach mutual understanding as we become clear on each other's point of view—or perspective."

"So there's only one reality, but multiple things can be true at the same time because each truth depends on your perspective?" Lisa stated.

Grandpa draped his arm around her shoulders. "You expressed that beautifully and very maturely."

"Seems I'm learning a whole new vocabulary."

"Indeed. Shall we go see the actual bike now?"

"What bike?"

"Very funny.

Ω

That evening, Lisa settled onto the sofa in the living room to write in her journal. Grandpa had started a fire in the fireplace, and Sera-cat was snuggled in her new favorite place, just beside Lisa's bare feet.

Journal: The Lisa Project:
The Secret of Life-Day 1-Concluded

It's evening now and I'm concluding my day. Today was packed! Grandpa taught me many things.

1. Our senses detect vibrations.
2. Each person's senses differ, so we pick up different vibrations.
3. Our senses register these vibrations, but our brain then converts them into an experience, such as an image or a taste. This conversion is based on each person's individual experiences.
4. Your position, where you are at a particular moment, is crucial in what your senses can perceive.

Sometimes things are present even if unseen-at least from someone else's viewpoint. And you don't understand them...

<u>Grandpa Added</u>:
Your literal or figurative position creates your
viewpoint-or worldview.

<u>And I said</u>: There's only one reality, but multiple
things can be true at the same time because each
truth depends on your perspective.

   I feel smart. But wow, there's a lot I don't know
.. or see .. or taste .. or smell .. or.. haha.

THE LISA PROJECT:
The Secret of Life

Day 2

CHAPTER 4 | Crawling Creatures

Creeping Assumptions

Lisa and Grandpa walked together at a quick clip from the lane, past the meadow to the gravel road. It was a crisp, jacket-weather day. Frank's farm neighbored Grandpa's, but due to a deep, water-filled ditch in between they could not easily cut through and decided to take the long way around to reach it.

As they were walking Lisa asked, "Grandpa, why don't you build a little bridge over the stream?" Lisa asked. "It would save a lot of time to get over to your neighbor's place."

"Well, I don't visit Frank that often. The *ditch* acts as a nice barrier between the properties. He's much younger and still has big plans for his farm. He'd like to buy the meadow and plant crops or maybe use some of it to raise cattle—make it a true working farm. I don't need all that, and really don't want that. I like the idea of preserving its beauty in its original form. I believe Frank and his parents, all born and raised as farmers around here, see it as a wasted opportunity. I'm the city slicker who moved in several years back. Still an outsider, I suppose."

Another matter of perspective, Lisa thought.

As they arrived at Frank's yard and opened the gate, they were greeted by a wolf-like dog who excitedly barked at them. Grandpa quickly pulled Lisa behind him and turned his back to the dog.

"Get! Go away!" Grandpa yelled.

The dog continued barking but kept its distance.

Lisa peaked around Grandpa. Despite his raspy bark, the dog had friendly eyes.

The dog is curious, not mean.

"Hey," Lisa called. "It's okay. We're friends. It's okay. Settle down." She stepped from behind Grandpa and reached out a closed hand.

"What are you doing, Lisa? He's going to—"

The barking gave way to a sniff of Lisa's hand, and he sat down, wagging his tail as Lisa petted his head.

Lisa looked over to Grandpa who still stood back warily when the man she figured must be Frank approached and nodded at Grandpa in greeting.

"And who might this be!" The man bellowed as he lumbered up. "You must be the granddaughter, Lisa. Welcome, young lady. I'm Frank. I see you've already met Little Wolf."

Lisa turned to Frank. "*Little* Wolf?"

"Ah, this old boy is harmless. Just protective when he gets scared."

"Scared?"

"Little Wolf is actually a wolfhound," Frank explained. "When I got him as a puppy, he truly resembled a little wolf. Now he's, well, you can see. *Big.* You seem to have a knack for handling him, Miss Lisa. Quite different from your scaredy-cat grandpa," he added, giving Grandpa a friendly pat on the back.

"I prefer cats," Grandpa smiled. "At least I can trust them."

"The felines are not for me, but to each his own," Frank said. "Well, are you coming inside? What would you like to drink?"

They stepped into the living room, with Little Wolf following. Lisa noticed it was more contemporary than Grandpa's, and the décor was decidedly masculine. The only framed photo was of Little Wolf. She wondered if there was—or had been—a Mrs. Frank. The room was full of natural light, and despite the cool day, windows were open allowing in fresh air.

"Your home is very pretty."

"Thank you, Lisa. I'm just a hard-working farmer with much of my time spent outdoors. So, when I'm inside, I like to feel a little more citified. Probably sounds like a contradiction. In any case, behind here, I have the old stables, which I now use for breeding and growing. The back part of the actual house is sort of my work shed if you want to call it that. There's a lot to see back there. Why don't you take a look around and I can discuss the *stream* with your grandfather."

Ω

Lisa decided to explore. She neared the back area of the house, the 'work shed,' and it seemed to emanate a lot of light. *Why? Skylights? Solar?*

The space looked like a giant terrarium with tons of plants and a lot of water misting. There were racks of jars and various tools. As she approached a row of tables with warming lamps hanging over tall, covered glass containers, Lisa hoped to find chicks but instead discovered tufts of cotton or something similar in which something was moving.

A *lot* of something was moving.

Spiders! She hightailed it back to the front room in time to hear Grandpa say, "I don't mind if you use the water from the ditch—okay the *stream*. Not at all! I was under the impression you wanted to—"

At the sight of Lisa, Grandpa jumped to his feet. "Lisa?! You look like you've seen a—"

"a ghost? No. Worse. Much worse. Spiders! Thousands of them!" said Lisa.

57

"You okay, Lisa?" Grandpa took her arm to steady her and looked at Frank. "I'm afraid she's a spider-phobe—arachnophobe."

"Aw, heck. I should have warned you before I sent you to scout." Frank stood and peered at Lisa. "So, you're not afraid of a big dog, but you're scared of little spiders? Please don't be distressed. I promise these are the helpful kind, not the hurtful. I get it though. Most people haven't heard about how valuable spiders can be. Come on back with me, and I'll explain what I'm doing here. I promise there is no need to be afraid—almost all the creatures are safely contained."

Lisa and Grandpa followed Frank to the sunroom as he began to explain. "I grow all sorts of vegetables in my gardens, and some hybrid breeds of corn and wheat. And I do it as naturally as possible, without pesticides or chemicals. They call it 'organic' these days, but to me, it just makes sense because all the poison you spray on food ends up in your body when you eat it, so you're essentially poisoning yourself."

Frank paused, then continued in earnest. "The reason why I am interested in utilizing some of your 'ditch water' to irrigate, is that it is spring-fed, pure. Now, without some form of defense against insects and bacteria, it's challenging to protect crops. So, I've been experimenting for years to find natural ways to safeguard my precious vegetables. By accident, I stumbled upon a particular spider species here that excelled at this task. They catch all sorts of pests and keep the vegetables remarkably clean. That's why I breed spiders and release them among my vegetable crops. It's effective."

"Who woulda thought," Grandpa said. "Well, Frank. I apologize. I didn't peg you quite right. I actually thought you might want that ditch—that stream—filled in for more growing area, more money making."

"I'm not against making more money, but that's not my primary intention. Not a chance. And no worries about the misunderstanding. It happens to me to be 'pegged,' as you say. My methods are not necessarily controversial, but they are different. My folks who used to own this place even say so. Unfamiliar to some and a change from tradition. You and I share something in common and that's the love of the land. Now, before I prattle on, welcome to my greenhouse or sunroom area. This is where some cool stuff happens. So, Miss Lisa if you will allow me to introduce you to my little darlings—"

"Hang on Mr.—"

"Just Frank," Frank said.

"Hang on, Just Frank. Little darlings is *your* viewpoint—his perspective, right Grandpa?"

"Or his perception of reality," Grandpa teased.

"Maybe, but it isn't mine. I see nothing darling about spiders."

Frank offered, "Well, maybe it isn't your viewpoint—yet."

"Do cats eat spiders?" Lisa interjected.

"Random question, but possibly so."

"Thought that might be why you aren't a 'fan of the feline.'" *Another difference in perspective. Another reason I like cats.*

Frank laughed. "Please let me show you what I do here. It might help you. Your greatest fear often conceals your greatest gift, if you're willing to explore it, of course."

Grandpa and Lisa chorused. "Sounds familiar."

Frank led them to the first row of glass aquariums. "Here's the breeding area," he pointed to a cotton and wool-filled box. "These are all eggs, wrapped in a silk-like substance, like an incubator or cocoon. And here," he gestured toward a second box, "the eggs hatched just a day ago." Tiny creatures scurried around. "These are still babies. Would you like to hold one in your hand? Okay, no. But how about a closer look?"

Frank opened the lid and lowered a cotton swab. A spider hopped on, and he lifted it out and let it crawl onto his hand.

Lisa took a quick back step, but observed the curious creature, which despite its small size, appeared complete in its own way. *How could such a small and amusing creature grow into a large, intimidating spider?* Lisa glanced at the glass boxes further down the row *Gross! Scary!—So many.* It gave her the jitters. *I hope he's right that they can't get out.*

"Frank, I do understand that these are your little darlings and that they serve a purpose. I can at least appreciate that. But I definitely still, just—don't like the bigger ones."

"A secret? I don't really like the giant ones either."

Lisa noticed Grandpa cringe a bit himself, before he turned away saying, "Thanks for the spidey class, Frank. How about we talk some more about my ditch—that stream? I think I'm about to get a lesson in irrigation. Lisa, I bet that big bad wolf dog would like to have some company."

CHAPTER 5 | A Change Of Heart

Grandpa's Dream

Upon return from their excursion to Frank's, Grandpa and Lisa entered the kitchen, draped their jackets over chairs, and Lisa put the kettle on for tea. A yawning Sera-cat strutted into the kitchen, stuck her head in the empty food bowl and plopped to the floor to stretch.

Grandpa sat at the table and clasped his hands together, satisfied. "Well, that was not predictable. I've had a change of heart with good ol' Frank and our *stream*. Didn't expect that."

"Sounds like a good outcome, Grandpa. Guess you're building a bridge after all, just a different kind of bridge."

"Astute, girl. Yes, there need to be a few changes around here I suppose."

Lisa nodded, "Yeah, and maybe we begin with the thermostat in here." She mocked fainting and then fanned herself. "It's seriously hot in here."

Grandpa went to the wall to turn down the heat. "I guess I don't have the thick skin I used to have. I definitely appreciate summer months and warmth. These days I dread autumn since it begins the chilly signs of the unavoidable onset of an unwelcome winter."

"And yet, you live in the north?"

"True. This has been home for a long time. A lot of seasons were spent here by your grandma and me."

"Why didn't you move to a warmer climate then?"

"Change. Moving again would have required change. And effort."

That also sounds familiar. Like me.

"To me, you've always been the same amazing Grandpa since I've known you. When was the last time you changed?"

"When was the last time I changed?" he mused. "That's easy. It was when you were born, and I laid eyes on you for the first time. It was like being struck by lightning. There was an instant connection between us, as if I had known you all along. It was a feeling unlike anything I had ever experienced before. I can't quite explain it, but it was a deep-rooted memory, something primal. It was as if, in that very moment, my heart opened up wider and made space just for you. Grandma used to say that you awakened a tenderness in me…," he trailed off, closed his eyes.

Lisa sat down. She waited.

"As I think about it, I experienced another change when a few years ago…when the…incident…happened with your father."

Lisa nodded, fully aware of what Grandpa was referring to, though the 'incident' had ever since been a taboo topic.

"When I received that phone call from the police," he continued, "it was like being struck by lightning once again. Looking back, it was the complete opposite of the feeling I had when you were born. It felt as if your father had been ripped away from my heart. And then, Grandma passed away a year later. Those two events changed me. Changed my life."

But how is accepting this hard for Grandpa? He's teaching me about change, but still seems confused by it.

Lisa's heart hurt for him. Always strong and now seeing him so vulnerable.

"I think I get it, Grandpa. We are actually a lot alike. It helps me to know that you've experienced things in life that you didn't want to or didn't choose. But you wouldn't let me give up, so I have to ask you: are there still things that you wish were different but aren't? Like a dream you had that never came true?"

Grandpa knew the answer she was looking for, and he wasn't ready to give it. He changed the subject from his only son. "Oh, yes, when I was young, living in a tropical country was my biggest dream. But I thought I had to establish something through hard work first, and that seemed more attainable in our country than anywhere else. And after going to college and finding a profession I excelled at, I met your grandma, and we started our life together. We laid down our roots, and after many years of the rat race and prevailing through the ups and downs, we moved here. She liked it here. Of course, back then, I didn't realize the cold would get to me so much."

"Did you ever talk about moving?"

"We did. When things got dull or we struggled, I suggested that we emigrate to a place where the sun always shines and start anew—again. However, she didn't want to. She loved this area, and especially the climate. She used to say, 'Every season is a unique piece of art.' I heard that often when I complained about the weather. While I bundled up with a warm coat and gloves, she didn't even need a jacket, similar to you. She handled the cold exceptionally well. It was the same inside the house. I'd crank up the heat, but she'd tell me I was going mad. She'd just put on an extra sweater. And going on vacation to tropical countries was out of the question for her too. Fear of flying."

"Looks like I'm a little like Grandma, too, except for the flying part. But hold on, that must have been a frustrating difference between you two. Where you end up living is sort of a big deal. How'd you work it out?"

Grandpa shifted in his chair and let out a deep sigh. "The short answer is that I had my priorities—they were Grandma, my work, and eventually, our son and you and your mom. Life happened and the tropical dream ended."

"Ended?"

"Okay, sidelined, and then it became a permanent hold."

"But Grandpa, Grandma is gone now."

"She is, and I have you and your mom close by after the situation with your dad, and because of what he did … well, no way I'm leaving you alone." Grandpa took a deep breath, and his thoughts went somewhere distant.

"Well, we don't see each other very often, but we have technology. I don't see why now isn't the time to pursue your dream. This is still your dream. I can tell. I want it for you."

Grandpa shook his head. "That's very kind of you to say that. But I'm getting too old now. Where would I go? I'm not sure I want to risk my savings to make it happen. And truth be told, I'm content right here. I can warm up the house whenever I please. I'm fine, honest."

Lisa tilted her head. "What about regrets? Saying you're old is an excuse. Contentment is good, but what if you could have more? I don't think you're being completely honest with yourself."

Grandpa placed his hand on hers. "Old soul. Already, the student becoming the teacher?"

"Well, you said The Lisa Project would turn my world upside down. Let's make your dream a project too. You need a change of heart. Let's turn your world upside down as well. In the coming days, we'll explore options and lovely places for you to move to and figure out a way to make it possible. Are you up for it?"

"I don't want to disappoint you, but it's simply not that easy."

"Who said anything worth having is? You told me I can't quit before I try. Shouldn't that apply to you?"

Grandpa shook his head. "What have I created in you! … Alright, we can take a look, but I won't make any promises."

"But you are willing to explore what might be possible?"

The tea kettle whistled.

"Saved by the proverbial bell."

"You might want to get a journal, Grandpa."

"You always have to have the last word?"

"Evidently."

CHAPTER 6 | Concerning News

Breaking Free

That evening after they finished dinner, Lisa settled onto the sofa and turned on the TV.

Grandpa put down the book he'd been reading.

The news flashed on with the headline story of a political dispute. Lisa intended to switch to Netflix, but Grandpa stopped her.

"Hold tight. We might find the news stories relevant to our project. Let's keep it on."

The headlines covered *uplifting* stories such as one of the wars going on, a murder case, concerns over a new virus outbreak, politics, a forest fire due to climate change, a fatal bus accident, reduced profits for a major company, and a fire in a migrant shelter.

"Asylum seekers, I think they are scary," Lisa said when she saw it.

"Why is that?"

"Just a feeling," Lisa replied. "They seem so different, and on TV they often appear mad or confused. Mom says they're a burden and only come here for money, which she has to pay."

"Have you ever encountered them in real life?" Grandpa asked.

"No, I haven't, luckily—But I've seen some homeless people, and they can be scary too."

"Now that you've seen some of the news, how do you feel?" Grandpa questioned.

Lisa sighed. "The world is a mess. Bad things are happening everywhere, and it's all getting worse."

"What if I told you that the world is actually doing well; that positive things are happening everywhere; that most places are improving and getting better?" Grandpa proposed.

Lisa was incredulous. "You clearly haven't been watching the news or reading the papers."

"That's right," Grandpa said, "because I haven't read the paper for years and the news doesn't typically interest me."

"Well, Mom always reads the news in the morning on her tablet while she's having breakfast, and it's always negative. So, where in the world are things going well?"

"That's the exact reason I no longer read the paper. It mainly contains news reports that make you worry."

"But there must be a reason for it. Apparently, we should be very worried or the world will end soon."

"Of all the things you've ever seen on the news or read in the newspaper, which ones have you actually experienced in your life?"

Lisa thought about it. "Not many, I guess. Homeless people when they are wandering around or begging. That does scare me—and honestly, so does Mom. She's so worried about all those things in the news. She's worried she'll be out of a job if the economy tanks. Or that she won't have any money when she's old. Or that a new virus will show up and everything will be locked down again."

"Well, your mom worries a lot. Most people do."

"Then it means they're probably right, doesn't it?"

"Well, it basically means that most people repeat what is said in the media and what other people say. The media has the greatest interest in making everyone concerned."

"Huh. Why?"

"Because people will keep watching to know if anything is getting better or if there is even more to be concerned about. If there was only good news to report, you could do without the news because there'd be nothing that could threaten you. But if you seem to be threatened, even if it's indirectly, then you'd want to check how things are going every day, or much more often. Then the more people want that information, the better it is for the media because they make money on that kind of attention. That was certainly very clear during the COVID years. Everyone hung onto all the news about new figures, new measures, new mutations, new vaccinations. A relentless stream of disturbing messages. And think about the result we now know! The stress that it caused turned out to be very harmful for many people, just as if stress was a virus as well," said Grandpa.

Lisa had never seen it that way. "But it all happened, didn't it? They don't make up all those bad things they report, do they?"

"No, you can't make up a virus. But there is so much news in the world that you can never address it all in one go. By choosing which events to report and how to report them, most media outlets create their own picture of the world and then present that to people. Take, for instance, the news about that company making less profit. Although it is still profitable, just not as much as before, the media often portrays it negatively, magnifying the implications for other companies. But it could also be seen as positive: the company is still making a profit, which could boost others. The problem is that most media opt for negative, sensational, and alarming news, which contributes to the perception of a negative and threatening world. And, as people, we are a lot less discerning—a lot less equipped, or a lot less interested in determining what is true, what is real," Grandpa elaborated.

"You get really worked up about this, don't you?"

"More people should. Just because it is said on TV or your iPhone—or any media—doesn't mean it's true or that it is the full story. I'm sorry, princess, if my take on it causes you discomfort, but that's actually good too. It's so frustrating to see a small group of people deciding what events the rest of us get to see in the world and with what biases. They prioritize negative, threatening, or sensational news because it sells better. Sure, there will be a new virus outbreak at some point in time. There will continue to be devastating and unfair wars around the world with the threat of nuclear weapons being used. Add to that the ongoing concerns about the environment, climate change, along with a constant stream of reports on shootings, murders, accidents, and scandals. It's a recipe for a lifetime of stress, anxiety, and fear of the world."

"But, Grandpa, I haven't heard you say anything positive now either. All you've done is make me stressed by the news."

"You're right," he muttered. "I got caught up in complaining and ranting, and that adds to the problem. It's not a solution." He continued, "Even this old geezer can let his frustration get the best of him.

"Of course, there are good and positive aspects of the news, too, where problems are being solved and things are changing. There are many outstanding researchers and journalists who expose abuses and terrible situations that need to be addressed.

"We can't live without the news either—

"It's just that at my age, I've seen and heard almost everything before. But for you, it's all still new and significant. I probably wanted to shield you from it, but I ended up doing the opposite. I'm sorry. All of this does wreak havoc on all of our senses, let alone the overall vibration of our world."

Our world…a changing world. Heck, my changing world!

They sat silently through the conclusion of the nightly news.

Grandpa shifted to peer at Lisa. "I have an idea. It could be an antidote—or a partial solution—to my laments just now and those on the news. What do you think it is?"

"A movie with kittens and puppies?" Lisa joked. "People would be hard pressed not to be happy seeing a kitten or puppy."

"Well, happiness is a gift, and it can be fleeting. What if I said there is a way to achieve some peacefulness amidst the chaos?"

"I'd say, bring it on."

"Good. How'd you like to see my practice space?"

"Your Zen Den? You mean the one place on this farm you haven't allowed me to enter? Heck, yeah. I'm in!"

"Great! I'm going to wake you early tomorrow and ask you to quietly come with me to the backyard and into the Zen Den where we'll create the experience. You said you brought your bathing suit for the polar plunge—put it on, but not for that kind of plunge. No! Don't ask, just be prepared."

"So, no puppies?"

"Go write in your journal and get some rest, Lisa. See you in the morning."

"Intriguing."

"Indeed."

———

The Lisa Project: The Secret of Life

Journal-Day 2

I learned that spiders can actually be helpful and some have a positive purpose. It depends on your viewpoint.

Frank also said, "Your greatest fear often conceals your greatest gift, if you're willing to explore it." Interesting that Grandpa said it too.

It's appearing like a lot-or in everything-depends on your perception of reality. Perceality? Did I create a word? Reminder to tell Grandpa.

Assumptions create misunderstandings. Communication clears them up. Bridges can be built.

Some people don't like the unfamiliar or change from tradition.

Change takes energy. It can be good or bad. A person can cause change or sometimes it happens unexpectedly.

It's so frustrating to see a small group of people deciding what events the rest of us get to see in the world. It is biased. The media has so much control over what we see and feel and think.

Just because it is said on TV or your iPhone-or any media-doesn't mean it's true or that it is the full story.

Be part of the solution. Complaining doesn't help.

Grandpa gave up his dream of living in a tropical climate. I understand his priorities-at that time. But now, I'm going to change that.

He taught me I can't quit before I try. Shouldn't that apply to him? It's not too late, no matter his age.

The Lisa Project is supposed to turn my world upside down. Same goes for Grandpa's world!

THE LISA PROJECT:
The Secret of Life

Day 3

CHAPTER 7 | Floating

Who are you without your senses?

As promised, the following morning Grandpa entered Lisa's attic room and found her sitting quietly on her bed. She motioned to let him know she was prepared in her swimsuit under her fuzzy robe.

He placed a finger to his lips to remain quiet.

She understood.

They walked outside into the mist and about twenty yards to a cabin with log-siding, many windows, and a backdrop of the farm's pond. It could be a scene from *Architectural Digest*.

Grandpa's Zen Den.

Lisa knew he practiced yoga daily and meditated and that he often entered this space to create his paintings. It was *his* space, and he'd made that clear since he built it sometime soon after he and Grandma moved here.

Lisa felt honored to enter and saw that Grandpa had arrived earlier to light candles, creating a gentle ambiance. His yoga mats were rolled and stored, and there were decorative bowls and statues, which she imagined served some purpose. A separate door was ajar and led to his painting room. His easel stood in the center and a painting in progress was on it. The meadow and pond shimmered in the early morning panorama. Lisa could envision the natural light shining in as he created his art.

Grandpa opened a second door and Lisa saw a sizable hot tub. No bubbles were whirling. The water was still. The room was windowless.

In a hushed voice, Grandpa explained, "When you get into the hot tub, you will experience a unique sensation of floating. You will be in salt water, which will make you buoyant. The water is warm, matching your body temperature, so it will feel like you're weightless. Once you're in, I'll turn out this light, step out, and close the door." he put his finger on a button on the topside of the tub. "It will be pitch black inside, but you can press the light back on whenever you are ready. Just feel for it. It will be right here. Stay in the darkness if you can. This room is made to be very quiet, but if you need me, I'll be on the other side of the door."

Lisa nodded, understanding the instructions, but feeling a little uneasy.

"The experience will simulate the absence of your senses as much as possible. You won't see, hear, or feel much. It might be a bit unsettling at first but focus on your breathing. Slowly inhale—count to four, then exhale, counting to four. I'll be right outside the door, and it will not be locked. You can exit if you need to. Ready?"

Lisa carefully immersed herself in the water. Grandpa quietly closed the door. The room was black. The water enveloped her body, and a gentle force lifted her. She lay back and closed her eyes and experienced the sensation of complete weightlessness.

It was a strange feeling. With the darkness and quiet, it was also a little—unnerving. She reached out for a side.

The water swayed and again became still.

How long am I supposed to stay in here?

Remembering Grandpa's words, she focused on her breathing. After fidgeting and several more breaths, her body calmed, and her mind began to 'talk' raising thoughts from her first days with Grandpa.

Without my senses, I am not my body anymore. The thought sent a shiver down her spine, but she managed to stay quiet. *I am not my body, yet I still exist because I can think and experience emotions. So, who am I? What am I?*

She realized, like the water, the thoughts were pleasant. *If I am nothing, then I can also be everything. What does it mean to be nothing? And what does it mean to be everything?*

Something peculiar began to occur. She felt as though she was splitting in two. One part of her was her physical body, while the other was her mind. She recognized this sensation from when she had fallen in the barn and lay on the ground. Even now, despite the darkness, she could observe her body from a distance.

The concepts of nothingness and everything-ness swirled in her mind. *How can I be nothing?* And rapidly she thought, *If I am nothing, then there is nothing else. Do I still exist? Yes, my thoughts are still present; otherwise, this makes no sense. I know I am here. But there is nothing else. Nothing to worry about, nothing to fear. Yet, I'm alone. And what am I exactly? Is it different when I am everything? How can I be everything?*

She sensed an expansion, as if she had exploded and became as vast as the universe and beyond. It felt strange, yet familiar. Everything was simply—

Me. Lisa.

If I am everything, then there is nothing else. And in that case, I'm still alone, she realized. *Even now, I have nothing to fear. But I still don't know who or what I am. So, everything is the same as nothing. Where am I now? Am I alone?*

She opened her eyes, greeted by absolute darkness. This startled her, and she suddenly became aware of her physical body. She thrashed, and found her footing on the bottom, only to begin floating up again.

It wasn't deep and she couldn't sink. She held onto the side and tried to relax, calm her panic, her heart.

The same sense didn't fully return. Her thinking mind was thinking, and the short burst of serenity was elusive. Maybe, at least until next time. She hoped there would be a next time.

It felt like an eternity had passed when she finally turned the light on, stepped out, took the towel from a chair and wrapped herself in it. She sat in silence. *What just happened?*

She opened the door and Grandpa, sitting cross-legged on his yoga mat, opened his eyes and arched his brows. "And?"

"And you better feed me before I try to explain that."

Ω

Lisa entered the kitchen with her journal in hand, finding Grandpa frying eggs and peeling an orange.

He paused upon seeing her in the doorway. "If you screamed in that tub, I didn't hear you."

"I suppose if I was as afraid of the dark as I am of spiders, I may have screamed. But it was different. I felt disoriented more than truly scared. It was the disorientation that caused me to feel scared."

"Do you know why you felt that way?" Grandpa probed.

"Before that, I felt safe and relaxed. I guess that was a little of the out-of-body experience I've read about, but when my thoughts came to my situation and my physical body not being in control, I wigged."

"You actually knew you were safe. But you began thinking— imagining—you weren't safe, which made you feel unsafe. So, your senses provided a sense of security?" Grandpa summarized.

"Not sure I follow. I mean, I am realizing that I am not solely defined by my physical self."

"And who or what are you without your senses?"

"I am my thoughts," Lisa replied, "but it felt as if I was observing myself from a distance."

"Wow, you've experienced a profound aspect of ancient wisdom," Grandpa revealed as he walked their plates to the table and sat. "A quick lesson on Eastern wisdom—or ancient wisdom—is in order."

"Will there be a test after?" Lisa grinned.

"Only in life. Now, okay, here it goes. May I have your journal? A picture might help." Grandpa bowed over the page and began to draw as he spoke.

"In Eastern philosophies, as well as others, humans are described as threefold beings: body, mind, and soul."

- *Your body represents your physical manifestation and the source of all sensory experiences.*
- *Your mind encompasses your thoughts and consciousness, processing and interpreting sensory input.*
- *Your soul is the perceiver, the connection to the universal source.*

"The soul is a little hard to draw as you cannot actually see your soul. I've shown it in the heart and all around the physical self for explanation's sake. What you experienced floating was the realm of your mind, your thoughts. While most of your senses were temporarily diminished, your consciousness remained intact. You tapped into the understanding that you are not just your body. It offered a sense of safety and reassurance, a realization that you'll never truly cease to exist."

Lisa looked at Grandpa's drawing and the words to depict the mind, body, and soul—and their connection. "That's deep. Well— because of what I know now, I would at least realize that if I had no senses, I would miss them a lot. I would never see or hear or taste anything again. It would be similar to someone who has gone blind after knowing what it is to see. You know what you're missing and you can never experience it again. So, I might feel trapped within my physical body. However, what I felt was also soothing, as if someone or something was assuring me, 'You're not merely your body.' It felt secure in a way."

"You mean like, 'I will never truly die or cease to exist'?"

"Maybe, but I also realized that without my senses, I wouldn't be able to experience anything again. And that felt really sad. So, without senses, I wouldn't exist within the world, and the world wouldn't exist for me," Lisa concluded, blinking as she turned her gaze toward Grandpa.

He clapped his hands in appreciation. "You did something incredibly brave, and your words were profoundly beautiful. I'm proud of you."

"I need to write all of this down. I don't want to forget anything."

"Take the time you need and meet me in the living room. There's something I've been working on that I want to show you."

Something more…

The Lisa Project: The Secret of Life
Journal-Day 3

I'm not exactly sure what just happened-but I liked it!

I got to visit Grandpa's Zen Den. He had me float! The hot tub was filled with salt water. It was pitch dark and quiet. At first, I was sort of scared. My mind went so fast-Grandpa called it Monkey Mind.

I remembered to breathe. Inhale for four. Exhale for four. Repeat. I kept thinking things like:

- ▶ Without my senses, I am not my body anymore.
- ▶ So, who am I? What am I?
- ▶ If I am nothing, then I can also be everything.
- ▶ What does it mean to be nothing?
- ▶ And what does it mean to be everything?

Wild! I felt like I was split in two—the physical me and my thoughts! Maybe that's the out-of-body thing people talk about.

I was alone, but not afraid.

I knew I was safe.

Was I really alone?

If I am everything, then there is nothing else. And in that case, I'm still alone, but not afraid.

But I still don't know who or what I am. I am realizing that I am not solely defined by my physical self.

CHAPTER 8 | Life

Rolling Forward

Lisa stepped into the living room and immediately noticed the new painting on the wall. She'd seen a portion of it on the easel in the Zen Den. It depicted a large, red ball perched precariously on a narrow beam. The ball appeared much larger than the beam and seemed like it could tumble off at any moment. However, it also conveyed the impression that falling wasn't its purpose. The beam had a slight downward slope, causing the ball to appear as if it were rolling to the right, toward the end of the beam where it met a wall with a small, round hole. It was as if the ball was meant to vanish through that hole.

"Wow, Grandpa, impressive new painting." She sat at Grandpa's feet in front of his favorite chair and opened her journal on the coffee table, gazing up at him and the painting behind him.

He looks rather regal. And I bet—here comes the something more...

"It's actually an old painting. I decided to touch it up again last night. I brought it in here as part of our project. Do you like it?"

"I really like the colors, and it feels like something significant is happening—some action," Lisa remarked, "but what does it represent exactly?"

"That's life."

"Life?"

"Yes, life. It represents my life and your life as well."

"I don't understand. My life is a ball on a beam?"

"Symbolized by a ball on a beam. Imagine you are the ball," Grandpa began, "but you can't look around. You can only look downward. What do you see?"

"I see the beam I'm standing on and the space beneath it."

"Exactly. You only see the beam you're standing on and the depths below. You can't see anything else. How does it make you feel?"

"Well, I think I'd be afraid of falling off, so I'd want to stay on the beam," Lisa ventured.

"Correct. You try to balance yourself as best you can. And you feel yourself rolling forward because you move into the next day of your life, and the day after that, and so on. You grow older, you develop, you experience new things. But you can't see the beam ahead of you and certainly not the hole in the wall in the distance. You can only imagine where you're going and what lies ahead. For some people, that's enjoyable because balancing can be fun. But for many, it's also a bit frightening. They don't know why they're on that beam or what the future holds. They're simply aware that they could fall off at any moment, that something bad could happen. And so, they worry."

"*That's* life?" Lisa asked, her voice filled with a mix of horror and disbelief.

"For many people, indeed, that is life," Grandpa nodded. "Often, they aren't even aware of it, but they are constantly concerned about their financial situation, their job, their relationships, their children, their friendships, their health, and what's happening in the world. They view the world, and especially other people, with a certain level of anxiety."

That's exactly what Mom does.

"But in everyone's life, there comes a special event. An event so powerful and significant that, for a moment, you stop looking down. Usually, it's a moment of profound insight or deep crisis. If you were that ball and momentarily forgot to look down, you would roll over, and your eyes would naturally focus on the beam behind you. This invites you—or even compels you—to look back, and that's when you see the beam from the moment of your birth. It's a straight line. You discover that line within everything that has happened in your life. All the experiences and occurrences that seemed unrelated, separate points, suddenly align into this clear, straight line—the path you have traveled up until that moment. This present moment.

"And then it all becomes clear: your entire life has led you to this very moment and this particular point. The line was always there, but you didn't see it. It's only by being on that beam, rolling forward with all the uncertainties, fears, and excitement that come with it, that you can experience things, that you can experience life."

Grandpa paused and placed his hand on Lisa's shoulder and pointed to her journal, encouraging her to take notes. "And that is when your life changes. By looking back, you can now look forward. Suddenly, you see the beam stretching out in front of you, as the same straight line. Your future is connected to your past. They both possess meaning and purpose.

"You no longer need to fear falling off the beam. You realize that everything has perfectly fallen into place leading up to that point, and it will continue to do so in the future, for the rest of your life.

"In that moment, you gain boundless confidence in life. You no longer need to fear anything, and you can surrender to what lies ahead. In the past lies the present. The 'now' holds what will become."

Lisa reread her notes:

By looking back, I can now look forward.

Everything has led up to this point, and it will continue.

My future is connected to my past.

I no longer need to fear.

I can surrender to what lies ahead.

In the past lies the present. The "now" holds what will become.

She looked up, lifting her pen. "I don't understand that last part."

"It's from an old poem by a Dutch poet and scholar named Willem Bilderdijk who had a difficult life. He posits that there are three moments: the past, which is the past; the now, which is the present; and the future, which is what will be."

Lisa began scribbling and Grandpa sat down and idly stroked Sera-cat as he recalled more.

"I'll paraphrase and use some of my own words: in essence the past is gone, but it has shaped the present. Similarly, the now influences what lies ahead. If you've always worried, you will continue to do so unless you can see that your past worries have led you nowhere. They have only hindered and restricted you in your life. Everything that has transpired in your life seems to form a straight line, a narrative, a purpose.

"Nothing happens without reason. It all makes sense. The moment you realize this in the present, both the past and present change, and, as a direct result, your perception of the future transforms immediately as well. *You* are the continuous connection between the past and the future. In the present moment, you always have the choice to alter your thoughts about something. By doing so, you can shape your future. My motto is: '*Embrace and live life forward with confidence, knowing that eventually, afterward, everything makes sense and falls into place.*' That's what I wanted to convey with this painting."

Lisa held up the 'hold on a minute' signal and wrote furiously. "Wow," she exclaimed after a few moments, "so my life has a line like that too."

"Everyone's life has it," Grandpa smiled. "And so does yours. Call it whatever you want: your destiny, your purpose, the goal of your life. Once you see it, you understand it and the notion of your life and the future changes drastically. Your life and future gain significance, and you will know why you're alive, why you're here, what your life is about. However, many people only discover this later in life, after experiencing a transformation. Sadly, some never do. Not many people realize it early on, and only a few are born with this knowledge, this certainty, this confidence."

Grandpa fell silent for a moment.

"When did you have that moment in your life, Grandpa?"

"It was when you were born, and I saw you for the first time," he said softly. "I've told you it was like being struck by lightning. I saw a little angel. It might sound strange or exaggerated, but that's exactly how it was. I didn't just see you. I could also feel you. I sensed your energy, your soul, your essence.

"Up until that point, my life hadn't held much greater purpose. I was still learning so much about life and gaining a broader perspective, but I had also endured some sad and painful experiences and I couldn't comprehend the purpose for them.

"When you were born and I felt an overwhelming love for you, I just knew that my life had meaning because you were the result of it. From that moment on, I understood that my purpose was to help you grow, to assist you in discovering what you needed to fulfill yourself in this world, to facilitate the experiences you wished to have. What we are doing right now is a wonderful outcome of that."

Lisa felt an overwhelming sense of love for Grandpa and a sense of safety in wellbeing with the knowledge that his love for her ran so very deep. Tears were in Grandpa's eyes, and Lisa took his hand in hers and squeezed.

She looked him directly in the eyes and began, "I really want to discover what I need to fulfill myself in this world, but when I'm being bullied at school, it feels as if I'm not worth it, as if I don't matter. That feels so unfair, and so unjust! I want to matter. I want to be of use with a purpose. I want to help this world become a better and nicer place.

"Also, to me it feels as if being a girl, being a woman, is a tougher starting point than being a boy or a man. Not only do I need to prove myself to everyone, it's even harder because the girls pull each other down instead of push each other up. Mom is pulling me down! Madison is pulling me down! But why? It makes no sense."

Lisa took a deep breath and continued, "Grandpa, I truly want to know right now what the straight line in my life is, what it is that I am here for, how I can contribute to something beautiful. I want to have that moment you described!"

Grandpa placed one hand on her cheek and squeezed the one he held. "That moment will come when it's your time, princess. You can't foresee it or force it. It will arrive unexpectedly, and its power will be undeniable. However, even then, it might take some time before you fully grasp its true meaning, and years may pass before you can accept it and appreciate it."

"Is there only one of these moments in a person's entire life?"

Grandpa contemplated. "No, it doesn't have to be just one. You may very well have several such moments throughout your life. But that initial and genuine moment of crystal clarity, I believe that only happens once. Because after that, you gain confidence, and your life undergoes a transformation."

"This really is deep stuff, and I'll admit I'm not sure I get it all or at least not yet." said Lisa.

———

"For what it's worth, I'm not sure any of us 'get it all' and certainly not at once, but it is a lot to think about." Grandpa wiped his hand over his face and looked away.

Lisa noticed. "And, it's time for a quick break. I am off to update my journal."

"Yes! How about we meet back here in an hour or so. I have a video I think you'll find interesting. What say you?"

"To the movies with Grandpa it is."

And I'm guessing it won't be a comedy.

Ω *Conflicted* Ω

Grandpa retreated to the sanctuary of his bedroom, softly closing the door behind him. There, perched on the edge of the bed, he surrendered to his reflections, cradling his head in weathered hands.

Through tears, he quietly whispered, "I miss you so much, honey. Your voice, your warmth, now absent, leaves an aching void. How am I to guide Lisa when I am adrift in my own turmoil? The past is so hard to release and re-release. I know this. I know how. Yet I can't, and here I am in the present with it present."

Grandpa's voice trembled as he continued, "The wrongs I've done to you, to our son, weigh heavily on me. I *know* guilt and fear are the twin destroyers. Yet I cannot help but feel guilty, not being able to release or resolve, and fear the day it will all be brought to light. I fear moving on. 'To acknowledge is the first step to address it,' my own teachers would say. But—I struggle. I struggle with my own reflection."

Clutching the quilt, a tapestry of memories lovingly crafted by her hands, he felt her presence linger where she once lay beside him. Drawing in a deep, steadying breath, he mustered a resolve, whispering, "Embrace life; move forward with confidence. In the grand tapestry of time, each thread has its place, together revealing a pattern of profound beauty and meaning."

He opened his eyes and looked up. "I beseech you. Let whatever must unfold do so now. Do not spare me, I deserve it. Grant me strength. Illuminate my path. For Lisa, for the world she is about to inherit."

Ω

In her attic room, Lisa wrote in her journal, unaware that Grandpa was beginning to write a new script for his life. Each, in their separate efforts, were joining to bring forth a grander inheritance of learning, loving and growing.

Journal: The Lisa Project:
The Secret of Life-Day 3-continued...

Grandpa and I are going to watch a video soon, but I have to write down things before I forget!

I looked up the Dutch poet and scholar, Willem Bilderdijk, because Grandpa quoted him as "positing" that there are three moments:

The past, which is the past;
The now, which is the present;
And the future, which is what will be.

Paraphrase: the past is gone, but it has shaped the present. It now influences what lies ahead. Everything that has transpired in your life seems to form a straight line, a narrative, a purpose.

Nothing happens without reason. It all makes sense. The moment you realize this in the present, both the past and the present change, and then your perception of the future transforms immediately as well.

I am the continuous connection between the past and the future. In the present moment, I always have the choice to alter my thoughts about something. By doing so, I can shape your future.

I asked Grandpa to write his motto down for me: embrace and live life with confidence, knowing that eventually, everything will make sense and fall into place.

Everyone's life has it: your destiny, your purpose, the goal of your life. Once you see it, your life and future gain significance, and you will know why you're alive, why you're here, what your life is about.

The best part of the day so far: grandpa told me when I was born, I gave his life meaning and purpose.

I cried a little. I think he did too.

CHAPTER 9 | The Brain's Sandpit

Life's Patterns

Grandpa found Lisa already in front of the television, the screen dark as she was lost in a book. He watched her quietly for a minute before saying, "You are going to turn into a book, princess."

"Nothing better to transport a person to the past, present and future—barring any apocalyptic—"

"Okay, you're ribbing me, but you'll see one day. For now, ready to watch this mini-movie? It's a documentary of sorts." He flipped the TV on and pressed start on the remote.

On the screen, Lisa saw three children, slightly younger than herself, playing in front of thatched huts with a few tin cans and a broken ball as their makeshift football. Surprisingly, their modest surroundings didn't dampen their spirits as they burst into laughter. Eventually, they ventured into what seemed like a forest but looked more like a jungle.

"That's a tropical rainforest," Grandpa informed Lisa.

The children maneuvered effortlessly, running and jumping through the dense forest. They settled on a fallen tree trunk at a clearing. One of the girls grabbed a long branch and started poking a hole in the trunk. Curiously, the other two watched, waiting for something to emerge.

Lisa let out a scream as the first glimpse of furry legs belonging to a large black spider. As the children were playfully teasing the spider, Lisa covered her eyes, "You didn't mention it was a shocker, Grandpa."

"It will soon prove a point that fear is relative. Keep watching."

As the video continued, the large black spider emerged completely, and the children began tapping it with sticks, laughing with delight. It was obvious that they considered the spider a toy.

"They are actually playing with that thing and … Oh gross!" Lisa yelped as one of the boys impaled the spider with a sharp branch, pinning it to the ground. After a minute, the spider's wooly legs grew still and the boy holding the stick hoisted in the air. The scene then cuts—to a village and a handful of children around a fire, each holding a stick over it, a spider roasting at the end.

Grandpa stopped the video before the 'meal' started. "Looks like they had a good hunt today," he said. "Thought I'd spare you the next bite—"

"Stop! Definitely not my kind of marshmallow roast."

"Mine either. That BBQ would require hot dogs, buns, corn on the cob, potato salad, not just roasted spider—not even spider soup."

"Sick."

"To us. To them, it's a delicacy. Dinner. It was probably all they ate." Grandpa shut off the TV.

"And the moral of the story is …? Because I know you showed me this for a reason."

"Of course I did! What you witnessed were a couple of boys fearlessly playing with the very thing you're scared of. To them, the spider represents joy and goodness—fun and food. They were raised in an environment where it's considered normal. This example illustrates that if you had grown up in that same place, you wouldn't fear spiders," Grandpa explained. "You'd still need food. That simple need connects us to them. A human need is food. You're connected to the spider too."

"I highly doubt that."

"Have you ever wondered about the life of a spider? For instance, did you ever consider how a spider's heart is beating?"

Lisa looked bewildered. "Does a spider even have a heart?"

"Of course, almost all animals have a heart. The spider in this video has a heart in its abdomen that beats just like yours, fueled by the energy of the universe. Remember our discussion about vibrations? It's the source of all life and everything that exists. So, the next time you encounter a spider, you might want to remember that you both possess a heart, and your hearts beat through the same energy. In a way, you're *connected* to each other," Grandpa explained.

"I think I understand, but I don't want to see a spider for a while."

"Come on, let's go outside. I have another point to make and I want to explain something fascinating to you."

Ω

Grandpa led Lisa to the garden to stand before the old tractor tire sandbox. It was still lopsided, sloping with the ground below. The metal awning still sat over it and had provided protection from weather and wind when she played outdoors as a little girl.

"Take a look," Grandpa said. "You can see that the sand is flat. Imagine this sand represents your brain when you were a baby. When you're born, a large part of your brain is like this pristine sand," Grandpa explained.

"I'm sure you have a point?"

Grandpa picked up a watering can and let a small stream of water trickle onto the sand at the top end of the sandbox. The water formed a meandering stream, flowing downward. They watched it trickle and stop. Then Grandpa poured more of the water from the can, starting at the same point at the top. A winding channel formed in the sand, twisting left and right following the same path until it reached the bottom.

"What do you think will happen if I pour more of the water?" he asked.

"It looks like it will follow the same path as the river the other water created," Lisa replied.

"Let's watch." Grandpa poured and the water indeed followed the pre-existing winding stream. "Notice how the river becomes deeper. With each successive pour, the river grows wider and deeper. The water has fewer opportunities to deviate from the river and create a new channel."

Lisa nodded. "You mentioned a baby's brain. Is that what you're trying to explain?"

"Exactly! For a baby, every new experience is a first. We all start with a blank canvas so to speak, and each experience creates a similar kind of river channel in the brain—a connection between different parts of the brain. Repeating those experiences causes the water to flow through the same channel again, deepening it. Do you understand?" Grandpa asked.

"I think I do."

"Another example: let's consider smiling. When a baby smiles at someone, they smile back. Every time—well almost every time—because the baby perceives this as a positive response. Thus, the baby learns that when they smile, others will smile in return. In a way, others become their mirror."

"So, every time a baby smiles and someone smiles back, that channel in the brain gets deeper and wider?" Lisa asked.

"Exactly! Babies are incredibly adaptable and learn quickly. As you grow older, most of these channels become deeper and the sand becomes more compact, making it harder to change."

"So, at a certain age, it becomes difficult to do things differently?" Lisa wondered.

"It's not always so absolute, but essentially, yes. It's harder to break established patterns and feelings as you age. That's why children and young people can deal with change much more easily than older people."

"Then it makes sense to establish good patterns—or habits—early."

"Yes, you need to remember that habits and emotions form through repetition. As we know, there are some habits, which are not so good. So, how can you *break* this pattern? Let's say you've been smoking cigarettes for twenty years. It has become deeply ingrained in your life. But now, you want to quit because you're increasingly aware of the harm it causes. How do you go about it?" Grandpa inquired.

"I'm not sure if this is right, but I think you have to make a conscious decision to do things differently? You have to want to change or quit smoking in this example."

"That's very astute," Grandpa praised. "Indeed, you must consciously choose to change. Then, you need to redirect the flow, just like this."

Grandpa poured more of the water in the same spot but placed his hand in the sand to divert the stream. The water followed a new path, bypassing the existing channel. "If I keep my hand there long enough, a small barrier will form—a levee. The water will naturally flow in the new direction, creating a new feeling or habit. But, as you said, it requires a conscious decision. It requires you to develop new habits, and that takes both time and discipline."

Grandpa walked over to a bucket resting beside the garden. It was filled with recent rainwater. Returning to Lisa he said, "There's also another possibility—a significant experience that leaves a lasting impression. It could be something overwhelmingly frightening or a sudden realization that hits you like a bolt of lightning." He emptied the bucket over the sandbox all at once. "What do you see now?"

Lisa observed that all the old channels had disappeared, replaced by a single new one. "There's only one river now. It's larger and deeper."

"And what do you think will happen if we pour water slowly from another can?"

"The water will follow the new channel."

"Correct. Suppose this result was triggered by a terrifying event. For instance, imagine you had a severe car accident and spent a month in the hospital as a result. Once you've fully recovered, you get back behind the wheel. What do you think will happen?" Grandpa asked.

"You might feel afraid to drive, fearing another accident."

"Yes, your experience of driving might have radically changed. Do you think a conscious decision can alter how you feel in such a situation?" Grandpa probed.

Lisa gazed at the sandbox, "I don't think so. Regardless of where you pour the water, the channel is so wide that the current won't run off elsewhere. It feels like you're stuck."

"Fortunately, there are still possibilities, though they become more challenging. This is what people who have experienced trauma go through, as well as those dealing with constant stress or burnout. Sadly, more and more people in our society are facing this. Do you see how this applies to fear too? Like your fear of spiders?"

"I see. So, my fear of spiders originated somewhere and created a deep channel. Even though I learned the value of some spiders, my first reaction in seeing that giant one in the video was to freak out. I reverted to my old reactions, following the wide and deep channel."

"Well said. Now, you understand how challenging it is to overcome deep-seated fears."

"And since some people, like Mom, have had more experiences to deepen a habit or a way of thinking or doing things, it's harder for her to change."

"That's right, but there's also a positive variant. You may gain an insight that turns everything in your life upside down. Your life has been the same for years, and suddenly you hear an inner voice that urges you to follow your heart, to do what you really think is important in this life now. You feel that voice is right, so you say goodbye to everything that you thought was very important for years. Status, money, your job, possessions, maybe even your relationships. This is such a huge moment that you, as the ball on the beam, look around and behind you, and for the first time see that everything in your life is a straight line until today—or leading up to today."

"Now, I get your motto more. You said something like, '*Embrace life confidently knowing things will make sense and fall into place.*'"

"Good memory and good paraphrase." Grandpa bowed his head. "Know, however, that those sudden moments are perhaps not as frequent. In real life, research shows that significant transformations rarely happen after the age of forty-five. It's not impossible, but it's less common. That's why people often experience a midlife crisis between the ages of thirty-five and forty-five, realizing that time is running out. It's now or never. Do you know what a midlife crisis is?"

Lisa nodded. "I think that's when men buy a motorcycle or a sports car, and they want to look younger."

Grandpa laughed. "Yes, that's a common stereotype, but women can also experience such a crisis, and it can happen at a younger age too. It's a way of shaking up deeply ingrained patterns—the river channels. The word 'crisis' sounds negative in our language, but you can also regard it as a gift. Originally it means 'moment of truth'—a time when a decision with significant consequences must be made, with a major impact on the future."

They moved together toward the house. "I think I have it, Grandpa. To connect the sandbox to the painting—you wanted me to learn that *the future is shaped by the present and the past and that our conscious choices impact the path we follow.*"

He draped his arm around her shoulder, "Have I told you how amazing you are lately?"

"Well, it seems like with all our conversations, things just seem easier to see and say. Clearer." Lisa hugged his waist. "You can tell me I'm amazing again, and again, and—"

"All right, all right. Tomorrow, shall we take a glimpse into the past?"

Tomorrow is the future—which we are shaping, right now.

Journal: The Lisa Project:
The Secret of Life—Day 3...my evening notes:

At my old sandbox, I learned about patterns and habits. Grandpa poured water into the sand, and it flowed to create a river or a channel. This demonstrated that we all start with a blank canvas and each experience we have creates a kind of river channel in the brain, a connection between different parts of the brain.

Repeating those experiences causes the channel to deepen. This forms how we look at things, like my fear of spiders. The more I have an experience of fear, the harder it is to change that.

Older people have deeper 'channels' sometimes making it harder to change. Younger people may adapt more easily. (Note to self: Try to create good channels early in my life!)

<u>Habits and emotions form through repetition.</u> Some habits are bad habits and hard to break. It's hard to get unstuck. We have to make a conscious decision to do things differently. You have to want to change. Then, you need to redirect the flow. It takes time and discipline.

Some experiences are so strong—like a lightning bolt—and they turn your life upside down. You go from the same to different—fast. This can happen with a traumatic experience or a really good one that shifts your way of seeing the world and being in it.

The word 'crisis' is sometimes perceived as negative, but it can be a gift. It means 'moment of truth' when a key decision is made that may majorly impact your future.

I learned that the future is shaped by the present and the past and that our conscious choices impact the path we follow.

My plan is to be really conscious about my choices. I really want to create a positive path. And soon, I hope that leads to my understanding of my purpose.

I wonder what my destiny is?

THE LISA PROJECT:
The Secret of Life

Day 4

CHAPTER 10 | Written Wisdom

Yesterday, Today, and…?

Grandpa's study—or library—was spacious, three of the walls completely lined with bookcases, overflowing with books. The fourth 'wall' was floor to ceiling windows facing the pond. This was Grandpa's domain, and Lisa's favorite place. It carried the scent of wood and aged paper. Lisa gazed at the multitude of books in awe. Some bookcases housed only old books with worn brown covers, while others were organized by genre. In the center of the room stood an antique desk with a storied presence. On it lay a decorative old quill and parchment.

"Have you read all these books, Grandpa?"

Grandpa nodded. "Some of them I've read multiple times because I couldn't grasp their meaning on the first attempt."

"Why do you have so many? I mean, what do they contain?"

"You could say these books hold a wealth of wisdom. They delve into topics like philosophy, religion, history, spirituality, astrology, and paranormal phenomena."

"Sounds complicated. Wouldn't you rather read a story?"

"Stories offer distraction and entertainment, and we can learn a great deal from them. That's perfectly fine. But throughout my life, I've been plagued by questions about existence: *Why are we here? Who are we? Who am I? Why must we face death?*

"If you genuinely want to comprehend these matters, you need to read beyond just stories. These books have helped shape and expand my worldview. It was primarily through them that I uncovered the secret of life," Grandpa explained.

"Really? So, if I read all these books, will I discover the secret too?"

Grandpa shook his head. "A secret contained within a book cannot be easily unveiled. You need your own life experiences for that and time. Moreover, you may not be able to read many of these books. They are too antiquated, and you're accustomed to a completely different writing style. However, that's precisely why we're undertaking this project. I'm introducing you to the secret in a different manner. Whether you uncover it or not will depend entirely on you."

Lisa was disappointed. "Are you saying that I might not even learn the secret?"

Grandpa nodded. "If the outcome were certain, why bother with the effort? But when nothing is certain, anything becomes possible."

"Sounds like a riddle." Lisa went over to where he sat at his desk. "I *will* discover the secret," she declared, "nothing can hinder me."

"Excellent! And that determination brings you one step closer to the secret. So, let's raise the stakes!

"Now, I'd like you to peruse the books in all these cabinets. Just scan through the titles and select five that captivate your interest or pique your curiosity. Then bring those books downstairs, and we'll discuss them. This way, you'll effectively have five book reviews today. I'll leave you to it." Grandpa left the room.

Lisa put her hands on her hips and stared after him. "Five book reviews? I haven't done that in five years of school," she muttered.

But—I said I would, and I will. I will discover the secret of life.

I've been entrusted with a mission of exploration.

She commenced with the first bookcase, examining the titles of the books it housed, shelf by shelf: *The Secret Doctrine, The Geometry of Creation, Bhagavad Gita, The End of Time* and interestingly, an aged copy of the *King James Bible.*

When she finished inspecting the last shelf, overwhelm set in—as did the realization this could take all day! Since she was unfamiliar with the titles or their wide-ranging subject matter, it was hard to know where to begin with such an arduous task but she *had* accepted the mission. She walked over to the desk, settled into the chair, and repositioned it to gain a comprehensive view of the library.

She picked up the quill, which was a replica, and put it down. She opened her journal to the next blank page and said, "I'm no scribe, but I do have my own version of pen and parchment."

She smiled as she wrote:

What do I love about books?

Words—I love words. Phrases that inspire me too.

I love the idea of learning something I can apply.

I'm interested in why stuff happens.

Then, she raised her head and as if by some inexplicable force, a book caught her attention. Lisa rose and approached a thick, blue book, and upon glimpsing the gold-embossed title, she removed it and continued to scan the shelves. Her fingers quickly land on four more books with appealing titles, making her collection of five. Happy with herself, she went to find Grandpa.

Ω *Titles and Tomes* Ω

Discovering him at the dining room table with his head bowed to his own book, Lisa made a production of placing the books in front of him and coquettishly sat down to open her journal.

Grandpa's eyes flickered to the journal. "I see that you are ready to take good notes." He then looked at her selections …

"Excellent choices. How did you manage to do it so swiftly?"

"I found the words and the topics that interested me. Sort of simple, but I was just drawn to each of these somehow. I didn't overthink it. Trusted my gut."

"Nicely done. You added your own touch to my assignment, and that was the only way you could have found these books. Let's examine them." He took off his reading glasses and looked at her, "First we have *A Course in Miracles*.[2] Now this is an extensive tome that essentially posits that life, our world—or the universe—is merely a dream. We all dream of being here, in a world rife with pain and sorrow, but in reality, we are safely asleep with God."

Lisa made a face. "I know nothing about God. Mom says we're atheists, and God doesn't exist."

"If we substituted the word 'God' with 'the source of all life' or 'the vibration encompassing this world and beyond,' would it sound more agreeable to you?" Grandpa proposed.

Lisa allowed those words to sink in.

Yes, calling it a source works, and I'm not sure I'm actually opposed to the word God.

She wrote that down.

"Okay, as I said, this book posits that we exist in a dream from which we seem unable to awaken. We endure death, reincarnation, and find ourselves trapped in an endless, futile cycle. The solution lies in perceiving the world and our lives as a dream, as a fantasy. Consequently, we need not fear or grow incensed about the actions of

---

others because none of it is real either. Once you master this art, you no longer need to be reborn in this realm, and you can escape what this book deems *an insane place*," Grandpa explained.

Lisa shook her head. "I don't quite grasp it. So, it claims we live to ensure that we no longer have to live—or live again?"

Grandpa regarded her with surprise. "That's a powerful interpretation! But I may have oversimplified in my summary. The book also contains nuggets of wisdom, such as ..." He flipped through pages and stopped. "Here we go, this one, *'Nothing real can be threatened. Nothing unreal exists. Herein lies the peace of God.'* It asserts that fear is never necessary because life itself is merely a dream. Moreover, it's considered a miracle if someone can shift their perspective from fear to love, altering their perception of the world."

"I think I'm going to need more than a book review. I need to read it."

"Good idea. This is one I've read more than once. Okay, moving on ... Interesting that you chose *Conversations with God: An Uncommon Dialogue*.[3] This book aligns well with this notion that it's a miracle if someone can shift their perspective from fear to love, altering their perception of the world. Yes, that's right, God makes another appearance. The intriguing aspect of these two books is that they appear to contradict each other entirely. This book is essentially a dialogue between the author and a voice he claims to have heard. He contemplates why we exist and what our purpose on Earth entails. In response, the voice asserts that the world is like a playground, with every person embodying a fragment of God. In this playground, we can experience and remember our divine nature."

Lisa interjected, "And yet, we saw part of the news—real or not, it was sad. How does the book explain the abundance of pain in this world?"

"Great question. The author also queries this. The voice maintains that everything in the world is perfect, every occurrence possesses meaning. Pain is indispensable for growth, yet suffering is optional—not essential. The crux of the matter lies in each individual recognizing the divine essence within themselves, within others, and within the entirety of the world. Once you grasp that, suffering dissipates."

"So, what exactly is the contradiction between these books?"

"The first book suggests that the world is a mistake, an insane place where we ought *not* to linger longer than necessary. It serves as a guide for an escape route, a means to avoid returning here. Conversely, the second book posits that the world is intentional and perfect, a realm meant for us to experience and remember our own divinity. Which one resonates with you more?" Grandpa asked.

Lisa contemplated for a moment. "I do understand the perspective of the first book. The world appears far from perfect with all the calamities, violence, and suffering. However, as you mentioned the day before yesterday, perhaps it only appears so bad because the media predominantly highlights such aspects. So, maybe it's not as terrible as it seems. The second book appeals to me more. I prefer perceiving the world as a beautiful, flawless place, and I wouldn't mind being divine."

"Even though you have limited knowledge of God?" Grandpa winked with a smile.

"Yes, it's simply not part of my upbringing, but I appreciate the concept of 'the source of life.' By the way, you mentioned the first book provides guidance on avoiding having to be reborn. I don't quite grasp that," Lisa admitted.

"That pertains to the concept of reincarnation. You are not solely your physical body, and your existence will never cease. You experienced a glimpse of that in the Zen Den's hot tub. Reincarnation suggests that your soul is eternal, and after death, you will eventually be reborn into a new body. It also means that you have lived through past lives prior to this one."

Lisa nodded. "This morning at the Zen Den, I sensed that I am more than just my body. But when you put it that way, I still find it challenging to understand because it raises numerous questions. How is all of this possible, who was I in past lives, and why don't I remember them?"

Grandpa placed his hand on her arm. "We'll delve into these matters in detail during a future project. For now, try to trust your intuition from your experience of 'floating.' *Feeling holds more power than reasoning.* As for reasoning, you've indicated what books resonate with you the most. But which of these two books do you consider to be right?"

Lisa remained silent, reflecting on one of day one's lessons. "Is it similar to the bicycle situation? You could see it in your mind's eye, but I could not from my vantage point. Can both books be right, depending on one's perspective?"

"Yet again, very astute. If you perceive this world as hell, you will likely consider the first book as true and find numerous insights to alleviate anxiety. However, the second book might cause you to learn to view everything that unfolds as perfect and divine. Both books emphasize that you always have only one choice."

"And what is that choice?"

"It is the choice between fear and love," Grandpa replied.

"That seems like it is a simple choice."

"*Deceptively* simple. We—people—often just don't consciously realize we have that choice. From now on, you can apply it to any situation in your life: do I choose fear, or do I choose love?"

"Can I also choose sadness, anger, or something completely different?" Lisa asked.

"Of course, you can choose any emotion you desire, but all other emotions stem from the fundamental choice between fear and love. Fear promotes exclusion and stands in opposition to love, which encompasses inclusiveness. In perfect love, fear ceases to exist. Fear is merely a lack of love. Actions such as anger and aggression arise from this absence of love, from fear of scarcity. Do you follow?"

"I do, in concept, and I think I may understand Mom a little better."

Grandpa smiled, "And yourself, I hope. Now, let's move on to the third book, *The Alchemist*.[4] It's rather slim compared to the others, isn't it? Misleading as it is chalked full of good stuff. *The Alchemist* is one of my favorites."

"What exactly is an alchemist?"

"An alchemist is someone who endeavors to transmute base materials into gold. It's a metaphor for seeking to enhance life's beauty. The alchemist quests for the ultimate substance, the philosopher's stone. With that stone, one could transform everything into gold, heal all ailments, and even attain immortality. This book tells a tale set in ancient times, revolving around a young shepherd who yearns to explore the world. He departs his hometown and embarks on a journey, driven by a dream of a hidden treasure. Along his odyssey, he encounters various individuals who impart wisdom about life and the world. He scours far and wide for his treasure, only to discover in the end that the treasure has always been buried in the very village where he originated, right where he slept beside his flock of sheep."

"And what's the message behind it? Nutshell it for me, Grandpa."

"The crucial message is that countless individuals spend a significant portion of their lives pursuing something external, believing it will bring them happiness: wealth, status, recognition, power, and the like. They assume that by possessing these things, they comprehend the world and life itself. They feel in control. However, the genuine treasure lies not outside but within oneself."

Lisa stopped him, "But—wouldn't the pursuit of money, status, and power create the experiences a person needs to have to understand that—to understand that the treasure is within? I mean, you mentioned to me an hour ago, that you—or people—wouldn't exert effort if we already knew the outcome is certain."

"You're right. It's tough to tell people that the stuff we are often defined by isn't the most valuable. Money, success, status, and power hold great significance in our world. Without money, survival becomes arduous. Without success, one is deemed a failure. Social and economic status indicates the extent of achievements, and power empowers one to dominate others. All four—money, success, status, and power—can become addictive individually, and collectively they are interlinked, mutually reinforcing one another."

Grandpa continued, "Power grants the ability to acquire wealth and success. Money empowers individuals to enact their desires. That's why the super-rich or the powerful can be dangerous. With great power, the world bends to their will. They can impose their desires upon the world and countless individuals. This manifests in a coercive manner, infringing upon the free will bestowed upon humanity, constituting a violation of the greatest gift bestowed by the source of life."

Lisa added, "The greatest gift is free will."

"And that brings us to this little book, *The Secret*,[5]" Grandpa said.

"I couldn't resist it. This book called out to me. Given our project goal is to uncover the secret of life, I figured it might have the answer," Lisa grinned.

"No short cuts. However, it does lift the veil slightly. It revolves around the *law of attraction*. According to this law, you can draw everything you desire to yourself through your thoughts. This book essentially asserts that in life, you can possess and become anything you want. You merely need to envision it, believe it has already been achieved, and act as if it's already yours. This is how you attract it," Grandpa explained.

"So, by simply thinking I can attain or become anything?" Lisa asked, astounded.

"Yes, it sounds effortless, doesn't it? Much like that philosopher's stone in *The Alchemist*. By doing so—by simply thinking—you exert influence over the world. After all, you can possess and become anything you desire. This form of energy is positive since it aligns with the fundamental structure of the universe. The key message is

---

that through your thoughts alone, you can impact the world beyond yourself. It's called manifesting."

"But isn't everyone always manifesting? Don't we always experience certain emotions?" Lisa wondered.

"In most individuals, their emotions operate unconsciously, and thus their manifestations remain unconscious as well. Many people are oblivious to what they unconsciously manifest, and often, fear-based emotions dominate, particularly in our western world.

"Have I ever told you about how my father died?"

Lisa shook her head.

"I actually believe it began with his own mother—my grandmother. She was a strange or troubled character\. She was the perfect example of loving kindness to the outside world, but within the four walls of her home, she wasn't nice. It seemed that from time-to-time straight evil would enter her. At least, that was what my father and my aunts told me.

"Then, at quite a young age, she died of cancer. It was September 4th, a year before I was born.

"My father lived his whole life afraid he, too, would die of cancer. As far as I remember, this fear was omnipresent for him, though he refused to see a doctor for any pain or ailment to find out facts or dispel his own fiction. Luckily, he had no critical need for doctors until he retired.

"From that moment on, he started to delve into the past, and at the same time, he lost all interest in real life. I don't know what caused it, but soon after, his body started to fall out and act crazy. He had to be taken to the hospital where he was finally diagnosed with a lethal form of cancer. His lifelong fear became reality. He deteriorated quickly and died eventually—on the 4th of September—the same date as his mother. Isn't that a powerful example of unconscious manifesting?"

Lisa nodded. "It's almost as if there was something passed on from your grandmother to your dad."

"That has been my notion as well. But I never gave it more attention."

"Couldn't people just say it was a coincidence that they died on the same day?"

"Sure, and I think most might. At the same time, being aware—conscious of—our thoughts, becomes much more important when we consider the possible outcomes."

"It's going to make me think twice when I start spiraling into negative thinking."

Grandpa nodded his approval. "For now, let's proceed to the final book: *Through the Looking Glass*.[6] It's remarkable that you chose this from the shelf, and especially since you just mentioned spiraling. You know the power of going down that veritable rabbit hole."

"Yes, a few days ago, I watched the movie *Alice in Wonderland*. But isn't this just a nice story? Is there a deeper meaning behind it?" Lisa inquired.

"You might be surprised," Grandpa responded. "Both the book and the movie depict an alternative world into which Alice ventures. Through her encounters in that world, she learns valuable lessons about herself. Lewis Carroll, the author, is a master. For now, I won't divulge any further details, but with this book and the movie, *Alice in Wonderland*, you've come closest to the secret of life."

Lisa's eyes widened. "Does this mean we're nearing the end of the project?"

Grandpa shook his head. "Not yet. It's like the young shepherd in *The Alchemist*. The secret is, metaphorically speaking, right before you on the table, but you don't see it. Not yet."

Lisa's face momentarily fell, and she put her head on the table dramatically.

"Princess? All okay?"

She turned her face, cheek on her hands, "Yes, but I need a break."

Grandpa laughed. "Info overload! No problem, my dear. Go outside and enjoy yourself. Frank mentioned yesterday that his nephew was visiting. I think he's around your age. Maybe you can find him."

CHAPTER 11 | The Cause Of It All

The Power to Change

Grandpa was busy preparing dinner in the kitchen when he heard the screen door slam.

Lisa entered from the porch tears streaming down her face.

"What's the matter? What happened to you?" He wiped his hands on his apron and moved in.

"Frank's stupid nephew, Jacob, that's what happened!" Lisa sniffed and pulled back to look up at Grandpa. "He said all sorts of dumb things. He was bragging about himself and his rich grandparents, and then he started insulting you. He called you a lazy man and said a real farmer should be actually farming to live here. I got so mad. I told him he was wrong, and then he pointed out my bruises on my cheek from my fall in the barn and then he called me an ugly, fat, city girl!"

Lisa flopped into a chair and Grandpa grabbed a Kleenex box. He waited silently for her to continue.

"I was so mad, Grandpa. I punched him in the gut."

"Did he strike you?"

"No, too busy doubled over."

Grandpa cleared his throat unsure whether to be angry, remembering she was only thirteen. "So you hit a boy? You hit Jacob? Lisa, that's not good. That's a serious thing and a knee jerk response!"

"Well! He called *you* names and then *me*! He poked fun at my face. He had it coming. I had to show that bully—"

Grandpa held up his hand to stop her. "Hold on, hold on. Before you say things you may not mean, first things first. You are by no means ugly, and your scrapes from that 'accidental fall' are barely visible. And you are not fat, but who cares if you were."

"Really? Then why did he say that?"

"He might need glasses," he teased. "You're the most beautiful girl I know."

"You're only saying that because you're my grandpa. It's sweet of you, but maybe I really am ugly."

"I know you know that's not true. Jacob was just trying to hit you where it really hurts. He struck out at your family—me. Not to worry about that though. I am aware of his grandparents' belief that I'm just a lazy, yoga wu-wu man who shouldn't live here. They see Frank who is much younger than me and at a different place in his life working hard on the land every day. The boy is simply imitating what he's heard. He tried to hurt you with his words, and unfortunately, it worked."

"He's still an idiot."

"Maybe. But shift your perspective. You can choose how you decide to feel. I mean, what do you think of me saying 你的衣服很丑 to you?"

Lisa looked at him blankly. "What did you say? I don't—"

"你的衣服很丑," Grandpa repeated, scrunching up his face.

Lisa laughed. "I have no idea what that means, but it sounds funny, and you look funny."

"Do you see now that you can also laugh when someone says something mean to you?"

"I don't get it."

"Exactly. You didn't understand what I said. I said in Chinese, '*Those are some ugly clothes you're wearing.*'"

Lisa stared at her grandfather but before she could say anything he continued. "Of course, I don't mean it. Your clothes are fine. I just wanted to show you that you could laugh at it initially when you didn't understand. You see, it doesn't affect you or hurt you if it doesn't register in your brain. If you don't allow it to."

"But what's your point? Should I pretend not to understand when someone says something mean to me?"

"That's not necessarily the only approach. You can also reverse it. By accepting that every situation starts with *you*. If *you* weren't there at that moment, it wouldn't be an issue for *you*, would it? *You* allow yourself to be a part of it. Something happened that affected *you*, that hurt you, and that's why *you* got involved."

He continued, "When you reverse it, you must learn *not* to see yourself as a victim or a part of the situation, but as the cause of it. You caused it. Even if you didn't think you caused it, you did. *By acknowledging that you caused it, you have the power to change it. If you have the power to cause it, you can also change it, and what you change is your reaction to it.* If you *point* to the other person as the cause of the situation, nothing will change."

Lisa felt confused. "So, are you saying that all the nasty things that boy said to me are my fault?"

"Hold on, I said cause, not blame."

"What's the difference?"

"A cause is neutral, but blame is a judgment. If you look at the situation and yourself without judgment, you can change it."

"Well, how do you explain that to someone who has been abused, for example?" Lisa asked.

"That's an extreme." Grandpa crossed his arms and stared at her intently. "It's also a little out of the blue. Why would you specifically ask about that topic at your age?"

"One of Mom's close friends was attacked last year, almost abused. Mom wanted me to understand and be cautious. There are boys in my class who are two or three years older than me, you know."

Grandpa took a deep breath and blew it out. He gestured for her to follow him to the living room where he pointed to the piano and waited for her to sit. "You're still having piano lessons, right?" Grandpa picked up a music book, opened it, and placed it in front of her.

She looked at him questioningly.

"Play it, please," he said.

Surprised, Lisa stared at the complex arrangement of tiny black notes. "This is too complicated, Grandpa. I can read sheet music, but this is super difficult."

"I understand, princess. You can't expect to play the piano at an advanced level right away. So, don't expect to understand all topics instantly either. If you want to comprehend how the secret of life works, you must start with the basics, with simple and clear situations. Once you understand those, you can tackle more complex issues.

"Abuse is something terrible and repulsive, and it should never happen. You can never tell someone who has been abused that they caused it. You can never even imply that someone caused something to happen to them. Passing judgment on others is something you stop doing once you know the secret."

"I get the point. One step at a time."

"Yes, and one situation at a time. We simply don't understand everything or ourselves all at once or just once for that matter." Grandpa closed his eyes and sighed before continuing. "Let's return to your situation with Frank's nephew. Consider that you are the cause, and you can change it. How will you do that?"

Lisa shrugged.

"Well, you think about it, and I'll get back to preparing dinner."

After a few minutes, Grandpa heard Lisa leaving through the front door. He smiled.

Ω

Lisa found Jacob throwing stones into the stream. She observed from a distance and noticed that he kept wiping his face with his shirt sleeve. Was he actually crying?

I didn't think I hit him that hard.

A small voice inside her then whispered, *Maybe it wasn't the physical punch that hurt.*

"Jacob?"

He turned around slowly, not startled at her voice or her standing there. His shoulders were slumped. "You are the first person I've talked to around here and look how that turned out. I was sent here for some *nature* and quiet. This place is sort of extreme."

Lisa stood straighter and put her hands on her hips, a smile spreading across her face. *Maybe he isn't so bad. Maybe we have more in common than we think.* "Yeah? Well, I guess you got all your loudness out at once. Also, guess you've never been in the same room with Grandpa—or Grandpa and Frank! Sometimes I'd like some peace."

Jacob walked toward her and handed her a stone. "Guess we pick and fight our battles in different ways."

Lisa nodded and quietly said, "So said the sage."

"Who's that?"

She elbowed him. "Come on. We'll make our own noise!"

Ω

After dessert, Grandpa turned to their guest at the table. "Well, Jacob, I think it's time for you to head back to your uncle's place. It was nice of Frank to loan you to us for an evening. Lisa and I still have some things to discuss for our project, and then we'll be turning in early."

"Yeah, Lisa told me about your project. That's pretty cool. But you go to bed this early?"

Grandpa nodded. "When you go to bed early, you can have a fantastic night's sleep and wake up early to get started on creating a great day. What time do you usually go to bed?"

"I don't know, around eleven."

"And do you wake up at seven?"

Jacob looked shocked. "No, not on weekends or during the summer. Usually around nine or nine-thirty. If I have school, then yes, but I'm always glad when the weekend arrives."

"What do you usually do at night?"

"Just watch some videos and play on my phone, that sort of thing."

Grandpa grinned. "Next time you're here, maybe I'll lend you a book. In addition to our debrief for the day, Lisa still has some homework." Grandpa pointed to her journal. As he did so, he didn't miss the looks or eye rolls exchanged between Jacob and Lisa.

"That's your cue. I'll see you out." Lisa walked Jacob to the door.

Ω

As she returned to the living room, Grandpa started in, "So did you notice that he has a little crush on you?"

Lisa blushed. "Him? Have a crush on me? This afternoon, he called me ugly and fat!"

"Boys can do strange things when they like a girl."

"Yeah, well, he goes home in the morning. Maybe we'll hang out next time."

"That would be nice, but tell me, what did you do? How'd he end up at our dinner table?"

Lisa sat down once more. "Well, I thought about what you said, and I gave it a try. I walked out to find him. Turns out he was feeling bad too. I apologized for my reaction and for hitting him. I also told him it had nothing to do with him, but I just wanted to let him know. Then I said that I thought he was nice, even though he called me fat and ugly."

"Well done! How did it feel?"

"It felt really good, actually. It sort of cleansed me, as you would say. I caused the problem, but it wasn't my fault, and then I resolved it. It didn't matter what he would do or say. For me, it was over. But then he was genuinely surprised and asked me if I wanted to come in. We played with Little Wolf, had lemonade, and talked for a while. We even played some of his video games, and then I asked if he could come over and have dinner with us. I invited Frank too, but he said he'd better catch up on some paperwork."

"Do you see how you completely changed the situation by accepting responsibility? And once again, you were the cause, in a good way!"

Lisa smirked. "Yeah, I admit it might have felt good to punch him—and it felt pretty good to see his shock when I said I was sorry. I think I knocked the wind out of him twice!"

Grandpa laughed. "Probably best to let the young man catch his breath, and speaking of breath, that's how we are going to start our day tomorrow."

"Come again?"

"Breathing."

"Yeah, I sort of do that anyway, breathing."

"Funny. We're starting the day in the Zen Den—with some meditation."

The Lisa Project:The Secret of Life
Journal–Day 4

<u>WHO does five book reviews in a day?</u>
<u>Grandpa and me, evidently!</u>

I said I would, and I will–I will discover the secret of life.

Books can give me information, but the unveiling comes with experience.

Grandpa asked me to pick five books from his hundreds of them. I didn't know where to begin, so I wrote these notes:

- What do I love about books?
- Words ... I love words. Phrases that inspire me too.
- I love the idea of learning something I can apply.
- I'm interested in why stuff happens.

I didn't overthink it. Trusted my gut.
"When nothing is certain, anything becomes possible."

I chose:

- ▶ A Course in Miracles by Drs. Helen Schucman and Bill Thetford
- ▶ Conversations with God: An Uncommon Dialogue by Neale Donald Walsch
- ▶ The Alchemist by Paulo Coelho
- ▶ The Secret by Rhonda Byrne
- ▶ Through the Looking Glass by Lewis Carroll

A Course in Miracles-suggests that the world is a mistake, an insane place where we ought not to linger longer than necessary.

Conversations with God-suggests that the world is intentional and perfect, a realm meant for us to experience and remember our own divinity.

I liked the second one better, but both can be right, depending on your perspective.

Grandpa asked me, if you substituted the word 'God' with 'the source of all life' or 'the vibration encompassing this world and beyond,' would it sound more agreeable to you?

I think my answer is 'yes.' Calling it source works, and I'm not sure I'm actually opposed to the word God.

I learned we always have one choice-the choice between fear and love. Most people don't realize they have that choice-or don't think about it consciously.

Do I choose fear, or do I choose love?
Well, duh. I personally choose LOVE!

The Alchemist-the crucial message is that so many people spend a lot of their life pursuing something external, like money or recognition, believing it will bring them happiness or control. However, the genuine treasure lies not outside but within oneself.

The greatest gift is our free will.

The Secret-according to this law of attraction, you can draw everything you desire to yourself through your thoughts. The key message is that through your thoughts alone, you can impact the world beyond yourself. It's called manifesting. But you have to be very specific and conscious of what and how you manifest.

Through the Looking Glass-I recently watched the movie, Alice in Wonderland. Just like Alice, I am learning

valuable lessons about myself. Grandpa says with this
book and the movie, I've come closest to the secret of life!

I CAN'T YET SEE IT! WHAT IS THE SECRET OF LIFE!!!??

I will discover the secret of life! I will change the world!
Day four continued in a weird way.
I think boys can be stupid. So, I punched Jacob in the
gut and called him an idiot—after he called me names first
and criticized Grandpa.
Still, I learned I needed to shift my perspective.
I can choose how I decide to feel. That's worth
writing twice and remembering every single day.

I CAN CHOOSE HOW I DECIDE TO FEEL.

Things do not affect you or hurt you if they don't
register in your brain. If you don't allow it.
Accept that every situation starts with YOU. IF YOU
weren't there at that moment, it wouldn't be an issue for
YOU, would it?
Learn not to see yourself as a victim. By acknowledging
that you caused it, you have the power to change it.

And what you change is your reaction to it. If you point to the other person as the cause, nothing will change.

"A cause is neutral, but blame is a judgment. If you look at the situation and yourself without judgment, you can change it." -Grandpa

Passing judgment on others is something you stop doing once you know the secret.

Just like I can't expect to play the piano at an advanced level right away, I can't expect to comprehend how the secret of life works.

Start with the basics, with simple and clear situations. Once you understand those, you can tackle more complex issues.

I get the point. One step at a time.

Anyway, I apologized to Jacob for my reaction and for hitting him. I told him it had nothing to do with him, and I just wanted to let him know. Then I said that I thought he was a nice boy, even though he called me fat and ugly.

It felt really good. For me, it was over. I completely changed the situation by accepting responsibility.

I was the cause! In a good way!

THE LISA PROJECT:
The Secret of Life?

Day 5

CHAPTER 12 | Namaste

The light in me sees the light in you.

Grandpa had promised her a great way to start the day.

As the sun was rising, he led Lisa to the Zen Den. The morning was fresh, the birds were chirping, and a dewy breeze floated the scents of fall. The world was awake, but Lisa wasn't quite. Grandpa had been up awhile, preparing the room with candlelight and two yoga mats with round seat cushions on them.

Besides her brief experience floating, she hadn't tried to meditate. *I thought only monks did that or those people who sit together and chant 'om.'* Grandpa had assured her there was no true right way to do it, and that it is called a practice because that's what it takes—practice. When he told her it might help her calm her thoughts, she was willing to try it.

"Sit down," Grandpa whispered and took a seat beside her. "Cross your legs like this and rest your hands on your knees. Keep your back straight, head held high as if there's a string from the ceiling supporting it. Now, close your eyes. Make sure you're comfortable. In a moment, I'll ring a bell, and then the meditation will begin. Remain silent. Just focus on your breath. Breathe in and out slowly. If thoughts arise, that's okay. Don't dwell on them too much. Instead, stay centered on your breathing. Continue this until you hear the bell again. When you hear it, return to the present but keep your eyes closed. I'll then guide you through something else."

With her eyes shut, Lisa listened to the faint, high-pitched ring of the bell. She honed in on her breath, inhaling and exhaling slowly. Almost immediately, her mind became cluttered with various thoughts. *Did I forget my journal? I didn't write all I should have yesterday. I wonder what Mom is doing? What day is it? Can I truly uncover the secret of life in just a few days? What have I actually learned? Why am I here? Am I breathing right? Oh—breathing. I need to calm down.*

Thoughts flooded in and out. Her breath rose and fell. She waited for the bell which felt like taking forever to ring until she forgot about it. Eventually the onslaught of thoughts ceased. Darkness and silence enveloped her, and Lisa floated in a state of blissful nothingness. It felt strangely familiar, as if she had been here before, sensing a deep primal connection.

Ting! The bell chimed, startling Lisa. It was as though she needed to awaken once more. Following Grandpa's instructions, she kept her eyes shut. A tingling sensation traveled through her legs, a strangely pleasant feeling.

Ω

Grandpa spoke softly. "This is now a guided meditation. Lisa, envision yourself as a baby, just born into this world. See yourself from a distance as they place you in your mother's arms. However, in this alternate life, your mother is entirely different from the one you have now. You were born in a poor country, to a mother facing hardships. Your father is absent and will never return. Your mother must shoulder all responsibilities alone: providing for you, maintaining the household, earning money. As you grow, you find yourself frequently alone as your mother works tirelessly.

"Early on, you learn to fend for yourself, often playing in the streets with other children who are also without supervision. Some of your friends possess nice things, and you yearn for them. They teach you how they acquire those items—through theft. Eventually, you too, engage in stealing.

"Your mother's boyfriend, unconcerned about your actions, encourages you to steal even more. No one suspects a young girl. He rewards you with sweets and delicious treats. Your skills improve, and you pilfer more and more. It feels exhilarating, challenging, and strangely gratifying."

"Grandpa, can we stop?" Lisa interrupted, opening her eyes to find daylight seeping through the windows. "You said this was supposed to be a great way to start the day."

"I did, didn't I?"

"Yes, and it took a while, but I enjoyed the first part. I was settling into it when the bell chimed, and we moved on so fast. What was the purpose of the second? I didn't like it. I could vividly imagine what it would be like if I were born somewhere else, as that girl. And then, I thought about Mom, and it made me sad."

Grandpa nodded. "That's understandable. I didn't want to make you sad, but I wanted you to feel what your life could have been like."

"Couldn't you have chosen a more pleasant example?"

"You didn't enjoy it, but did you realize that up to that point, it was quite thrilling for that girl? She excelled at something—stealing—and someone important in her life took notice and encouraged it."

"Yeah, great. This girl was becoming a thief."

"Indeed. You know that now, but that girl wasn't fully aware of it. She emulated those around her and received approval for her actions. It seemed normal to her, even positive."

Lisa contemplated for a moment. "Yes, I think I can understand that. It means she wasn't born bad."

"Exactly. You've experienced how circumstances can shape who you are and what you become. I could have chosen a wealthy family, or a poverty-stricken country in Africa, a family with children subjected to frequent abuse, and so on. Can you imagine children growing up in any of those circumstances?"

"I'd rather not."

"And yet, that is real for many people. You are just not present to it. Can you fathom that those circumstances could lead to different behaviors each time? And that you would exhibit the same behavior if you had grown up in their shoes?"

"Yeah, I guess I could have been anyone, depending on where and to whom I was born."

"That's right. You could have been born as Jacob or as Madison."

Lisa was taken aback. It dawned on her that Grandpa was correct. It made complete sense. Suddenly, she felt a vibration coursing through her body and mind. "Grandpa, I had a really strange thought. I considered the possibility that I could be anyone in this world. But that also means every other person could be me, Lisa. And that implies every person in the world has experienced life as I would have, but in different bodies and with distinct pasts. You're a Lisa too!"

"*Namaste,*[7]" Grandpa exclaimed with admiration, and placed his hands together at his heart and bowed to her.

"What? What does that mean?"

"*Namaste* is an ancient greeting from the Far East. It signifies something like *the light in me sees the light in you*. Or some say, 'the divine in me bows to and honors the divine in you.' Some people use the word celebrate—I celebrate you, as I celebrate myself. The gesture you saw me use is a yoga tradition, a sign of respect and as a simple greeting of peace. The point is that Namaste expresses the notion that you and the person you greet originate from the same source and therefore belong to the same family. Whatever name or version of definition we give it, we all share a common origin, whether it be a creator or a big bang, and whether our creation was intentional or coincidental. By definition, all people are forever interconnected from day one."

Grandpa paused as Lisa processed. "Imagine that. We are all connected."

Grandpa continued, "The ancient Maya used *In Lak'ech Ala K'in* as a greeting, which translates to *I am another you* or *I am you, and you are me*. Well, that's precisely the thought that just crossed your mind—that you could have been anyone in the world or they, you. It's a beautiful, ancient, and profound concept. It's remarkable that it emerged in your thoughts."

"It actually makes sense," Lisa remarked, "but what were you trying to teach me with this example of the girl stealing?"

"I wanted you to experience the fact that you truly could have been anyone in the world. And that you can never pass judgment on someone else's behavior because, under different circumstances, you would have exhibited that same behavior yourself."

"So, if I were Jacob, I probably would have done the exact same thing yesterday. And if I were Madison, I would have been mean and resorted to bullying too. I understand, but I need time to adjust. I'm not sure if I want to be understanding all the time. If someone bullies me, I want to be able to fight back."

"That's perfectly fine. There's no need to suppress yourself and refrain from standing up for yourself. Having boundaries is completely appropriate. Anger is a flame, and sometimes, it's necessary to defend yourself and stay resilient. However, always remember: *What happened to the other person could have happened to you. What the other person does, you could have done as well.*"

Lisa thought of her father. She hesitated but knew she couldn't—or must not—refrain from expressing her thoughts. "Grandpa, you say that we should always keep in mind that things could have happened to us. That applies to what happened to Dad too."

Grandpa tensed and took an audible breath. He bowed his head and closed his eyes.

"Grandpa, it could have happened to you. So why don't you want to see him anymore?" They sat quietly.

"Yes, it could have happened to me in the past. You can empathize with someone and acknowledge that it could have happened to you, but that doesn't mean you have to accept or condone everything. Remember what you said earlier: *I'm not sure if I always want to be understanding.* Well, in this case, I couldn't be understanding, considering the damage he caused. I still can't."

Grandpa rose from the meditation cushion and extended his hand to Lisa, his conflict written on his face.

As he helped her up, she wrapped her arms around his waist. "I love you, Grandpa. Thank you for being patient with me, and for taking your time to teach me."

Grandpa kissed her head. "Ah, I love you, too, and we have only begun. There's so much life will teach you. Next, however, let's get ready for the day. I have a big one planned. We're heading into Old Town."

The Lisa Project: The Secret of Life
Journal-Day 5

Grandpa taught me how to meditate! Well, sort of, because it really takes practice. During the first part my monkey mind went bananas! I was thinking about so many things, but I was so relaxed by the time the bell chimed.

Then Grandpa did a guided meditation. I didn't like it because he had me visualize a girl who was taught to be a thief to survive. For her it was normal. That girl wasn't born bad. I experienced how circumstances can shape who you are and what you become.

Imagine being in that life! I'm sure glad I have the one I have. I could have been anybody, and they could have been me.

Remember: what happened to the other person could have happened to you. What the other person does, you could have done as well. Do not pass judgment. Under different circumstances, I may have done the same thing.

Namaste: the light in me sees the light in you.

It expresses the notion that you and the person you greet originate from the same source and therefore belong to the same family-share a common origin. All people are forever interconnected from day one.

You can empathize with someone and acknowledge that it could have happened to you, but that doesn't mean you have to accept or condone everything. It's okay to have boundaries, especially to defend myself and stay resilient.

I asked Grandpa about Dad. Grandpa is still not choosing to be understanding. It makes him sad. It makes me sad too.

CHAPTER 13 | Our Journey

What You See Isn't What You Get

They drove through light fog toward Old Town and whatever excursion Grandpa had planned. The weather was gloomy, with intermittent rain showers. A cloud was hanging over Lisa too. She felt the conversation from her meditation experience was incomplete.

"Grandpa, earlier you mentioned that we should always keep in mind that things could have happened to us." She opened her journal. "You specifically said, 'What happened to the other person could have happened to you. What the other person does, you could have done as well.'" She looked over at Grandpa. "That applies to what Dad did too. It could have happened to you. So please tell me why don't you want to see him anymore?"

She noticed Grandpa grip the steering wheel.

He shifted in his seat, and stiffened, his jaw clenched. "I understand your concern. Yes, it could have happened to me in the past. Honestly, drinking and driving happened much more frequently when I was your dad's age. People did what they wanted, and sometimes things went terribly wrong. But as your father grew up, it became strictly forbidden and socially unacceptable. He should have known better. I also said to you that, 'You can empathize with someone and acknowledge that it could have happened to you, but that doesn't mean you have to accept or condone everything.' Well," he raised his voice, "in this case, I can't be understanding or forget the damage he caused!"

"Grandpa, you're driving too fast!" Lisa said, pushing her feet at an invisible brake on the passenger side.

"Sorry. I apologize, sweetheart," Grandpa said, taking his foot off the gas as they entered a small town. "I didn't mean to scare you. You're right. I guess it still affects me. But I'm afraid we are going to leave that topic for now ... We've arrived!"

Grandpa hurried to park the car and get out, opening an umbrella as he did. Lisa pulled up her raincoat hood thinking, *Alright, Grandpa, I'm afraid we <u>are</u> going to raise that topic again—when the timing is right! What's going on in him?*

Ω

They were in a dated and somewhat dilapidated residential area, the street lined with identical gray townhouses and a few rundown vehicles. "Where are we going?"

"This way. You'll see."

As they walked, Grandpa explained that this neighborhood had been one of the pioneers, serving as an example for future developments. However, much of its former glory had faded, and most residents had no other place to go due to the high prices elsewhere. There were discussions about demolishing the houses and revitalizing the entire area. Lisa hoped it would happen as soon as possible.

They reached the rear of a large building with dirty siding. A fence surrounded the property, and there were some dumpsters nearby. A man was rummaging in one of them as they passed. Lisa felt a shiver run down her spine.

"What do you think of this building?" Grandpa asked.

"I think it's ugly and depressing. Are you sure your car is safe back there?"

"Safe enough. Let's keep going."

The sun began to peek through the clouds. Lisa could feel the warmth of the rays, so she removed her raincoat and tied it around her waist. They continued walking around a corner, entering another neighborhood. This new area seemed like the complete opposite of the one they had just left. There were beautiful, spacious houses with impressive and well-kept landscaping. The old cars from the previous district had been replaced by shiny, luxurious vehicles. Grandpa informed Lisa that the people living here were financially fortunate, allowing them to afford such a lifestyle.

Lisa realized they were walking toward a private club. The lane was lined with majestic trees, leading to a breathtaking grand classical building, entirely painted in white.

They entered through elegant wooden doors and moved through the chandeliered lobby toward a maître'd standing at the entry of a restaurant. He greeted Grandpa by name and escorted them to a table. A waiter quickly came to them and filled their water glasses.

"So, what do you think?" Grandpa inquired when they were settled.

"It's beautiful, really beautiful. How is it you've never brought me here before? And—how is it they know you?"

Grandpa grinned. "I pulled in a little favor. This is a stark contrast from the other building we saw earlier, isn't it?"

"Absolutely, like night and day."

"Like black and white."

Lisa nodded. *I get it, but what's Grandpa up to?*

After enjoying breakfast, Grandpa paid the bill and walked over to engage in a brief conversation with the maître'd who nodded and waved a waiter over.

"Come on, Lisa. There's a back exit that will get us back to the car faster."

They followed the waiter through the kitchen. He opened a door to the outside for them and closed it behind them quickly. Lisa took a moment to get her bearings. Her heart skipped a beat when she recognized the fence and dumpsters. She turned and saw the same rear view of the building that had appeared so unappealing an hour ago. However, now it didn't seem as bad, and the siding didn't appear as dirty. Even the sun had emerged from the clouds.

Grandpa joined her. "Do you understand now?" he asked.

"Well, I think I understand that when we first arrived here, it was raining, and we walked through an unattractive neighborhood. That made the back of this building look sad. But now, it's not that bad," Lisa concluded.

"You see how our perception of something can be influenced by our previous experiences. But there's one more thing. This side of the building isn't nearly as impressive as the front, but it's the same building with an exquisite interior. The same principle can apply to people. Sometimes we initially see an unflattering side of someone, but that doesn't reflect who they are inside. Buildings and people can be ugly and beautiful simultaneously. And our past experiences play a significant role in determining whether we focus on the negative or positive aspects."

Lisa gripped Grandpa's arm.

"What's the matter?"

In a hushed tone, Lisa whispered, "There's that man rummaging through the dumpsters!"

Grandpa saw the man with unkempt hair and dirty clothes sifting through the trash. "Let's go talk to him." He began walking, Lisa in tow.

"Are you crazy!?"

"You're seeing the outward appearance that seems unappealing," Grandpa explained. "What did you learn about buildings?"

"I just find him scary! Isn't this unsafe?"

"I understand, and you should never approach a stranger on your own. But I'm here with you, and looking at this man, I'm pretty sure he's not a threat. I actually know he is not since my friend inside, the maître'd you met, knows this man. But I'll admit that I'm not opposed to walking up to anyone who is homeless and in fact, I've been surprised by some delightful discussions. In this case, my friend gave me a heads-up that there was a special person back here who frequents the place. Plus, we're close to the restaurant and other people. So, come on."

Reluctantly, Lisa followed Grandpa's lead and they stopped beside the man who looked up, surprised.

"May I bother you for a moment?" Grandpa asked in a friendly manner.

"Well, you're the first person to ask me that in years," he half-smiled, revealing yellowed teeth. "Usually, I'm the one who has to ask people for help. So, go ahead. What can I do for you? Need some money for coffee? Sorry, I don't have my wallet on me," he laughed.

Grandpa laughed with him, then said, "This is my granddaughter."

Lisa stared at the man in silence, edging a little behind Grandpa.

The man glanced at Lisa and took a step forward with a slight limp. "Don't worry, I'm used to it. You're not the only one, young lady. Almost everyone is afraid of me. When I'm on the street, most people look the other way. They try to ignore me."

Lisa regarded him warily. "That doesn't sound very nice." *That's how I feel when I'm bullied at school.* "So, why is almost everyone afraid of you?"

"Perhaps you can tell me first why *you're* afraid of me?"

"Well, I guess I've always been told to be afraid or cautious of homeless people. And I apologize, but if I'm truthful, it is also because … well …"

"Because my hair is messy, and my clothes are dirty, and I'm guessing I don't smell pleasant either. That happens when my grocery store is a trash bin, and my bedroom is outside, typically on the ground, beside a cart filled with stuff I may or may not need someday."

Lisa averted her eyes. "It's just that a normal person doesn't do those things."

"Careful, Lisa," Grandpa warned.

"No, no, it's okay. I'm not offended. Once upon a time I was a teacher. I know how direct young people can be." The man smiled sadly. "Normal? There are a lot of ways to look at what's normal. But, miss, you are mostly right. Most *normal* people have a house, a job, food, a shower, and clean clothes. I had all those things, too, until four years ago."

Lisa looked at him in surprise. "So, what happened?"

"I'll tell you, but first, let's introduce ourselves. What's your name?"

"I'm Lisa, and this is Grandpa."

"I'm Rick," he said, extending his hand. They shook and Rick continued, "Thank you. It's been a long while since I've shaken hands with a *normal* person."

Rick began recounting his story.

Until four years ago, he had been a teacher, leading a very ordinary life. One day, he went fishing with a friend, and they got caught in a thunderstorm in their boat. Rick woke up in the hospital, having been struck by lightning—a random and obviously unexpected experience. Miraculously, he survived. His friend did not.

Rick paused, struggling to get his emotions in check and find the right words.

"I lost my best friend. I eventually also lost my job. The lightning strike affected my speech for a while and it—and my guilt—affected my ability to think or to process what I felt or what I was doing. I couldn't think clearly, and I worked around kids, so I was eventually fired. None of that's really that normal either, is it?" he shrugged. "And there's more. I couldn't find other employment. Admittedly, I didn't really care if I did. I got kicked out of my apartment. I was not a person anyone wanted to be around, including my girlfriend. Eventually, friends grew tired of me sofa hopping and drinking and eating off them, and I knew I was a burden to my family too. I gave up. I hit the streets and learned what it takes to survive out here. Look around. You've witnessed some of what that is."

After a few moments, Lisa said, "So, it's not your fault you're homeless."

"Fault? What does that even mean? I felt like a victim for a long time. Very few people are struck by lightning, but I was. And my friend died to boot—instead of me.

"Afterward, some people tried to help me, but I was mad. I didn't know where to place blame, so I blamed them—or took it out on them by just behaving worse. Then, no one wanted to help me anymore. They couldn't anyway. I escaped to the streets where I feel I get what I deserve. To be treated like a filthy animal or just invisible. Do you know what that feels like?"

Lisa shook her head. "No. I am bullied, but no, not like that."

"Good, make sure you never experience it. It's terrible. It makes you feel worthless, as if you don't deserve to live. I only exist within my new circle of fellow sufferers. Yet, even there, everyone has their own problems. Every one of us has fallen."

Lisa jolted, recalling her intentional 'fall.' "But, Rick, you don't have to—"

"Hold on. Not done. There's more and it's worse," Rick took a deep breath. "Since the lightning strike my body constantly ached, and my mind was plagued by a constant buzzing. It drove me crazy. So, a year ago, I felt like I had only one option left."

Silence.

"Taking my own life. Freeing myself from my body, pain, and sorrow, and freeing humanity from my presence."

Lisa's breath caught in her chest. It wasn't the first time she had heard someone talk about suicide, but it was the first time in person—

from a *real* person in front of her. "But you're still here, and you're speaking so clearly, so—normally. How is that possible?"

"This is where the story becomes unbelievable, but I swear it's true. On the day I planned to end my life, as some prefer to call it, I was standing on top of a bridge. Below me, there was a highway and a railroad track. I had the choice of jumping in front of a car or a train. It felt empowering to have that choice, at least. And it would traumatize others—car drivers or the train conductor. That thought felt oddly satisfying. It was time for others to experience my trauma. After all, they were the ones who hadn't noticed me.

"I stood there, deliberating between the two options, when I noticed dark clouds approaching in the distance. I recognized that sky all too well. 'Okay,' I thought, 'let's go with that. Works for me. Bring it on!' I climbed a small hill beside the bridge, reaching the highest point in the area. I spread my arms, closed my eyes, and awaited what was to come. The wind picked up, rain poured down, and at a certain point, it genuinely felt like I was alone in the world, engulfed in a massive storm. I could sense the power of the elements—of nature, of the earth, of life itself. Then, I realized I didn't want to die. I wanted to live again! In that moment, I heard a sound, as if God were speaking to me. But just as suddenly, the sound disappeared because I lost consciousness and collapsed onto the ground."

Lisa stared at him, expectantly. "What happened?"

"Well, at some point, I woke up lying at the bottom of the hill. Turns out lightning does strike twice. I noticed the ringing in my head had ceased. I could stand up without much difficulty, and my body didn't ache as intensely. I felt like I had mostly returned to my old self, except for a torn ACL in my leg—thus, this reminder limp."

"Rick, if I wasn't right here before you, I'm not sure I could believe all that. But here you are. If I may, why are you still living on the streets?" Grandpa asked.

"Because it's easy to fall out of society, but it's not so easy to reintegrate. Where should I start? Based on my history, it is unlikely I'll ever find a teaching job again. If I want any kind of work, I need to look outside of the profession I know. But to make that change, I need first to make a choice to try and move on. Also I'd need money for a program to develop new skills. Mainly, I could use someone to care about me. It's just so difficult to get back on track."

Lisa felt a gentle touch on her shoulder, a signal it was about time to leave. She realized that her fear had dissipated, and she no longer viewed Rick merely as homeless, as less than. She was the one who felt helpless.

Grandpa was ready with an offer. "Rick, if you'd like a cup of coffee and something to eat, feel free to go inside. I've arranged something for you. And, if you are willing, I want you to talk with the waiter who opened the door to the outside for us. He has walked in your shoes and is willing to tell you about what is available to you and what he did to get himself back on track."

Rick studied Grandpa's expression. "Are you serious?"

"There are people who care."

Rick covered his face with his hands. "It's incredibly kind of you to do that for me. A little overwhelming. Thank you." Rick lifted his chin, "But the best part is that you saw me as a person, not just a dirty drifter. And I had the opportunity to share my story with Miss Lisa here. Thank you, Lisa."

Ω

Rick headed into the restaurant while Grandpa and Lisa made their way back to the car. As they walked, they passed through the first neighborhood once again. This time, Lisa noticed various other details. People were walking their dogs and greeting each other.

The area seemed more vibrant. It felt far more real to her than the neighborhood filled with grand houses and expensive cars.

"You know, Grandpa, I felt a connection to Rick. In his way, he's been bullied too. I feel like I can find a way to stop the mistreatment of each other at school."

Grandpa took her hand, "It only takes one sometimes. One to care. One to make a difference. No reason why it can't be you."

They walked along thinking in silence until Grandpa remarked, "Struck by lightning twice, huh? Rick's story. Can you believe it?"

"I think I do. But even if it wasn't true, it's still his story, and for him, it's true. Besides," she winked at Grandpa, "you've been struck by lightning twice in your life too, haven't you?"

Once when I was born. And the second time when the police called regarding your son and the incident—the accident. What is it that you're hiding, Grandpa?

CHAPTER 14 | Blessings In Disguise

Responsibility and Fault

On their way home, they took a detour through a smaller village. Lisa was in the middle of saying something when Grandpa suddenly slowed down. "You're driving really slow now, Grandpa. Are you tired?"

"Not at all but take a look ahead. There are a few kids playing on the road. We always need to be extra careful around children and traffic."

BANG!

Grandpa had barely finished speaking when a young child on a bike collided with the passenger side of their car. Grandpa immediately stopped and quickly saw that Lisa was not hurt. He opened his door and hurried over to the crying boy.

Lisa sat frozen for a moment, then stepped out to see Grandpa trying to console the boy and assess him for injuries.

The boys' friends watched in shock, and a frantic woman rushed over, shouting, "Billy! Oh my God! Billy!" She dropped to her knees beside her son.

"I'm okay, Mom. Really. It just hurts a bit."

The mother turned on Grandpa, "What have you done? Did you hit my boy? This is your fault!" She bumped Grandpa aside.

"Ma'am, I'm truly sorry, but our first priority should be ensuring the boy receives care," Grandpa said calmly. "I have first-aid training. If you'll allow me, I can check him over and determine if we need to call an ambulance."

The woman calmed down slightly, and Grandpa placed his hand on the boy's leg. Another car turned onto the street and the driver pulled quickly to the curb and hurried over. The boy and his mom obviously knew her.

"Move away! I'm the neighbor. I'm a nurse. What happened here!"

By this time the boy was sitting up, still crying.

Billy's mother turned her attention back to Grandpa. "You were driving way too fast. This is your fault. You have to pay for his damaged bike, and any medical bills. I should sue you!"

The nurse interjected, "There is no need for police. He has scrapes, but nothing is broken."

Grandpa softly said, "Miss, everything will be alright. I'm relieved that your son is okay. That's the most important thing. The rest is just money for his bike, and I'll ensure you're fully reimbursed. Please don't worry about that."

"You better," she continued her tirade, "and you should give up your driver's license. People like you, old folks, shouldn't be allowed to drive anymore!"

Grandpa nodded and reached into his jacket for a small notebook and pen. "If you inform me about the damages, I'll immediately reimburse you." He scribbled quickly, tore out a page, and handed the mom the paper. "These are all my details, so you'll know where to reach me. Come on, Lisa, everything will be alright. Let's head home."

Grandpa carries a notebook and pen? Guess I'm not the only one who takes note of the day's events—or surprises.

Ω

As they resumed driving, Lisa looked at Grandpa with great astonishment. "You know this isn't your fault, right?"

Grandpa shrugged. "Then whose fault is it?"

"It's the boy's fault! He rode right onto the road between those parked cars. Luckily, he didn't ride directly in front of our car!"

"Yes, he was fortunate. I'm glad I noticed them playing and was driving so slowly."

"Yeah, but his mom blamed you and called you old."

"Well, 'old' is relative. She'd think that since she's younger than me," he half-smiled.

"And," Lisa continued, "she said you were driving too fast. And you agreed with her! And now you have to pay for a bike? How is that fair?"

"Of course, I can understand your perspective. This incident actually aligns perfectly with our project. You noticed that the mother was extremely upset. It's natural for her to be in shock when her child had an accident. My primary concern was getting the boy help as quickly as possible, and that wouldn't have happened if his hysterical mother continued to scream. So, I agreed with her because she wouldn't have accepted any other response. From her standpoint, that was her truth. Even when it turned out he wasn't injured, there was no point in trying to change her mind. I willingly took the blame to ensure the boy and his mother could return to normalcy as soon as possible."

Lisa furrowed her brow. "I don't quite grasp how that fits into the project. I'm thinking about how Mom would have reacted if she were driving. She would have freaked out more than that mother and would have immediately explained what really happened."

"That's certainly a possibility, but there's a good chance she and the boy's mother would have engaged in an argument, which wouldn't have been beneficial for the boy. Even when it became evident that he was unharmed, your mother would have continued arguing with that woman, prolonging the resolution of the situation."

"But by doing it your way, you'll have to spend money, and now they believe it's your fault. I remember Dad's lawyer advised never to admit guilt, even if you are guilty, as it leaves you vulnerable to being sued. You did the complete opposite!"

"First, I'm immensely grateful that it turned out this way. As you said, it could have been much worse if he had ridden onto the road just a little earlier, right in front of our car. Who cares if it costs me some money? The alternative would have been truly dreadful, and I would have given anything to prevent it. It's a blessing in disguise! This is my way of expressing gratitude to the universe and helping these people. As you learned yesterday, this situation wasn't my fault, but I was the cause. If I hadn't been there, there wouldn't have been a situation. Do you understand?"

"It's still odd."

"I acknowledged that I was the cause," Grandpa continued. "And by doing so, I could change the situation. I altered my response, which in turn, changed the mother's reaction." He held up a hand to give Lisa's next remark pause. "Now, you have me going! Let me jump on a stump for a second. I despise how our legal system operates—just as you described your father's lawyer's advice. If you know you've done something wrong, you should take responsibility and act accordingly. I firmly believe that trusting in the ability to resolve an event in the right way is how we make the world a better place. There are numerous individuals in high positions, representing companies, corporations, or the government, who will always publicly deny any wrongdoing, despite everyone knowing they're guilty. I loathe them, but I also acknowledge that they are victims of the system. To transform the system, you must take clear and courageous actions. So, if I have done something wrong, I will always accept blame. In this case, I also assumed responsibility for the reasons I just explained to you. I trust that the universe will yield an outcome that benefits all parties involved. Many ancient philosophies embrace this approach, such as one from Hawaii called *Ho'oponopono*.[8]"

Lisa didn't even bother asking about the peculiar word. Grandpa was on a roll.

Journal: The Lisa Project: The Secret
of Life-Day 5-continued...

We visited Old Town today.

I saw a neighborhood that was run down on one side and the other side was very nice. The same was true of the beautiful restaurant where we had lunch. The outside was unflattering, but the inside was beautiful. I learned that this can be true of people.

Our perception of something can be influenced by our previous experiences which play a role in whether we focus on the negative or the positive aspects.

A highlight of our journey is that I met Rick, a homeless man. At first, I was scared and then we had a conversation. Rick was struck by lightning-twice! (I believe him.) The first time, his friend was killed. The second time, Rick's injuries from the first strike were healed (a miracle?). Rick used to be a normal teacher, but he couldn't function.

(I also learned there are a lot of ways to look at what's normal.)

After his accident, Rick got mad and blamed others and behaved badly. He lost everything. People tried to help, but he pushed them away. He said he escaped to the streets where he feels like he gets what he deserves. People ignore him and mistreat him. In my perspective, it's a different sort of bullying. He nearly took his own life. He felt like he had only one option left, but now, he has another chance. He says it's "easy to fall out of society, but it's not so easy to reintegrate. It's just so difficult to get back on track."

Before we left, he said the best part is that I saw him as a person, not just a dirty drifter. That made me feel good. And I am so glad he shared his story with me. It's given me courage-I feel like I can play a role in stopping bullying at my school. Mistreatment of others, no matter their circumstances, is not okay.

Grandpa had planned to help Rick before we even got there. It only takes one sometimes. One to care. One to make a difference. Grandpa said to me, "No reason why it can't be you."

Lightning does strike twice-for Grandpa too. Once when I was born, and once when the police called about Dad and the accident.

Later when we were driving home, a boy ran his bike into the car! Believe it or not-it was a blessing in disguise.

Grandpa said it gave him a reason to give thanks to
the universe for being there and being able to help.
I think the other blessing is that it helped me to
understand that trusting in the ability to resolve an
event in the right way is how we make the world a
better place.

It was not Grandpa's fault, but he accepted the
blame—even with the mom yelling at him. He said it was
to calm her down and take control of the situation. The
mom said some mean things, and there was no point
at that time in telling her the truth—she'd created
her own truth. And, from her standpoint that was
the truth. (Her channels, the patterns. Her experience
caused her to associate the events and react.)

Grandpa was the cause because he was there.
If he wasn't, there wouldn't have been a situation. If
you know you've done something wrong, you should
take responsibility and act accordingly. (Even though
Grandpa wasn't at fault, by acknowledging he was the
cause, he could change the situation.)

P.S. Grandpa REALLY doesn't like our legal system.

CHAPTER 15 | Truth And Reality

Perceality

Grandpa may have exhausted his energy on law and politics, but Lisa was brimming with excitement and renewed vigor. She dropped her raincoat on the kitchen table and tugged Grandpa's arm to drag him toward the library.

"Now! We can finally start working on your project!"

This time, it was Grandpa's turn to look surprised.

"Oh, did you conveniently forget already? We're supposed to figure out which warm country you could move to and how you could make it happen." She pulled an extra chair behind his desk and opened his laptop.

Grandpa chuckled, though not entirely wholeheartedly. "That's right, we were going to do that. What do you suggest? Tea first?"

"Tea next. I suggest we research warm countries where you could relocate."

"We will, but if it's not financially feasible, it would be a waste of time. So let's first explore how it could work. Is that okay?" Grandpa proposed.

Lisa let out a sigh. She had an urge to browse through images of tropical beaches, but Grandpa was right. It had to be a realistic possibility, otherwise there was no point in pursuing it.

"How much money do you have in savings, Grandpa?" she asked.

Grandpa laughed. "Direct approach. Enough to handle unforeseen expenses."

"But how do you manage to support yourself?"

"I receive a monthly pension, and I can live off of that. But how would I afford a house if I were to move to another country?"

"Just the same way you pay for your house here. How do you manage that?" Lisa pressed on.

"I don't pay anything. This house is fully owned. The mortgage was paid off a long time ago," Grandpa revealed.

"So, your savings are tied up in the house, right? If you sell the house, you'll have some money."

"What would this house be worth then? Your mom is a real estate agent, so she should know, and maybe you do too."

"Well, we can check out the houses for sale in the area. That way, we'll get an idea of the value of this place. Also, you have the acreage—the farmland—and we'd need to explore the value of that. Frank's place might be a good comparable."

"Seems you've listened to your mom at work."

Lisa sat at the computer and began her search. She showed Grandpa the available houses and farms in the vicinity and their asking prices. She entered the details and prices into a spreadsheet, gradually estimating the potential value of Grandpa's farm. It turned out to be quite a substantial amount.

"I am impressed, Lisa, with you—and your mom for that matter. But really, I don't intend to—"

Just as he opened his mouth to explain, the doorbell rang. Lisa went to the window and peered out toward the front. She ducked. "Hide! It's that kid's mom—and that kid!"

Grandpa calmly walked to the front door, and Lisa could hear him welcoming the woman and her son. She peeked down the hall and saw Grandpa leading them into the living room. Grandpa called for her to join them.

To Lisa, the mom looked completely different from before. She had brought some flowers. Tulips! A good sign! And her son shyly held a drawing in his hands. Before they took a seat, the mom turned to Grandpa and said, "I'm truly sorry I yelled at you. But most people drive recklessly on our street. I've feared something terrible would happen for years! Just a few weeks ago, there was an accident involving the little boy next door, and it really shook me."

Grandpa glanced at Lisa. "Can you now see how it works with the sandbox?"

Lisa nodded. *The channels, the patterns. This mother's experience caused her to associate the events and react.*

Not knowing the meaning of this exchange, the mother continued, "Billy and his friends explained what happened and that you were not at fault. As far as I know, you were driving very slowly. So, I want to apologize, and you don't have to pay for Billy's bike."

"Well, you didn't have to do this," Grandpa responded, gesturing toward the flowers and the drawing made by her son. "But thank you. Very thoughtful."

"But I'm sort of confused. I mean, you were the one who apologized and offered to pay when you knew it wasn't your fault. Why did you do that? Most people wouldn't do that."

Grandpa smiled. "I'd like to believe most would—or at least be a part of the world in which they would—be generous with their understanding. If I were in your shoes, and Lisa was lying on the ground, I may have reacted similarly. As it were, I wanted to steer the situation away from crisis and fear, and into a solution that calmed us all down, especially you and Billy."

"I still don't fully understand it," the woman admitted, "but it worked, and I'm grateful to you."

"For me, that's the best outcome," Grandpa replied. "And, I may just have another solution."

Grandpa turned his attention to Billy, "Son, I imagine your bike is pretty beaten up, right?"

"Yes, sir. I can't ride it anymore."

"I tell you what, Lisa here is a little older than you and has outgrown the bike I got her a few years ago. It happens to be sitting in the barn just waiting for a new rider."

Billy's eyes widened, and his mom placed her hand on his arm.

"Lisa, how about you and this young man go get that bike. I'll be out in a minute to help put it in the trunk to be taken to its new home."

Grandpa…changes someone's world…again. Is the type of stuff he does to change how he feels about his own?

Ω

When he returned, Grandpa joined Lisa in the library where she was working again on her laptop at his desk. "You see, princess, sometimes things can turn out even better than expected when you change the perspective."

"What do you mean? It would have been foolish if she hadn't done that. Her initial reaction after the accident was completely wrong," Lisa argued.

Grandpa looked at her seriously. "How do you know that?"

"Well, you were there."

"Didn't I explain to you in the car why I reacted the way I did?"

"Yes, you did it to prevent the situation from worsening, even though you knew what really happened while Billy's mom didn't," Lisa recalled.

Grandpa nodded. "You're right, that was my primary goal. But do you remember the bicycle inside the barn? I could see it—from my perspective. You could not see it—from your perspective."

"Yes! I wanted to ask you something about that."

"You are not upset I gave that bike to him, are you?"

She smiled. "No, Grandpa. Very nice and he was really happy." She picked up her journal and began flipping through the pages. Grandpa patiently waited.

"Here it is. You mentioned that there can be multiple truths depending on where a person stands. But as I thought about it later, I couldn't help but wonder why there seems to be only one reality in the end. And apparently, truth is different from reality. Why is that?" Lisa inquired.

"Great question and I believe this is a good time to revisit the topic of our senses," Grandpa suggested.

Lisa didn't seem thrilled. "Is it going to be boring? Haven't we covered that?"

Grandpa chuckled. "You're in the midst of uncovering a profound secret. How can it be boring? Just trust me not to bring up anything you wouldn't enjoy. And I'll try to keep it concise."

"I'm ready to finally know what the secret is, so I'm in."

"Good. So far, we've described our senses as antennae that pick-up vibrations, remember? Well, what if our senses not only receive signals but also transmit them?"

Lisa stared at him blankly.

"Okay, an example. Do you know how bats navigate in the dark?"

Lisa remembered learning about it in biology class. "I think I do. They continuously emit very high-pitched sounds and listen to the echoes bouncing back, right?"

"Exactly. Now, imagine if humans were to do something similar with our senses. What would that imply?" Grandpa inquired.

"Um … We'd continuously annoy each other?"

"Funny, but no. It would mean we can hear the reflections. And what causes us to perceive things differently?" Grandpa probed further.

"Our senses, of course. They vary from person to person, and we are never in exactly the same position. So, we see and hear different things. And, our life experiences shape our perception. As you've taught me, we construct our thoughts based on what we've seen."

"Very impressive! Now, what if our senses also transmit signals and then receive them again?" Grandpa continued.

"Are you suggesting that what I see is because my eyes transmit a signal and then receive it back?" Lisa asked, trying to grasp the concept.

Grandpa nodded.

"Then it must matter what signal I send out …," Lisa trailed off.

"Exactly! Your thoughts on something influence the signal you transmit."

"So, by changing my thoughts, I can influence the signal I transmit," she concluded.

"Bingo! Indeed, your previous thoughts—your mindset—play a crucial role. And your thoughts are shaped not only by past events but also by recent experiences. The boy's mom's story about accidents in the neighborhood is a prime example. Also, you found the back of the country club building ugly and depressing because we walked there in the rain through a dilapidated neighborhood, saw rundown cars, and rundown people. Those events influenced your feelings, and your perception adjusted accordingly. You were influenced without even realizing it. But now that you understand this, you can actively decide how you want to feel about something. You can intentionally choose or decide how to feel. On the flip side, it also means you send out different vibrations when you're not intentional about it. In that case, the vibrations stem from your subconscious, often driven by fear. Consequently, you tend to notice things that instill fear in you."

"So, let me get this straight. When I've made up my mind to be happy, I will literally see different things?"

"Yes, perfectly put. The signals received by your nerves are colored by your consciousness and subconsciousness. When these are positive, you mainly notice the positive aspects of life. When they lean toward negativity or fear, you predominantly see things that worry you. Therefore, instead of the law of attraction, which was the focus of *The Secret* book, there is the law of ..." Grandpa trailed off, waiting for Lisa to fill in the blank.

"Transmission?" Lisa guessed.

"Splendid! You transmit something and what you transmit determines what you see, hear, or feel," Grandpa affirmed. "Perhaps the simplest example is that of a smile. When you smile at someone, they may more quickly warm up to you and smile back. You've created a 'transmission' without saying a word. This is true of your inner smile too. It shows—or is visible to people—by how you show up in the world. People are attracted to positive energy, but most of us can red flag someone's negative energy quickly based on their body language and facial expressions."

"But not everything changes just because of my thoughts. Many things remain the same. They're still things," Lisa pointed out.

"Yes, that's true. However, your perspective, your emotions, and your judgments do change by shifting your mindset," Grandpa clarified.

"No, I still don't fully grasp it. Some things are either true or not true. There's no middle ground," Lisa argued.

"Come with me to the kitchen."

Ω

Lisa found it slightly amusing how Grandpa often responded to her questions by demonstrating rather than answering directly. *I mean he could have just said that by changing my thoughts, I can influence the signal I transmit, but no, he had to involve bats.*

Lisa was grinning when Grandpa turned around from arranging a platter, a bowl, water, and a small dropper on the countertop.

He wrinkled his brow. "See, you are thinking something amusing. Well, I can only guess, but let's continue. Now, watch." Grandpa sucked up water from the bowl with the dropper and dropped two drops onto the platter. "You would agree that this is: one plus one equals two?"

Lisa nodded. "Those are two drops, not zero, one, or three."

Grandpa repeated the action, dropping two more drops onto the same spot on the platter. "How many drops do you see now?" He then dropped two drops into the bowl of water. "And where can you see these drops now?"

"But Grandpa, they aren't drops anymore. They're part of the water itself."

"Can you think of an example where one plus one becomes four or even more?" Grandpa challenged me.

Lisa was blank for a moment. Then she noticed Sera-cat, peacefully sleeping on her mat. "You have Sera, and that's one animal. But if you add a tomcat, they could have kittens, resulting in multiple animals."

Grandpa smiled approvingly. "Mathematics is a human-made system of agreements. In math, one plus one is always two. However, in the world beyond that system, much more is possible, as you witnessed with the drops and just imagined with the kittens."

"May I use your journal?" Grandpa spoke as he wrote, "You saw this in action:"

Perception → Truth → Reality

What you seem to perceive, shapes your truth about it, which determines your reality.

"So, everything around me is a perceived reality, a kind of *perceality*," Lisa jokingly remarked.

Grandpa looked straight at Lisa.

"What's the matter?" she asked, puzzled.

"Do you realize what you just said?"

"Yes, Perceality. I actually thought about that word once before!"

"You've just coined a powerful new term that accurately describes how this works! It acknowledges that there's no absolute reality. Each person has their own version of truth. It's a fantastic expression!" Grandpa said.

Lisa puffed up and then collapsed her elbows onto the countertop. "But it feels like reality doesn't exist because no single person possesses all knowledge, can observe everything, or is omnipresent. And no one can read minds," she said.

"You're right. That part is reserved for God or the source," Grandpa replied with a wink. "*Reality*, as we perceive it, doesn't exist on the level of our world. *People*, by definition, have limited perceptions and, in addition, always carry judgments, opinions, or at least preferences. *Absolute reality* has no judgment, opinion, preference, desire, guilt, or victim."

"But yesterday, you redirected me to the piano when I brought up someone who had a terrible experience with abuse. Yet, I still wonder how all of this applies in such a case. I mean, I can't play that musical piece or know what it is to have her experience, but I can listen to it when someone else plays it, right? I haven't had the experience but can respect and appreciate it."

"My dear, you continue to impress me with your ability to articulate your thoughts—and your questions. I believe it's time to ask my friend Theo if we can visit him tomorrow morning. With his experience, he may be better suited to address reality and truth—and now, your creation: *perceality*."

"It's a lot to digest, Grandpa. Your friend, Theo, will have a lot of explaining to do. Right now, I better capture the day."

"Seize the opportunity."

"Last word—no, many words, thoughts, ideas! Journal, here I come."

Journal: The Lisa Project:
The Secret of Life-Day 5-continued...

This afternoon we started to make some progress on
figuring out Grandpa's next destination (he seems like he's
dragging his feet?)-and ..? He tells me to 'shift,' yet he
resists.

GET This! The mom and the boy actually came to the
farm! And apologized. We found out that another kid had
been hit by a car a few weeks earlier, and the assumption
was that Grandpa was going too fast in the neighborhood
where kids play. The mom was really scared, and acted
out in anger because she loves her son and didn't like
seeing him hurt.

Anyway, happy ending-Grandpa gave Billy my old bike.
Changed his world and his mom's for sure.

This led to a whole new discussion because I wondered
why there seems to be only one reality in the end-and
that apparently truth is different than reality-even
though there can be multiple truths depending on where
a person stands.

<u>Grandpa wrote</u>:

Perception → Truth → Reality

What you seem to perceive, shapes your truth about it, which determines your reality.

Everything around me is a perceived reality: <u>PERCEALITY</u>.

It acknowledges that there's no absolute reality.

Each person has their own version of truth.

Our senses cause us to perceive things differently. Sometimes things can turn out even better than expected when you change your perspective.

Life experiences shape our perception. We construct our thoughts based on what we've seen. My thoughts on something influence the signal I transmit, and by changing my thoughts, I can influence the signal transmitted.

Thoughts are shaped, not only by past events, but also by recent experiences. Our thoughts, feelings, and perceptions can be influenced without even realizing it.

I CAN ACTIVELY DECIDE HOW I WANT TO FEEL ABOUT SOMETHING.

I can intentionally choose or decide how to feel.

(Note: If I focus on fear, I will think about it and not feel good. We tend to notice things that instill fear in us, e.g., spiders!)

<u>Law of Transmission</u>—what you transmit determines what you see, hear, or feel (and what others see, hear, or feel from you!)

Example: a smile. And also how you show your 'inner smile.'

People are attracted to positive energy. I can tell when people have negative energy.

Not everything changes just because of my thoughts. However, my perspective, emotions, and judgments do change by shifting my mindset.

I had to have Grandpa repeat and write this for me:

<u>Reality,</u> as we perceive it, doesn't exist on the level of our world. <u>People,</u> by definition, have limited perceptions and, in addition, always carry judgments, opinions, or at least preferences. <u>Absolute reality</u> has no judgment, opinion, preference, desire, guilt, or victim.

It feels like reality doesn't exist because no single person possesses all knowledge or can observe everything. And no one can read minds. Reserved for God or Source?

I can't play that musical piece or know what it is to have that experience, but I can listen to it when someone else plays it, right? I haven't had the experience but can respect and appreciate it.

I may not understand someone else's perceality—but I can listen.

MIDDLE Ground? Not sure about this. Tomorrow, we are visiting Grandpa's friend, Theo, who is supposed to be able to address reality and truth—and now, my creation: Perceality.

So by changing my thoughts, I can influence the signal I transmit. I'm thinking Grandpa and Dad should talk. I'll keep thinking that.

CHAPTER 16 | Shooting Stars

Lessons in Infinity

Lisa was exhausted from the day's events and groggy with a full stomach after dinner. She just wanted to relax on the couch without having to think. A movie would do. Maybe popcorn after her salmon salad settled.

"Will you clear the table?" Grandpa asked as he rose from his chair. "I'm going to get something from the attic that we'll need in a minute."

"What is it?" Lisa asked, feeling a bit disappointed.

"Well, I won't tell you just yet. You'll have to be patient. You'll see it outside."

Grandpa headed up to the attic, and Lisa audibly sighed. *Be patient? Why do older people always say that?* Patience wasn't her strong suit.

She could hear Grandpa's words in her head, *Just trust me that I won't come up with something you won't like.* She gathered the plates from the table and took them to the sink, feeling sulky.

"What could Grandpa have in mind? Outside? It's already dark, and there's nothing left to see anyway."

"Nothing left to see?" Lisa was startled by Grandpa, who suddenly appeared behind her. Unbeknownst to her, she had apparently been talking to herself out loud.

She noticed that Grandpa was carrying two sleeping bags and a backpack, had a headlamp bound to his forehead, and there was some kind of large binoculars on a strap over his shoulder.

Lisa giggled, "Are you joking, Grandpa? We're not going to sleep outside, are we? I won't, you know. There are creepy crawlers out there."

"Visions of spiders crawl in your head. I know, I know. And no, we won't sleep outside. You know I find it chilly during the day, let alone at night. Forget about cleaning up. It's perfect outside right now." He turned off the lights and motioned to the porch door.

Lisa walked out into the yard, with Grandpa following. They made their way to the lounge chairs he had set up on the back patio. He handed her a sleeping bag. "Here, lie down in the sleeping bag on the chair and get comfortable. I'll pour us some hot chocolate."

He took a thermos from the backpack and filled two mugs. "Three marshmallows for you, princess." They took sips and began to relax.

Grandpa knew exactly how to make Lisa happy, even when they were about to do something she might initially not like. He looked at his granddaughter affectionately as she settled into her sleeping bag. She resembled him in many ways. He recognized her impatience, her occasional stubbornness, and her vulnerability. But her wisdom, her strength, and her intuition? Those were qualities he hadn't possessed at her age.

He wrapped up in the other sleeping bag on the adjacent chair. "Now, close your eyes," he instructed. "Are you comfortable? Now focus on your breathing. Place your right hand on your stomach and take a deep breath of this wonderfully fresh evening air. Hold it for a moment, and then exhale. Now, open your eyes."

As she opened her eyes, she was immediately greeted by a sight she had not noticed on the way out and perhaps had never seen so brightly before. The sky was pitch dark and filled with stars. There were so many of them! She could even see the Milky Way.

"Wow," was all she could manage to say.

Grandpa remained silent, enjoying the breathtaking view with her. The cloudless sky, the stillness of the evening, and what was to come, made it the perfect moment to be there.

"How many stars do you think you can see?" Grandpa eventually asked.

Lisa began counting in a small square, a technique she had learned from her dad. Define an area, count the objects within it, and then determine how many of those defined areas fit into the overall object you're observing. At some point, she stopped. "I don't know, Grandpa. There are too many to count. There must be thousands, maybe even tens of thousands."

"Experts claim that there are at least a hundred times more stars in the universe than grains of sand on Earth."

Lisa let that sink in for a moment. "I can't even imagine the vast number of sand grains on the beach, at the bottom of the ocean, and in all the deserts."

"Yes," Grandpa replied, "for every grain of sand on Earth, there are approximately a hundred stars in the observable universe. What lies beyond that, nobody knows."

Lisa couldn't help but gasp. *What lies beyond?* "Is there an end? No way, because what would be beyond that? Can it go on forever? Is it possible, Grandpa, that space never ends?"

"It's quite possible. In fact, I think it's the only possibility. If something is infinite, there is no end and, therefore, no beginning. The beginning is the end, and the end is the beginning. That's where the joke comes from that says you're the center of the universe. In an infinite space, every point can be considered the center."

Lisa fell silent, gazing at the sky with even more awe. The longer she looked, the more stars she saw. Some twinkled faintly, while others shone brightly. The Milky Way resembled a trail of filmy light in the air. It was truly a remarkable sight.

"If there are so many stars, there must be other places where life exists, right? There must be aliens. And perhaps people really do see UFOs from time to time." Lisa commented.

"It's more irrational to assume that we're the only living beings in the universe than to believe that there are several inhabited planets out there. Astronauts are convinced of this, and they have actually been to space, even if it was only a small part of the grand whole. So, yes, it could be true that genuine UFO sightings occur on Earth."

"But why is the universe so vast?"

"Would you prefer it to be a bit smaller?"

"Well, no, it doesn't really matter, but I just can't comprehend it. What's the reason? Why is it so immense? This place already feels huge when you drive through it. The entire world is much larger, and it's just a tiny part of the universe. And I'm just a teeny-tiny part of the world. So why am I here? I'm insignificant in all of this. What is the purpose of my life?"

"The sun might ask the same question," Grandpa remarked.

"Huh?" Lisa replied, surprised.

"Yes, the sun is gigantic, much larger than Earth and much bigger than you. Yet, the sun is just a tiny part of the universe. In fact, there are at least tens of trillions of stars in the universe. The sun is merely one of them. In all likelihood, there are only eight billion people like us in the entire universe, and you are one of them. So, you are billions of times more unique than the sun."

"I understand, but I don't really," Lisa grumbled.

"It all depends on how you look at it and what you compare it to. Everything is relative. It's up to you to discover the purpose of your life. No one else can determine that for you. If you seek it and search for it, you'll find millions of people who have shared or want to share their experiences and insights about this. But ultimately, the decision is yours. I can tell you that you are unique in the entire universe, but it's up to you whether you embrace that or not. If you find yourself getting stuck in these thoughts, it can be helpful to consider the opposite. For example, what's the smallest particle you know?"

Lisa recalled her science lessons at school. "An atom."

"Do you know what the inside of an atom looks like?"

Lisa fell silent.

"No, no one truly knows," Grandpa continued. "But the inside of an atom is somewhat similar to the universe. Atoms are mostly empty space, consisting of protons, electrons, and neutrons. And those particles, in turn, are made up of even smaller particles, and it continues infinitely. Within each of those particles, there's an entire universe waiting to be explored. The universe is infinite, and the quest for the smallest particle is infinite as well. There's no distinction between the largest and the smallest. Every particle, every part of the whole, is equal to the whole and just as significant. You are as important as the universe. And so am I."

"Everyone is equally important. Therefore, everyone is equally unimportant," Lisa reasoned. "That doesn't help. I want to understand the universe. I want to be special, unique. I want there to be a reason for my existence."

"There is a reason. You are unique. No one has experienced the same things as you. No one has lived the exact life you've lived or seen the world through your eyes. You are a one-of-a-kind expression of life energy, of vibration, and you always will be. Throughout the history of mankind, no other girl like you has existed, nor will there ever be one," Grandpa assured her.

Lisa fell silent, contemplating how the world would be without her. Grandpa's words had evoked both happiness and a touch of melancholy within her.

Then, she spotted a streak of light in the sky. "Wow, Grandpa! Did you see that shooting star? Now I can make a wish."

"Yes, you can. What will you wish for?"

Thinking back to their conversation, she wished for her life to have a clear purpose. She also longed to be special and desired recognition from others. But she couldn't pinpoint in what way she wanted to be unique. She also wished for Rick to find his path again, for harmony between her parents, and for Grandpa to pursue his dreams. *Argh, it was all too much! So many wishes at once.*

"If your wish was for a second cup of hot chocolate, your wish has been granted," Grandpa said with a smile as he filled Lisa's cup.

"I couldn't decide. I wanted to wish for something for myself, but also for others. And honestly, I just wish for everyone to be genuinely happy."

"That's beautiful! But how can the one granting this wish fulfill it?"

"What?" Lisa looked at Grandpa, taken aback. "Are you suggesting that there's someone out there who listens to wishes and makes them come true?"

"What do you think?"

Is Grandpa being serious? What if there really is someone capable of granting wishes? Who could it be?

She tried to envision herself in the role of wish granter. *It certainly wouldn't be an easy job. My wish for everyone to be completely happy seems almost impossible, doesn't it? Wishing for a new phone or new clothes is one thing, but happiness? And sure, I could wish for a new phone, but I know it won't simply materialize out of thin air. So what is the point?*

"Grandpa? I think I understand that wishes aren't magically granted. Actually, I don't think wishes are granted at all. If I wished for a new phone right now, it wouldn't happen. So, it seems that wishes are just a matter of chance, and the same outcome would occur even if no one made a wish." Lisa felt satisfied with her mature analysis of the situation.

"But if there *were* someone capable of granting wishes, who do you think it would be?" Grandpa inquired.

"It would have to be God, right? But then it would only work for those who believe in God, right?"

"What was another name we mentioned for God?"

"The Source. The source of all life—that's what you called it when we were going through the books."

Grandpa nodded. "Or, you could say all vibrations in this world and beyond. And now, look up."

Lisa gazed upward once again, captivated by the vastness of space.

"Are you saying," she asked slowly, "that everything is connected to the source of life? That we originated from space?"

"A beautiful and profound name for space is the *universe*. Yesterday when we were in the library and reviewing the five books you chose, do you recall the book we discussed that covered the law of attraction?"

"*The Secret*?"

"Exactly. I told you then that many people are oblivious to what they unconsciously manifest, and often, fear-based emotions dominate, particularly in our Western world. I also said I'd share a simple solution. While the book, *The Secret*, may not directly address the secret we're exploring in our project, it contains a kernel of truth. This truth is that your thoughts alone have the power to influence the world beyond yourself. It's the concept of manifestation, remember?"

Lisa nodded, and in that moment, they witnessed another star flash.

"Look, I'm manifesting," she joked, prompting Grandpa's laugh.

"Manifesting is essentially making a wish. And when done effectively, it becomes a wish that always comes true."

"Do you mean all my wishes can come true? I find that hard to believe."

"Well, it's the truth."

"But if that's true, why are there so many unhappy people?"

"My dear Lisa, unhappiness primarily resides in your mind—actually, it's all in your mind. There are numerous terrible and unpleasant situations, big and small, that might make you unhappy or have already done so. How you perceive and think about these situations determines whether you experience happiness or not. It's a fundamental force in every event of your life. You determine how anything affects you and how you respond to it."

Lisa absorbed Grandpa's words.

"Many people who we consider 'poor' are actually very content," Grandpa continued, "while many 'rich' individuals are quite unhappy. People with perfect health and bodies can be unhappy, while those without limbs or sight can experience great joy. Numerous individuals believe that happiness can be obtained externally and quantified in the outside world. They think having lots of money, a luxurious car, a big house, or, in your case, the latest smartphone will bring them happiness. However, this happiness is short-lived. There is always something new, something different, something bigger, or something more beautiful to chase after."

Grandpa continued, "So if you adopt that mindset, you will forever be pursuing happiness, but you will never truly attain it. True happiness lies in being content and grateful, finding joy in the small and simple things: feeling the warmth of the sun on your face, being with your loved ones, the scent of freshly cut grass, the smile of a baby, or even a comforting embrace from your old grandpa." He wrapped his arm around Lisa in the chair beside him. "This doesn't mean possessions cannot bring you happiness, but if your sense of fulfillment and happiness does not depend on them, you can do without. It's all about intention, the underlying thought."

Lisa took a sip of her still-warm hot chocolate, tilted her head back again, and sighed.

Grandpa continued, "If you desire all your wishes to come true, you must understand and apply the principles of manifestation. You will tap into the primal power of the universe—the quantum field. That power is immense, which is why you must approach it with knowledge. Otherwise, it's like a young child playing with an electrical outlet, and that can lead to trouble."

"Are you saying that a wish that doesn't follow these principles can result in something truly negative?"

"Not exactly. The universe doesn't punish you with a sudden surge of power or anything like that. However, the outcome might be the opposite of what you desired, simply because you wished for it."

"I don't quite grasp it, Grandpa."

"Remember when you were a child and used to take things literally? For instance, if I asked you, 'Can you help me?' you would reply, 'Sure, I can!' and then you wouldn't do anything."

Lisa chuckled. "Yes, I remember. It was fun to take those questions literally."

"That's precisely how the universe works," Grandpa explained.

As Lisa remained silent, he continued, "The universe can only give you what you ask for. So, if your wish or question is, let's say, 'I want money,' the universe can only respond with, 'Okay, your wish is to want money. As per your request, I will let you keep wanting it.'"

Lisa pondered for a moment. "So, I keep *wanting* because that's literally what I wished for? Does it work like that?"

Grandpa affirmed, "Many people wish for something they lack. They desire more, believing it will bring them happiness. However, the universe can only interpret and fulfill this wish by perpetuating the sense of lack, by prolonging the desire."

"That's as unfortunate as fear attracting more fear."

"Yes, Lisa. When you understand the laws of the universe, everything becomes fair and logical. Once you truly comprehend these laws, fear will no longer hold power over you."

"Is this still connected to our project?"

Grandpa laughed. "Everything is intertwined with our project! What aspect of life can't be connected to the secret we're unraveling? The secret of life!"

And once again, they witnessed a flash in the expansive sky above. *Did Grandpa mention a meteor shower earlier today? Is the Universe listening?*

"Wow, another one! I'm going to make a wish this time! But what should I say? I know now I shouldn't say, '*I want.*'"

"A wish is born out of gratitude. Gratitude for what is yet to come. You make your wish from the future, as if it has already been granted. Essentially, you're expressing gratitude to the Universe or the Source for the situation in the future."

"So, I pretend that it has already happened?"

"Yes. However, it requires both gratitude and trust. You must firmly believe that it will indeed manifest. You have to visualize it vividly, see it before you. It takes practice. It doesn't usually come naturally. Your thoughts and words must be positive. Allow time to work its magic, and you must also make a sacrifice."

"A sacrifice?"

"Yes, because you need to take action yourself. You must do something to make your wish come true. That's one of the laws of the universe. There is always a balance. Every event disrupts that balance, and a reaction follows on a different plane. By taking action, you create an imbalance, and the universe responds to it. May I ask what wish you would like to make?"

Lisa contemplated. *What do I truly desire?* Suddenly, it became clear. "I'd rather not be bullied at school anymore!"

"Well," Grandpa said, "let's begin by eliminating the word *not.* The universe doesn't recognize it. Small children don't understand that word either. If you tell a child, 'Don't fall,' they're likely to fall. So your wording should be positive and focused on the future situation."

"Ah, I see. Wait, I think I have it," Lisa followed the steps in her mind that Grandpa had just explained. "I'm grateful that my classmates treat me kindly. I envision my class being enjoyable. Everyone is friendly toward one another, and I receive invitations to parties."

"That's very clever, my dear! And what sacrifice are you willing to make for this? What action will you take in return?"

Lisa fell silent. She hadn't considered this aspect. "I think I won't do anything at all. I'm being bullied because other kids spread rumors about me, and I can't change Madison. To overcome the bullying and fit in, I used to try doing what Madison wanted me to do. But then I wasn't being true to myself, and that's not right. So, I won't try to change myself anymore. I'll simply be myself and take pride in who I am. I'll be my own best friend! And anyone who wants to be our friend is welcome."

"*Oo-way*," Grandpa expressed, impressed.

"Oo-what?"

"*Oo-way*. It's written as *wu wei*. It means: *doing by not doing*. Ancient Chinese wisdom. That's a sign that it's time for us to head to bed. Through sleep, by doing nothing, your insights from today will embed as memories within your being and you'll always remember them. That will come in handy tomorrow when we see Theo!"

Grandpa stood up and started walking back toward the house.

Lisa took one final glance at the vastness of the universe above.

One day, I'll meet you—whoever you are. Wow—infinity is cool.

Journal: The Lisa Project:
The Secret of Life-Day 5-continued...

Shooting Stars! A Vast Universe-End of Day Five! (Biggest Day!)
Grandpa made the evening even more special than usual.
We took sleeping bags and hot chocolate outside and did
some star gazing.
I learned:

- If something is infinite, there is no end and no
  beginning. The beginning is the end, and the end is
  the beginning.
- Everything is relative-even happiness. It starts
  with my mind. How I think about things/
  situations/life determines how I experience
  it. (Also, happiness is not always the goal-it is
  a gift and not always permanent.) How about
  contentment and finding joy in simple things?)
- It's up to me to discover the purpose of my
  life. No one else can determine that for me. The
  decision is mine-and mine only!

- ▶ In all the universe-I am unique! It is the reason I exist!
- ▶ It is true that my thoughts alone have the power to influence the world beyond me.
- ▶ If you desire all your wishes to come true, you must understand and apply the principles of manifestation. (Go back to The Secret!)
- ▶ Manifesting is essentially making a wish-but, it has some rules.
    - Using the word want-or I want-means the Universe will keep you wanting.
    - I must declare my wish or intention as if it already happened.
    - I must take action myself to make it come true. It's a balance.
    - Requirements: gratitude, trust, firm belief. Be positive.
    - Declare the future. Allow time. Take Action!

<u>Bullying</u>—this is what I asked of the Universe: I'm grateful that my classmates treat me kindly. I envision my class being enjoyable. Everyone is friendly toward one another, and I receive invitations to parties.

My sacrifice (my action): do nothing but be true to myself. Be me. Take pride in who I am. Be my own best friend.

Oo-way (dictionary): wu wei. It means doing by not doing.

Ancient Chinese wisdom.

Maybe I'll study outer-space.

Time for bed. Maybe tomorrow we will define the truth. Well—maybe not.

THE LISA PROJECT:
The Secret of Life

Day 6

CHAPTER 17 | To See Or Not To See

Truth and Justice

The next morning, Grandpa and Lisa sat in the living room of Grandpa's long-time friend Theo who had moved to America from Holland after his retirement. He stepped away to fetch their refreshments, and Lisa's gaze was drawn to a large painting of an eye on the wall directly opposite her. The eye seemed to be looking straight at her, and Lisa couldn't quite grasp the message behind the artwork.

At first, the eye appeared stern and unyielding, but the longer she stared at it, the more it seemed to transform and soften. At one point, it even resembled the beautiful eyes of Grandpa and Mom, radiating warmth and comfort. Lisa felt a tinge of sadness, and the eye in the painting now seemed to offer solace. The iris resembled the familiar photograph of Earth taken from space. *I'm reading a lot through or in those eyes.*

"Do you like it?"

Lisa snapped out of her trance.

Theo stood next to her, also looking toward the painting. "It's special. Your Grandpa painted it for me. But I'm the only one who's never seen it."

At that moment, Theo turned toward Lisa, and she saw his unfocused eyes. They were cloudy, reminiscent of the Milky Way she had observed under the stars with Grandpa. His pupils were small, seemingly peering into the distance. *How had I not noticed this when we first arrived?*

"Oh, didn't your grandpa tell you that you were visiting the blind man? Sorry if I startled you, young lady," Theo said, as he effortlessly settled himself on the couch across from them.

How does he seem to know what I'm thinking or feeling?

"Your Grandpa told me you had a question for me. So, let's hear it."

Lisa felt somewhat awestruck by this man. During their journey to Theo's place, Grandpa had mentioned that Theo used to be a judge, but he hadn't mentioned his blindness.

"Well, Grandpa and I are working on a project to uncover the secret of life and I've been learning about the senses, truth, and reality. I'm a little stuck on the truth. I understand that there's no absolute reality or truth, but there are still some cases where I struggle to comprehend it fully. If someone does something really bad—something that is always wrong like abusing someone—then isn't there just one truth: that the perpetrator is always wrong, by definition?" Lisa asked.

"Ah, you've come to the right place," Theo replied, his tone serious. "I understand your question and your struggle. Maybe I can help you, but first, allow me to share a brief glimpse of my life story. Is that alright with you? Might take a minute."

Lisa nodded and settled into a more comfortable position.

"I understand your question very well," Theo began. "I used to be just like that, but to an extreme extent. Right was right, wrong was wrong, and there was nothing in between. I learned this from my parents, who spent their lives fearing making any mistakes. They approached life with utmost seriousness, rarely finding joy or laughter. Their motto was that 'You're on Earth to walk a straight path to your grave without making any mistakes.' That was the essence of their mindset."

"So, I followed their blueprint and graduated from university. I not only feared making mistakes myself, but I also became adept at spotting and judging others' mistakes. I pursued law school and eventually became a judge, which I believed was my dream at the time.

"I was an accomplished judge right from the start. I thought so myself, and others in the court seemed to think so too. I was decisive and unwavering. Wrong was wrong, and I saw everything in black and white. I applied the law faithfully, aiming to make the world a better place by upholding justice.

"But after many years, I started to notice that people in the courtroom were never truly satisfied with my verdicts. Not the defendants who were sentenced, not the ones who were acquitted due to the law, neither the winners nor the losers. It seemed that my court rulings carried the energy of my parents: serious, strict, and devoid of any cheerfulness or humor. I recognized it, but I did nothing about it because I believed it was my duty to serve Lady Justice," Theo explained, pointing to a statue of a blindfolded woman holding a sword and scales.

"Lady Justice wears a blindfold to symbolize impartiality and the objective consideration of facts, regardless of the individuals involved, and I excelled at that. I started handling more significant and controversial cases. Boy, did I feel important and skilled! Deep down, I yearned for my parents to acknowledge and congratulate me, to feel proud of me one day. But it never happened. It wasn't in their nature.

"And then, one winter evening as I descended the grand staircase of the courthouse, something inexplicable occurred. One moment, I took a step, and the next, everything went dark and quiet."

Lisa recalled her own fall in Grandpa's barn and the profound experience she had in the Zen Den hot tub. A floating sensation, suspended.

"Ahh, so you understand how it feels."

Lisa was caught off guard. *Okay, really. How does he know what I'm thinking?*

"Anyway, it was dark and quiet, and I had no idea where I was. I sensed that I was lying on a bed, occasionally feeling the touch of human hands. In reality, I had taken a terrible fall down those stairs, hitting my head multiple times. As a result, I lost both my sight and my hearing. I was unaware of this at the time, lying blind and deaf in a bed, making unintelligible sounds. After a few days, my hearing gradually returned, and I finally managed to communicate with the nurses at the hospital where I had been admitted. The attending doctor came to my bedside and delivered the news that I would never regain my eyesight. I remember his tone was casual as if ordering half a loaf of bread from a bakery.

"Well, to spare you a lengthy narrative, let's fast-forward. I learned to accept and adapt to my disability and eventually returned to work. Reading legal documents became a challenge, so I received them in braille. One day, as I sat there preparing for my first lawsuit after the accident, I had a thought. *Well, Theo, now you are Lady Justice, with your own blindfold!* And that thought made me smile. It was an extraordinary moment. I even laughed aloud. I may have howled. In any case, everything that had been bottled up inside me— everything my parents had instilled in me, was released. And I felt liberated and light. I returned to the courtroom with my cane, sitting down cheerfully and in high spirits. The case began, and something remarkable unfolded. I truly listened to both sides. I could hear them, understand them, and visualize their perspectives and pains.

"It was a divorce case, and the man and woman involved were engaged in a bitter custody battle over their daughter. I asked each of them to express their concerns and propose solutions. I allowed the woman to speak first, and she shared her story, which I comprehended completely. When she finished, I said, 'I understand, you're right.' I could sense that some people in the courtroom appeared surprised, but to me, it felt natural.

"During the man's statement, I could empathize with his perspective and understand his viewpoint. When he concluded, I once again said, 'I understand, you're right.' The clerk objected at that point. 'Your Honor,' he exclaimed, 'you're now suggesting that both sides are right. That's impossible.' And my response, of course, was, 'You're right.'" Theo burst into laughter, thoroughly amused by his own story.

"At that moment, I addressed the two spouses and said, 'You are both right. I order you to find a mutually beneficial solution that prioritizes the well-being of your daughter. If you fail to do so, I will make a ruling, but I can assure you that neither of you will be satisfied with it.' And from that moment on, that became my approach in most similar cases, whenever the circumstances allowed for it."

"I'm not sure if I fully understand," Lisa hesitated, "but I find it a beautiful and extraordinary story. Of course, I am sorry about your blindness."

"You may not completely grasp it, but my blindness has opened my eyes. When I had sight, I *looked* but didn't truly *see*. I perceived life in black and white, with great seriousness. But my accident allowed me to shed that seriousness and experience the infinite shades between black and white, all without relying on my eyes. I learned to listen, to feel, and my heart opened up. I became the real Theo, the one I had concealed due to my strict upbringing. So, I'm not pitiable. In fact, quite the opposite."

Lisa stopped him. "So, let me make sure I get it. You also believe there's no absolute reality?"

"Essentially, yes. In the courtroom, the pursuit of absolute truth is paramount. But since losing my sight, I've come to realize that truth is rarely black and white, and it's never absolute. In my previous view, truth could be discerned by uncovering objective facts. Yet, no fact is entirely objective. The observer's perspective colors the information, sometimes consciously but often unconsciously. Reality is often seen as the ultimate concept, the one and only truth. However, humans can never fully comprehend that reality. My experience aligns with a statement by Einstein, who said, and I paraphrase, that sensory perception indirectly informs us about the world around us, and thus, we can never fully grasp it.[9] Can you follow this line of thought?" Theo asked.

"Grandpa has already taught me about senses and vibrations, so I can grasp what you're saying." Lisa glanced at Grandpa who smiled and nodded.

"If you're surprised that I noticed your nodding or could sense your thoughts earlier, it's connected to this," Theo said. "Due to my blindness, I had to rely on my remaining senses, which became incredibly heightened. My sixth sense, intuition, and also my empathy are awakened. As a result, I sometimes 'feel' what others think or feel."

Lisa found his explanation sensible. "You mentioned the terms black and white a few times. Grandpa also talked to me about it. What do you think—can something be both black and white at the same time?"

Theo nodded affirmatively. "Allow me to share another brief story. Several years ago, a traditional children's festival in the Netherlands called Saint Nicholas, similar to Santa Claus, gained international attention. During this festival, Saint Nicholas would visit the Netherlands in December, delivering gifts to children. However, he was always accompanied by numerous assistants called Black Petes,[10] who appeared in blackface. Many people around the world found this practice discriminatory and demeaning to people of color. The debate surrounding Black Petes caused deep divisions among the adults in the Netherlands. One group demanded an end to the tradition, while another fiercely defended it as their cherished folklore. The situation even led to physical altercations between parents in front of their young children. The issue needed resolution, but how? Both sides seemed polarized."

Grandpa piped in. "Perhaps a wise person could engage with everyone involved and help them understand each other's perspectives?"

"That's an excellent approach," Theo agreed. "However, in the Netherlands, there was no one considered impartial enough to undertake such a task. So the idea emerged to bring the case before an international court, with an unbiased judge deciding the future of this children's festival. And who do you think they turned to?"

"You!" Lisa and Grandpa chorused.

Theo nodded. "Some people appreciated my approach to court rulings and considered me sufficiently impartial to tackle this seemingly insurmountable issue. When they approached me, I didn't hesitate because it felt like my soul's calling. So, with renewed energy, I delved into researching the Black Pete situation in the Netherlands. I discovered that the entire country was deeply involved, with everyone holding strong opinions that disregarded the perspectives of others. To truly comprehend the matter, I sought to understand all sides."

Theo paused as he considered his next words. "Lisa, what I have shared and am about to share incites a lot of controversy. I'm entrusting it to you because I feel you are mature enough to hear me out, and process why it is often a mishandled or misunderstood topic. Ready to listen for a bit?"

Lisa nodded solemnly. "Thank you, Theo. I'll do my best to listen and understand."

"Good. Now, you probably know about colonialism from your US history lessons. Large groups of people from most countries in Europe traveled the world hundreds of years ago, and often this included stealing valuable items and raw materials wherever they could—and abusing people of different origin or skin color. That has gone on for centuries. It is how Europe became wealthy. Also, America carries many scars from these practices. Roughly speaking, Europeans saw it as normal to think that people who looked or lived differently were inferior. This justified occupying their land, looting it, and exploiting and trading the original inhabitants as slaves. That's where racism and inequality came from. If you then look at the Saint Nicholas party, in which an old white man is helped by black servants deliberately acting clownish, you can feel how this can be hurtful to entire population groups.

"The supporters of Black Petes cited tradition as their primary argument. This is where I had an epiphany," Theo continued. "I delved into the history of the Saint Nicholas festival itself and discovered that it had been celebrated in the Netherlands for centuries. However, the inclusion of Black Petes only began around 150 years ago. That's when I believed I had found the solution. Since the proponents wanted to preserve the tradition, I thought they would eventually realize that a Saint Nicholas festival without Black Petes was the true tradition."

Theo fell silent for a moment, lost in thought. When he spoke, his voice carried a hint of uncertainty. "I thought I had the solution, but there was a small voice inside me, questioning whether I had become part of the problem and allowed my own judgment to cloud my perspective. I realized that the proponents of Black Petes wouldn't simply change their minds because of what I found in my research. It was true, and I needed to find a way to bridge the divide between both sides. However, I didn't know how to do that. I worried for days, but a solution eluded me.

"In my desperation, like I often do, I turned to your grandpa for help. He arrived with a small canvas, a brush, and only two tubes of paint. I pointed to my eyes and asked, 'What can I do with these?' Or really, I meant without these. I obviously couldn't see to paint. Your grandpa calmly replied, 'Once you understand, you'll see. And then you'll know exactly what to do. See it in your mind's eye.'

"Well, I sat down at the dining table with the canvas, the brush, and the tubes of paint, waiting for inspiration to strike. I held the tubes of paint in my hands, trying to guess the colors your grandfather had given me. And suddenly, it hit me like a bolt of lightning, and I burst into laughter. I believe you already know what colors they were, don't you?"

Lisa nodded. *Black and white? And I just nodded at a blind man…*

"I thought so," Theo continued. "I began painting on that sheet of paper, guided by how it felt to me, by how I imagined it looked. And eventually, with my own hands, I created this," Theo said, pointing to a painting hanging near the dining table.

Lisa hadn't noticed it before. For a blind person, it was remarkably well done, she thought. It reminded her of the symbol Grandpa had placed next to his front door.

"Familiar, yes? Mine is not exactly like the one your grandpa has, but that symbol represents one of the fundamental aspects of life here on Earth. You may want to write this in your journal, Lisa:

"Opposites are not absolute.

"They are relative.

"They share similarities and are therefore connected.

"They cannot exist without each other.

"In essence, they are different aspects of a whole that complement each other.

"Everything is in harmony with everything else, but also subject to constant change.

"Nothing remains the same, yet fundamentally, nothing truly changes.

"It was through this realization that I understood both sides in the Black Petes conflict were only focused on the past and the present, but not on the present and its future."

"In the past lies the present, the now holds what will become," Lisa recited.

"Ah, you remembered. Wonderful, Lisa!" Grandpa said.

Lisa continued, "'Yesterday is history. Tomorrow is a mystery. Today is a gift; that's why they call it the present.' It is not my creation. I found it online, but I like it a lot!"

"Yes!" Theo agreed. "I can hear your grandpa paraphrased, as he usually likes to quote dusty old books and poets! Nicely done."

Lisa glowed inside, truly feeling part of the conversation with these two wise men.

Theo went on, "The present is a product of the past. But if you solely focus on the past, you forget where you want to go, and as a result, your present suffers. In the Black Petes debate, both sides were only fixated on their present pain and not on understanding the roots of that pain in the past. That's why they couldn't envision a solution that would allow both sides to live in the present and create a bright future for their children—one that was colorful, not limited to black and white. That's the foundation on which I based my legal argument and subsequent ruling. I have a feeling that you grasp this concept, don't you?"

Lisa nodded. "I understand now, thanks to your story and what Grandpa has already shown me, but—"

Theo continued, "You see these contradictions all around the world. During elections, in wartime, or with humanity facing global climate change. Strong supporters and equally fervent opponents emerge swiftly, turning the discussion into a black and white battle, disregarding the other colors, the nuances. As a result, they fail to understand the other person's perspective or simply refuse to acknowledge it."

Picking up on his energy, Lisa quickly inquired, "But there are genuinely bad people out there, right? People who harm others for their own benefit or pleasure. How did you, as a judge, deal with that?"

Theo nodded. "You're right. There are people who make grave mistakes with tragic consequences. In such cases, it's often impossible to bring the perpetrator and the victim together to find a solution. Since I became blind, I've prioritized giving victims a voice. I let them express what happened and describe the actions of the perpetrator. It's not as simple as it sounds, but it's essential for the healing process. They need to be heard and taken seriously. I dedicated days to these conversations whenever possible.

"If the circumstances allowed and the victim consented, I sometimes allowed the perpetrator to be present. Remarkably, this approach led to some genuinely positive outcomes. The harm had already been done, and the pain had been inflicted. I couldn't change that, but if possible, I facilitated healing for the victim and provided insights for the perpetrator. However, there were times when I had to revert to my traditional role and deliver a black-and-white punishment."

Ω

Lisa took an audible breath and sat back absorbing Theo's words as her thoughts rushed along. *There is so much to think about. Isn't the unknown sort of a gray area? I mean how about Dad's viewpoint on what he did vs. Grandpa's? How different are their perspectives really? Do they even know what the other is thinking? Or feeling?*

"There is a lot on your mind, young lady. What would you like to ask?"

"Well, it's just that—I mean, you seem to understand everything so deeply. So, I wanted to ask if you know what happened to my father."

Lisa observed Theo's gaze shift toward Grandpa, his expression one of affection and compassion and … *Is that hope I see?*

"Your grandfather made me promise never to discuss this," Theo replied calmly.

"Why not?"

"Because it brings my dear friend great pain."

"But won't it remain painful if you never talk about it?" Lisa pressed.

"That's true, but—"

Grandpa interrupted Theo, "I just can't bring myself to talk about it. So, I didn't want Theo to discuss it with you right now, at least not with me here."

"Grandpa," Lisa said firmly, "if you don't want to hear it and I do, you have two choices: either close your ears or step outside for a while. In either case, you won't have to bear the vibrations that you don't want to encounter—seeing us or hearing us—and you won't be in pain. You taught me that."

Grandpa was outwardly shaken. "But knowing that you'll be discussing it already hurts me."

"You also taught me how our own beliefs influence our feelings about something," Lisa reminded him. "Maybe you should remember that I'm seeking personal advice from Theo. I need this. You can choose how you feel."

Grandpa's mouth hung open, clearly feeling the power emanating from Lisa, knowing she was absolutely right—she had utilized his own teachings and insights. Without saying a word, he rose from the couch, and left the room. Lisa heard the door open and close as he went outside.

After a few moments, Theo said, "I'm truly impressed with you, Lisa."

"Thank you, but it's bittersweet," she glanced toward the window, seeing Grandpa standing at the garden fountain. "When I believe something wholeheartedly, I can stand my ground—my truth, I guess. I've learned a lot from Grandpa, but I felt like these words came from somewhere beyond me. It seems to happen a lot—or a lot more anyway—during this project."

Theo smiled, "And thus, the student becomes the teacher. But now, to the tough topic at hand, ask me your question again."

"What would you have done if you were the judge in my dad's case?"

"And, why would you want to know that?"

"Grandpa has disowned Dad, his own son, and is condemning him for what happened. I know Dad made a mistake, but does that justify cutting off your own child?"

"But how does that relate to a judge's decision?" Theo asked, contemplating the connection.

"Well, at the trial, Dad wasn't sentenced to prison, but Grandpa clearly believes he should have been. He doesn't talk about it often, but when he does, it's pretty evident."

Theo let out a deep sigh. "This is closely tied to everything we just discussed, and it's certainly not a coincidence. What have you learned from your grandfather and me about contradictions?"

"That something can be both black and white, depending on how you perceive it."

Theo nodded. "So, can you imagine that the situation with your father appears black to you, but white to your grandfather?"

"Okay, I can entertain that possibility. But at the same time, I can't. It's his son!"

"That's true, but you can't peer into your grandpa's mind. You don't know what he has experienced that led him to view his own son as a villain."

"That's valid," she agreed. "And there may be others who think poorly of my dad too. I know he isn't bad. But even in this situation, it clearly depends on a person's perspective. So, what would you have done if you were the judge in my dad's trial?"

Theo looked saddened and shook his head. "Any response I give could genuinely hurt your grandfather. I accept him as he is and where he is with his choice. I do not have to agree with him to love my friend deeply anyway."

"And I do not have to agree that you won't answer, but I get it and respect you." A radiant smile lit up Lisa's face. "The bottom line is that what you two have is true friendship—or should I say truth in friendship. I do understand, even if I wish Grandpa could let go. I think I better go show him some love. Thank you so much, Theo."

Lisa planted a kiss on Theo's cheek before rushing outside to Grandpa who was equally surprised by the kiss on his cheek and her warm, forgiving embrace.

Each with a different perceality. All of them, connected.

The Lisa Project: The Secret of Life

Journal—Day 6

Grandpa and Theo are catching up after having lunch, and we just covered a boat load of stuff. So, here goes before the next stop on our project:

To see or not to see! Grandpa did not tell me Theo is blind, but he sees more than most people see. It was like he could read my thoughts!

He relies on his remaining senses, and they are strong. His sixth sense, intuition, and his empathy were awakened. This is how he knew what I felt and thought sometimes.

I now understand that there's no absolute reality or truth, but if someone does something really bad then isn't that person always wrong? Answer: Not necessarily!

Theo said he used to be extreme—right was right, wrong was wrong, and there was nothing in between. He learned this from his parents who lived in fear of making mistakes.

Truth is rarely black and white, and it is never absolute. I learned that before I 'judge' black and white I need to listen and create understanding of the perspectives of those involved.

Humans can never fully comprehend reality. Our experiences are individual to us, and we create our own reality-which is going to be different from someone else's in many (most?) cases.

Example of Black Petes and the St. Nicholas celebration: Theo's job was to find a way to bridge the divide between both sides of whether Black Petes should be part of it. To many it was disrespectful and to many it was part of heritage and culture.

He had me write this down:

- Opposites are not absolute. They are relative.
- They share similarities and are therefore connected.
- They cannot exist without each other.
- In essence, they are different aspects of a whole that complement each other.

- ▸ Everything is in harmony with everything else, but also subject to constant change.
- ▸ Nothing remains the same, yet fundamentally, nothing truly changes.

Both sides in the Black Petes' conflict were only focused on the past and the present, but not on the present and its future.

He quoted Willem Bilderdijk—

"In the past lies the present, the now holds what will become."

The present is a product of the past. But if you solely focus on the past, you forget where you want to go, and as a result, your present suffers. In the Black Pete debate, both sides were only fixated on their present pain and not on understanding the roots of that pain in the past.

There are people who make grave mistakes with tragic consequences. Theo tried to facilitate healing for the victims and provide insights for the perpetrators, but there were times when he had to revert to black-and-white punishment. It's never simply cut and dried.

I asked him how he would rule on my father. It hurt Grandpa's feelings and he stepped outside-but I had to stand my ground-my truth.

Theo said something like, "The student becomes the teacher." Am I Grandpa's teacher?! Haha.

I've learned that something can be both black and white, depending on how you perceive it. So, I know that Grandpa sees things one way where my dad is concerned, and I see it the other. But I don't know what Grandpa has experienced to make him feel this way.

Theo would not say what he would have done with Dad's case because it would hurt Grandpa. He is a true friend-a truthful friend too!

CHAPTER 18 | The Shelter

Lesson in Humanity

Grandpa and Lisa drove along a rural road enjoying a mosaic landscape of meadows, farmland, forest, and a smattering of homes and livestock. Occasionally, they saw wind turbines in fields and a few passing cars and trucks. It was mostly pretty, and a little remote.

In the distance, Lisa spotted the outlines of what appeared to be a town. "Where are we headed now?"

"We're going to meet some people I assist every week for an afternoon."

As they drew nearer, Lisa realized the structures were more like elongated barracks, and they were surrounded by a tall chain-link fence topped with coils of wire. The inside was bustling with people of various colors and dressed in clothes unlike any Lisa had ever seen.

Grandpa pulled the car up to report at a security shack. The guard greeted Grandpa with a broad, knowing smile. "Hello! Is your granddaughter joining in to help today as well?"

"I just want to show Lisa what it's like here, Sarge!"

"Well, Lisa," the guard said to her, "things can be challenging here at times, but ultimately, it's the most rewarding work one can do.

Please, feel welcome!" He raised the gate and they drove through and parked just inside.

"Okay, Grandpa, what is this place?"

Grandpa said nothing but quickly got out of the car and headed toward a large building. Lisa hurriedly followed, feeling the gazes of various people upon her.

These are all foreigners.

As Lisa glanced back at them, she noticed beautiful, sparkling eyes brimming with hope and determination, as well as eyes exuding a mixture of sorrow or deep happiness. It stirred a unique sensation in her stomach, as if she were connecting with her own emotions of determination, sadness, and joy.

Reaching the entrance of a reception building she asked again, "Where are we?"

Grandpa pointed to a sign next to the entrance, *Abacus Migrant Shelter.*

Lisa read it, and a shock ran through her as she realized where she was.

This is what Mom is so worried about.

Once again, she surveyed her surroundings. Her mental image of a dirty, foul-smelling place filled with chaos, raw emotions, and crowds didn't match what she was witnessing so far. In fact, it seemed completely different. A sense of order, peace, and tranquility enveloped her. She grasped the message Grandpa wanted to convey without him uttering a single word.

They stepped into a vast hall, and she couldn't believe her eyes. It was a spacious area divided into an assortment of cubicles. Hundreds of bunk beds were scattered throughout the hall, and people were walking, sitting, or sleeping everywhere.

"What are we doing here, Grandpa? Why do so many people know you?"

"I volunteer here. I talk to people, help with translations and paperwork, and often bring along some food, clothes, and toys that I've collected," Grandpa explained.

"Toys?"

Grandpa nodded toward the room and Lisa noticed tiny babies, young children, and boys and girls her age. "So, all these people are asylum seekers, right?"

Grandpa looked at Lisa, amused. "What, in your opinion, is an asylum seeker?"

"Mom always says that asylum seekers come to our country to take advantage of how well-off we are and the things we provide. But now I realize that, like Mom, I don't really know what an asylum seeker truly is."

"Why don't you come with me?" Grandpa led her to a spot in the room where three bunk beds formed at a right angle, providing a little privacy. Sitting on one of the beds were a dark-skinned man and woman dressed in vibrant, cheerful colors. They were delighted when they saw Grandpa. They stood and embraced him warmly. They began speaking in a mix of English and Spanish, which Lisa couldn't fully understand. When they glanced at her, she gazed into two pairs of bright green eyes. She was taken by their intensity.

A girl around Lisa's age approached and stood next to her. She possessed the same captivating eyes. "Lisa, meet Esmeralda. She speaks English quite well. Can she show you around while I talk with her parents?"

Lisa nodded and smiled back at Esmeralda. There was something about her that felt oddly familiar. "Come," Esmeralda said, "you will be safe. There is a lot to see."

Lisa fell in step beside her as Grandpa settled down with Esmeralda's parents.

Ω

Ninety minutes had passed, and Grandpa, done with his assistance, glanced at his watch. Lisa had yet to return. Suddenly, a commotion erupted in the distance. Grandpa instinctively tuned in and moved toward the noise to search for Lisa. The clamor grew louder, surpassing the realm of a mere argument. Reaching the scene, he witnessed two men locked in a heated fight. It was a fierce altercation, with a large crowd of people encircling them, screaming and shouting. Then he spotted Lisa alongside Esmeralda, clutching her hand, and standing too close to the brawling men. Grandpa wasted no time forging a path through the crowd. Instead of going directly to Lisa, he entered the circle where the two men grappled in headlock, spewing insults.

Ω

What happened next resembled a scene from a movie. Grandpa seized both men by the shoulders and forcefully separated them. Lisa's jaw dropped. She had never witnessed such strength from her grandpa. The clamor subsided, and all eyes fixed grandpa who had swiftly restored order.

Like a referee, Grandpa wedged himself between the two men and had quick words. "Interpreters!" he commanded. "English!"

The two men were from different countries and couldn't communicate with each other.

One of the men broke free, clearly intending to assault Grandpa. But he had anticipated it, swiftly evading the attack. In a split second, the assailant found himself pinned on the ground while the other man, Lisa, and the rest of the crowd looked on at Grandpa in confused relief, respect, and disbelief.

Lisa realized Grandpa had taken control of the energy in the room. Two uniformed men arrived, but Grandpa instructed them to keep their distance. Soon after, two interpreters appeared. The guards escorted Grandpa, the two men and the interpreters into a separate room, leaving the witnesses of the fight in stunned silence.

Lisa and Esmeralda returned to her family and waited for Grandpa's return.

Ω

As they drove toward the guard shack to leave, Sarge gave Lisa and Grandpa a thumbs up and raised the gate. Outside, protestors had assembled with banners reading, "No more $!#%! No more migrants!"

"Well," Grandpa said as he drove slowly through them and turned safely onto the main road, "You were afraid of asylum seekers and maybe now the protestors too. But in any case, would you want to go back and visit Esmeralda? Even after what just happened?"

"Yes. I would like to return. I really liked her." A serious expression crossed Lisa's face. "Do you know what Esmeralda's family has been through?"

"I do."

"I thought my life was tough, but compared to her, I'm fortunate. And they have a baby who is seriously ill and might not survive. I saw him. It is heart-wrenching."

"I know, but I'm confident the baby will make it. We'll ensure that he receives proper medical treatment at the hospital this week. That was part of my purpose for this visit."

Lisa exhaled in relief and turned more toward Grandpa. "You never cease to amaze. And speaking of, something extraordinary happened when you got involved in that fight. It was as if you anticipated it all and saw everything. And when that man tried to attack you, I couldn't comprehend it. It was like you were dancing and he couldn't lay a finger on you."

"Well put. We were indeed performing a kind of dance."

———

"We? He wanted to harm you, not dance with you!"

"What you witnessed was Aikido," Grandpa explained, "It's an Asian martial art that I've been fortunate enough to master. Aikido isn't about combat. It's more like a dance. It assumes the need for each other because without an opponent, you're alone. It also recognizes that there's an attacker, but as the defender, you take the initiative to regain control of the situation. Just as I've explained to you before, by acknowledging that you are the cause of something, you can change or resolve the situation. Aikido teaches that the attacker wants to give you a gift, and it's your task to accept that gift without causing harm to the attacker or yourself. Thus, you utilize the attacker's energy to express gratitude for their gift."

"I saw what you did. Otherwise, I wouldn't believe it and would think you're crazy."

"I knew it was crucial to facilitate a dialogue between both parties, somewhat like Theo's role in the courtroom. That's why I needed those interpreters. When we went into the private room, the men were allowed to express themselves, and eventually, they ended up embracing."

"Those guys who wanted to destroy each other—hugged?"

Grandpa nodded. "Initially, it was about something so small, yet very big. One thought the other was looking at his wife with a certain intention. And he was very sensitive to that because his wife had been abused in their country. The other lived an even more horrific experience, as his wife had gone missing after the flight from their country, so he was also very emotional. They misunderstood and an altercation ensued that led to a fight. They both had no idea of the other's situation and only reacted from their own pain."

Lisa sat there, speechless. *So much drama. I vow never to complain about my life again.*

"That's why incidents like this occur quite often in migration shelters, but also in correctional facilities and in jails. They house people from diverse backgrounds, languages, and cultures, most of whom have fled threatening situations and experienced traumas. It's like a powder keg ready to explode. And sometimes, things go wrong. The people living near such centers can become victims of these conflicts, and that's why those demonstrators outside the gates are protesting."

"From now on, I don't want to hear the term 'asylum seekers' again," Lisa declared firmly, "not even from Mom! They're people who need help. Thank you, Grandpa, for taking me there."

"Let's get back to the farm. After all the excitement of this day… it's time for a nap!"

Journal: The Lisa Project:
The Secret of Life-Day 6-continued...

The Abacus Migrant Center

I made a new friend today-Esmeralda. She lives in a migrant shelter with her parents and siblings. Yes-I now know asylum seekers!

Mom says that asylum seekers come to our country to take advantage of us, but she doesn't have the full picture. She's never met one in person. I don't plan to use that term again. They are like us-with hope, love, fears, families.

- Misunderstandings create conflict. It escalates when there are communication boundaries-like language.
- Misunderstandings also occur when you assume what someone is thinking, or you have no idea where they are coming from due to their experiences or their circumstances.
- Misunderstandings occur because people don't get their facts

Grandpa had to break up a fight. The men who fought both had situations-unknown to each other-and reacted from their own pain.

Grandpa knew exactly what to do because he is an Aikido master. Who knew!

Aikido is like a dance. It teaches that the attacker wants to give you a gift, and it's your task to accept that gift without causing harm to the attacker or yourself. Thus, you utilize the attacker's energy to express gratitude for their gift.

I thought this was nuts-but I saw it in action, and it works!

As I learned yesterday, by acknowledging that you are the cause of something, you can change or resolve the situation.

A migrant shelter can be like a powder keg ready to explode. And sometimes, things go wrong. The people living near such centers can become victims of these conflicts, and that's why those demonstrators were outside the gates protesting. I get that, but … it's not black and white.

I vow never to complain about my own life again!

CHAPTER 19 | Guilt

Love and Fear

When Lisa burst into the living room an hour later, her excitement was palpable as she clutched an old photo album in her hands.

Grandpa, who was still lounging on the couch, was roused from his nap. His eyes landed on the album, and he sat up abruptly.

"What do you plan to do with that?"

"I found it at the back of your closet. I was looking for—"

"Put it back," Grandpa said sternly.

Lisa looked at him in surprise. Grandpa's face had hardened, and there was a different look in his eyes. She had never seen him like this before.

"But just take a look. These are all pictures of you when you were little."

"I know what's in that album, and I'm telling you again to put it back."

In that moment, the sternness in Grandpa's voice stirred something within Lisa, as if a significant chord had been struck on a guitar. The vibration of his tone hit a nerve. "No!"

Grandpa looked at her, bewildered.

"You're working with me on this project," she continued in a resolute tone, "and it's important that you take me seriously. Mom and Dad have never told me *not* to ask any questions. And you've been encouraging me to ask questions these past few days. I want to know what you were like when you were my age and what your childhood was like. That's part of how you've become who you are! It's unfair to make me put this photo album back without us looking at it together. That's unacceptable." Her words had poured out effortlessly. It was as if she had been holding that 'guitar' her whole life but had only just discovered how to strum it.

Grandpa looked at Lisa, obviously disoriented and distraught. He finally sighed, and said, "You're right, Lisa, but the reason I reacted that way is because I didn't hide that photo album in the back of my closet for no reason." He paused, closed his eyes, and contemplated for a moment. "Okay, this is going to be tough, but it's time." He patted the sofa next to him. "Come and sit with me, and we'll look at these pictures together. I'll tell you everything."

Lisa walked over and sat beside him, handing him the album. He opened it.

Grandpa remained silent as he turned the pages. Lisa saw black and white pictures of a young boy dressed in a sailor suit, appearing almost like a miniature man. There were also photos of that little boy with his parents on the beach. As Grandpa turned another page, Lisa noticed a picture of him, around five years old, standing next to a crib. She looked at him questioningly.

"That's my little sister," he said, his lips pressed together.

"You have a sister?"

"Had," Grandpa responded, falling silent for a while.

Lisa immediately sensed that something had gone terribly wrong, and she gently placed her hand on his arm. "What happened?"

Grandpa took a deep breath. "I'll tell you the story, but then we won't look any further in this album, and it will immediately go back to where you found it. Can we agree on that?"

"Okay."

"Very well. My little sister's name was Mary, and she was born in the winter. I remember the day she was born. It was snowing heavily outside. I was five years old when she was born, the doctor told my mother that little Mary was very weak and needed to gain strength. She required special care. A few weeks later, she developed a high fever and started screaming at an ear-piercing pitch. I vividly remember that sound. It was terrifying. My parents were in a panic, and my father rushed to get the doctor in the middle of the night. He saved Mary's life that night, but he made it clear that my parents needed to be extremely cautious because it could happen again.

"From that moment on, my parents were solely focused on Mary. They worried every time she coughed or caught a cold, and I was forbidden from bringing friends home. This went on for years. Mary's health dictated everything. I adapted to that. She was incredibly cute, and I loved her, but there were times when I resented her too. I hated that she had come into our lives because, from that moment on, all my parents' attention was directed toward her. I felt like I no longer mattered, like I almost ceased to exist in their eyes."

Grandpa halted to gather himself. Lisa sensed that the story was far from over and remained silent.

"I had a love-hate relationship with my little sister. She looked so sweet when it was just the two of us. In those moments, she truly was my adorable little sister. But because of her, everything changed at home, and my parents were no longer my parents.

"On a beautiful summer day, the four of us strolled through the park. Mary sat in her stroller. My mother wanted to take a brief rest on a bench, and I offered to take Mary for a walk. At first, my mother hesitated but eventually agreed. I began walking, pushing Mary in front of me. The stroller seat was reversed. I distinctly remember her looking at me with such sweetness, and I'm almost certain I heard a small voice in my head saying, *Be free!*

"It felt incredibly special, and it filled me with joy. I started running with her across the grass as if we were about to take flight. She laughed and for the first time in a long while, I felt light and free. We ran and ran across the grass, and the remarkable thing was that time seemed to stand still. I felt a genuine connection with my sister. It was as if we were sharing something extraordinary. You know," Grandpa paused and looked at Lisa, "that same feeling of being incredibly close, that's what I felt again when I first saw you."

There was silence for a while. "What happened to Mary?" Lisa asked cautiously.

Grandpa gazed into the distance. "I kept running with Mary, as if in a dream, and we reached the sidewalk again, where I could run even faster. Suddenly, I heard loud barking nearby. I turned to my right and saw a large black dog charging toward us. I was shocked, and I tried to run faster, but I stumbled.

"The stroller flipped over with Mary in it. When I got up, my dad was holding her in his arms. There was blood on her little head, and she wasn't moving. She was unconscious. I saw the panic in my mother's eyes as she called for help. I blocked out the rest of what happened. It felt like everything took forever. Eventually, an ambulance arrived and rushed her to the hospital. We had to wait for what seemed like an eternity to receive any news about her condition. I sat helpless, consumed by guilt over the times I had resented Mary. I could only pray that she would recover. When the doctor finally came to us, he told my parents that Mary had passed away."

Lisa covered her mouth with her hands.

Grandpa had tears on his cheeks. "It was *my* fault. *My fault*. She was knocked over because of *me*. Although my parents never said anything, I felt that they never truly forgave me."

———

Once again, Lisa felt as if a symphony of emotions was playing within her. "And so, you can't forgive Dad either," she mechanically uttered.

Grandpa looked at her in shock. "It's not the same," he exclaimed firmly. "It's ab-so-lute-ly not the same."

"In my perceality it is."

Ω

Lisa put on her coat and stepped outside. She started walking aimlessly along the road, and the crisp, dry air felt like the harbinger of something new. Oddly enough, with Christmas still a good month away, it even carried a hint of spring. Her mind raced with so many of Grandpa's stories. Her response to him about her father surprised her. It felt as though her words had come from a place beyond herself, as if she hadn't generated them on her own.

But it had to happen, she reassured herself, or else Grandpa wouldn't have shared this painful secret. Of course, Mary's story was heartbreaking, and it was evident Grandpa was still saddened.

So why did I bring up the comparison with Dad? I didn't show empathy. Have I been too harsh toward Grandpa?

Panic began to well up within her. *What if Grandpa is angry with me now? What if he decides to end the project?* She quickened her pace, mentally envisioning scenarios of what might unfold.

And so you can't forgive Dad either, she had said. Those words had transformed a poignant moment of shared grief into a reproach toward Grandpa. Lisa started feeling guilty. *Poor Grandpa—first, he had shared an old and painful secret, and now his granddaughter has chastised him.*

The guilt intensified. *What if he sends me back to Mom before I discover the secret of life?*

Twilight fell, and she knew she had to return to the farm, apologize to Grandpa, and explain that she hadn't meant her words the way they came out. She turned around and began running. She had walked farther than she had realized, so she was breathless by the time she spotted the farm. Someone stood waiting for her at the top of the driveway.

"Grandpa!" Lisa called out and sprinted toward him, mustering every last ounce of energy. When she finally reached him, she didn't even get a chance to speak. Grandpa reached out and embraced her tightly.

They held onto each other… and let love conquer fear.

Ω

That evening there was no mention of the incident or the project. It was a night of simple, old-fashioned fun—pizza, popcorn, and movies. When they finally went to bed, Lisa fell asleep within minutes, physically and emotionally drained.

Ω

Grandpa wept—the right kind of tears.

Journal: The Lisa Project:
The Secret of Life-Day 6-continued...

<u>The Day's end...</u>

I learned Grandpa had a sister, Mary. She was very sick, and Grandpa's parents spent most of their time focused on her. This made Grandpa resent Mary-and his parents.

But then, there was an accident caused by Grandpa-and Mary died. He felt responsible. But it can't be changed.

I challenged Grandpa. How is this not similar to what happened with Dad?

I upset him and also myself. But I communicated my perceality!

Love trumps guilt. Love conquers fear. We hugged it out.

Grandpa forgave me. Maybe-he'll think about doing the same with his son.

This day-was emotional chaos.

Tomorrow, I hope I'm ready to see it-The Secret of Life.

THE LISA PROJECT:
The Secret of Life

Day 7

CHAPTER 20 | Mirror, Mirror

The Law of Reflection

The next morning, Lisa slept in later than usual. By the time she descended the stairs, the sun had already been up for a while. A donut and juice waited for her and a note. "Meet me in the Zen Den."

"Hm … Whatever will this day bring?" Lisa smiled, sinking her teeth into the doughy delight.

Grandpa was waiting for her, sitting cross-legged on his yoga pillow with a long, beaded necklace in his hand. "Well, it's time. Are you ready for it?" His voice carried a hint of mystery.

"The Secret of Life?" she whispered.

Grandpa nodded. "You've learned so much in the past few days, and you've shown incredible mastery at lightning speed. Today is the new moon, the perfect moment to change your life forever."

"Well, at least you're not putting too much pressure on me," Lisa smirked. "And what kind of necklace is that?" She sat on the mat beside him.

"This is a *mala*.[11] It's used in Buddhism and Hinduism during the recitation of mantras or prayers. It has one hundred and eight beads, and the traditional practice involves holding the necklace in your hand, starting at this larger bead—the mother bead—and then running it through your fingers, bead by bead." He demonstrated. "It's often used during meditation. I believe this necklace can help you find understanding."

Respectfully, Lisa accepted the necklace from Grandpa, and he helped her wrap it around her neck in three circles. "Thank you, but what am I supposed to do to uncover the secret?"

Grandpa smiled. "All the knowledge you need is already within you. All the puzzle pieces are there. Now it's up to you to put them together. You could spend all your time overthinking and worrying, but that won't bring you the answer.

"You need to get out of your head and into your heart. Your heart holds all the answers. You can meditate, take a walk, paint, or do whatever feels right to you. I know you can do this. And just in case you get stuck, I've written a clue on this card. It is for you to discover other clues. Listen."

"Listen? I do love a treasure hunt."

Lisa took the note from Grandpa and unfolded it. It read, *Where do you see yourself?*

Grandpa quickly took her hand, closing the note within it. "Focus on the question at hand. You have the entire day, including the evening. You can use anything inside or outside the house. Try something completely different first and see what comes up. When you have the answer, come to me." With that, he left her in the silence of the Zen Den.

Lisa felt anxious. Suddenly, she was tasked with unraveling the secret of life, but she felt like she had only just scratched the surface of understanding. Her heart raced, but she remembered Grandpa's meditation instructions.

She settled onto the yoga mat and focused on her breathing, taking slow, deep breaths. It helped to calm her down, and she closed her eyes. The words of the note echoed in her mind. *Where do you see yourself?*

Where do I see myself?

What did Grandpa mean?

How could the question lead me to the answer?

She continued breathing slowly, and gradually, her thoughts faded away.

Ω

Lisa opened her eyes, coming out of her meditation as she felt Sera-cat rub against her knee. Glancing at the clock, she realized she had been meditating for nearly thirty minutes. It felt like mere moments had passed. Stretching her stiff limbs, she stood up and walked outside to return to the house.

What should I do now?

Without a clear plan, Lisa went through the kitchen and living room, quickly eyeballing the perpetual fresh tulip in the mantle vase, and into the library. Grandpa was nowhere to be found. No clue cards either. Eventually she found herself in the long hallway. The one where she could not see, until the vibration of light illuminated her way.

Where do you see yourself? The words echoed in her mind once again and she said aloud, "Where do I see myself?" *If the answer I get doesn't help, I should try asking the question in a different way.*

Where do I see myself? Where do I see myself? Where do I see myself?

She took off the Mala from her neck and began running the beads through her fingers, calmly asking the question with each bead. She continued and suddenly, she felt the larger bead again, the one she had started with.

Have I repeated the question one hundred and eight times already?

Wait a minute, I need to try asking a different way. Earlier, I asked myself, "How could the question 'Where do I see myself' lead me to the answer?"

Wait! That is the second clue: How could the question lead me to the answer?

I was being literal in finding a clue. I needed to listen! It was within me.

Of course! I know where I see myself!

Standing in the middle of the hallway, she glanced around and caught sight of herself in the full-length mirror directly in front of her. *Where do you see yourself?* she murmured. It struck her—*how could I have missed it?* She looked at her reflection, a smile forming on her face. She decided to sit down and examine herself more closely.

As she stared at her reflection in the mirror, she initiated a conversation with her mirrored self. She asked the mirrored Lisa, "Do you know the secret of life? Why is a mirror significant?"

However, her reflection remained silent, responding only when the real Lisa spoke. This lack of response gradually irritated her, as did the idea of simply staring at herself and the remnants of those bruises from her fall from the hayloft ladder. She stuck her tongue out at mirror Lisa, realizing that perhaps she wasn't as smart as she had thought. Frustration built up, fueled by the reflection's imitative nature and its inability to offer any help. It felt as if the mirrored Lisa was mocking her, mocking her efforts to find the secret, implying that she would fail, disappoint Grandpa, and—

BANG! Lisa kicked her mirror image with her right foot as she began to stand up, causing the mirror to fall and shatter on the floor. Startled, she stepped back, shocked by her own action. *What have I done? Kicked myself?*

She sat back on the floor, motionless for a while, gathering herself, feeling bad about breaking the mirror, and worse, feeling she was still unsure of what to do. "I'll need to replace this for Grandpa. It's an odd place for a mirror." She reached for a piece of it and caught her image upside down.

Turn my world upside down. It's what I feel like—a big clump of chaos. But I wonder this: if things aren't how they should be—how do I create them as they could be? Or better yet, as they must be. I can create.

Aloud, she said, "I may have just given myself another clue." An idea came to mind, "As grandpa created a painting for Theo to help him with understanding his world, I will create one for Grandpa to hang here."

She had always enjoyed painting when staying with Grandpa, yet she hadn't picked up a brush this time. She felt drawn to return to the Zen Den and rose and glided outside. In the studio area, she found a blank canvas and placed it on one of the easels. With fresh brushes and paint, she began her work. Grandpa had taught Lisa that painting was about following her emotions. By engaging in the act of painting, she could awaken those emotions and decide whether to continue or start anew. So, she began playing with the brush, creating flowing and round shapes. Out of the corner of her eye, she noticed the Mala she had placed on a shelf.

Picking up the necklace, she examined the mother bead. It was a round bead with a blue stone, containing a myriad of colors within. Lisa felt an urge to start a fresh painting. She grabbed another canvas, and with the help of a drawing compass created a large circle. With the colors from the mother bead, she began painting the circle, meticulously recreating its intricate details.

After she felt it was complete, she stepped back to admire her work. She was satisfied with the beautiful result. And she noticed it resembled a globe, the world.

This project will turn your world upside down, she recalled.

Alright, then I'll paint the world upside down.

With the image of a world map in her mind, Lisa recreated her globe as comparable as possible. She recognized the Americas, Europe, Middle East, Africa, and the vast oceans.

I'm painting the world upside down because this project is meant to turn my world upside down. But where am I?

She took heed of her inner voice and quietly looked at her painting, picturing herself being painted into it. *A person's perspective on the world depends on where they've stood—where they were from and what they experienced.* She felt a surge of excitement. All the lessons from the past few days came rushing back, falling into place like pieces of a puzzle, just as Grandpa had said they would.

She envisioned the words in her mind's eye, the wisdom revealed in a montage of images—

I am my thoughts.

Everything in the world is vibration.

In the past lies the present—the now holds what will become!

The genuine treasure lies not outside of me, but within me.

I can intentionally choose or decide how to feel.

I manifest out of gratitude.

If I have the power to cause it, I can also change it. And what I change is my reaction.

Lisa's mind came back down to earth. She became still and heard within:

The truth is that my thoughts alone have the power to influence the world. It is up to me to discover the purpose of my life.

What is my perceality? There is no absolute reality.

Each person has their own version of the truth.

I could have been anyone depending on where and to whom I was born.

Lisa decided to place herself in North America, near where she actually stood, in her 'true' reality. She began painting herself in the picture. With intense focus, she began to paint her heart on her image.

As she hurriedly loaded the paint onto her brush, a small blob fell onto the globe. Lisa's heart sank. "Oh no! It was turning out so beautifully!" She attempted to correct the paint, only to create a smear. Frustrated and disappointed, she turned away and sank into a chair.

I can't fix it. I don't want to start a new one.

What would Grandpa say to me about now?

"Remember to always look for the beauty, the magic in what happened, even if things don't go as you planned. Maybe it even happened on purpose" *that's what he would say.*

Lisa closed her eyes, taking a deep breath. When she opened them again, she faced the painting and saw that the smear, the mistake, had transformed. It looked like a butterfly and to her it resembled a reflection of the Lisa she had wanted to paint in front of the world.

She saw herself.

I see myself in the mirror, exactly where I am, exactly as I am.

Her heart skipped a beat, and a surge of new energy coursed through her.

"Is this it? Is this really it? The secret is that the world is my mirror?!"

The world is a reflection of myself?

With a scream of exhilaration, she carefully lifted the still-wet painting and ran into the house.

Grandpa was still nowhere to be found.

Lisa sat in Grandpa's usual spot on the living room couch, feeling a mix of joy and confusion. She had searched and called out for Grandpa, but he remained absent. The encroaching darkness outside added an eerie ambiance, amplifying her sense of solitude on the farm. She felt her fear creeping in and reminded herself to breathe. Closing her eyes, she sought inner calm. When she opened her eyes again, the world didn't appear as menacing.

If I discovered the secret a moment ago, Lisa thought, *then that means I have the power to decide how scared I am. I don't have to be scared of anything if I don't want to be. It's how I choose to see it. Is it really that simple?*

The world is my mirror. It's a reflection of myself.

Lisa decided to experiment. Placing her hands over her heart, she asked herself, *Where is Grandpa?* In an instant, the words she had heard from him, and neighbor Frank flooded her mind: *In your greatest fear often lies your greatest gift.* Astonished by the rapid response and the significance of those words, Lisa understood that Grandpa must be at Frank's—and therefore close to the spiders.

A shiver ran down her spine, but she knew she had to face her fear, especially now that apparently the world had turned into being her own reflection. Encouraging herself, she murmured, "Come on, Lisa. Everything will be different now."

With some trepidation remaining, she decided to head for Frank's place. At the front door, a large spider rested just outside on the doormat.

Of course, you would be there at this time.

It was an impressively-sized creature. Lisa mustered her courage and decided to observe it, reminding herself that everything had changed. The spider remained still. Lisa watched it, feeling a mixture of goosebumps and clammy hands.

"Hello, Mr. Spider," she said, her voice wavering. "Or are you Mrs. Spider?" Instantly, a shift occurred within her fear. "I'm afraid of you because you have nephews and nieces who can be very dangerous. But fortunately, you aren't. So, there's no valid reason why I can't pick you up. However, I won't. I find you scary and unpleasant. I apologize for saying that. I recognize that your heart and my heart, beat with the same energy. You have just as much right to exist as I do. So, I won't harm you. But maybe you'd like to do me a favor. I need to open the door wider so I can leave, and I ask that you go somewhere else. I'll close my eyes, and when I open them again, you'll be gone. All right?"

Lisa shut her eyes and after seconds, blinked them open. The spider had vanished.

And I'm not at all surprised. Manifested.

She breathed a sigh of relief, stepped outside, and hurried to the neighbor's house carefully carrying her painting, excited to show Grandpa.

Ω

Frank and Little Wolf greeted her and invited her inside. Lisa dashed into the living room. "Grandpa! I've discovered the secret! Look!" She eagerly displayed her painting, expecting a grand reaction from Grandpa. However, he seemed unfazed, responding with a smile.

"You did that quickly, princess," he said quietly.

He was serene, knowing, and calm. Lisa felt a twinge of disappointment, anticipating a more enthusiastic response. Maybe even some pomp and circumstance!

"I wanted to show you immediately. Why did you leave me alone?"

"Because you didn't need me there. You had to experience it by yourself, in your own way. Remember, your perceality?" Grandpa continued, "The process you went through is unique to you. Only you could have done it. And you don't need my validation to know that you did it right or found the right answer. What you've discovered is the right answer for you, within your perceality—your perception of reality. Even the way you say it may differ and mean something different to you than to me: The world is your mirror. The world reflects you. You only experience yourself in this world. Everyone and everything in this world is you."

Lisa still felt a flicker of doubt, unsure if she had truly uncovered the ultimate secret. But then she reaffirmed her belief. There was no other way. It felt like the only possible answer. Instantly, her happiness and excitement resurfaced. A small voice inside her head whispered,

"So, you decide it all yourself." And there it was, the final affirmation she was looking for,

the Secret of Life: the world is a reflection of me. I am a reflection of the world.

Ω

On their way back home, Lisa danced alongside Grandpa. She was elated to have discovered the secret, relieved that she had not disappointed. A sense of fulfillment washed over her.

Yet, has the project really reached its conclusion?

New thoughts began forming in her mind. "Grandpa," she began, "what about things that happen to many people or the entire world, like the coronavirus? How do I view those situations from the perspective of the secret? Did I play a role in bringing COVID into the world? Am I to blame?"

Grandpa remained silent, veering off the path toward the familiar tree trunk. A large root rose in the grass. Curious, Lisa followed him.

"Would you mind pushing that root a bit?" Grandpa requested.

Lisa looked at him, puzzled.

"Why? I'll never be able to move it," she said, then realized that Grandpa intended to convey another lesson. Against her better judgment, she pushed against the root with all her might. Predictably, it didn't budge.

Grandpa joined her, pushing against it with her. Together, they managed to rock it slightly, but it remained firmly in place still rooted to the tree. After a few attempts, they stopped. Grandpa gazed at Lisa expectantly.

"Well?" he prompted.

"Okay … Your point … The point is—I can't do it alone, but with someone else, there's some movement. So, with even more people, it should be possible. Is that what you mean?"

Grandpa nodded, "What one person cannot achieve alone, a number of people can accomplish together."

"Yes, but does it mean that events like natural disasters are caused by the collective actions of many people?" Lisa asked incredulously.

"If the secret you've discovered holds true, then that's the case."

"But nobody wants that, right? Nobody consciously desires an earthquake or a flood."

"You're correct, Lisa. Nobody wants it consciously. Yet, it still happens. Do you remember when we discussed manifestation while going through the five books you chose? Do you recall what you said?"

Lisa contemplated for a moment. "Yes, I asked if everyone is always manifesting because everyone always experiences certain emotions."

"Exactly. Unconscious emotions lead to unconscious manifestations," Grandpa affirmed.

Lisa's mind raced, trying to comprehend the implications. "But no … Is it really *that* simple?"

"It's simple, yet it also appears complex," Grandpa replied, taking a seat on the tree trunk. "Once you discover the secret, it has far-reaching consequences, reshaping your perspective on everything in the world. Now you know that everything is vibration, energy. Everything is interconnected through a matrix field. *Actions have reactions. Small actions can have significant consequences.* Just as a multitude of butterflies flapping their wings can cause a storm, all individuals collectively shape the events on this planet through their thoughts and emotions. It's called the collective consciousness. Ancient societies understood this secret and lived in harmony with the world around them, maintaining a balance of giving and receiving with deep respect for all that exists. Today, most of humanity has lost touch with this knowledge. We address problems merely at the surface level, treating the symptoms instead of addressing the root cause. *That's why your discovery of the secret is so crucial. With the insight it brings, we can restore balance to the world.*"

Grandpa resettled his position on the tree trunk and forged on. "Much of how the world operates today—whether in government, media, or even in our homes—is based on masculine energy. I don't mean man vs. woman. I mean masculine as characterized by doing and achieving—making these things of highest importance. Whereas the feminine energy brings a more intuitive approach and one that is more accepting and encouraging of how we are being in the world— or how we can or must be in our lives. Lisa, we all need more of this balance—the doing and the being. It is what will be the root of change and the cause of fulfillment. Sorry for rambling on, but I want you to know that your discovery is not just something. It's a very significant something."

Lisa gave Grandpa a heartfelt hug. "Don't apologize. I love it when you get carried away about these things. I am beginning to see."

And one thing I do see clearly is that it is time to restore some balance in your world, Grandpa.

~~The Lisa Project: The Secret of Life - Day 7~~
THE GIRL WHO CHANGED THE WORLD PROJECT

JOURNAL–DAY 7

I Discovered the Secret Today–I can change the world!

I am already changing the world. Can you feel my energy that I'm sending out to the universe?

THE SECRET OF LIFE:

The world is a reflection of me. I am a reflection of the world.

As I am writing, I am holding my new Mala that Grandpa gave me. I used it and it's 108 beads on my treasure hunt for the secret. Grandpa had said that all the knowledge I need is already within me and that the puzzle pieces are there for me to put together myself. He told me to listen, and gave me the clue: <u>Where do I see myself?</u>

But I <u>listened to my inner voice</u> and it told me to ask a better or different question (it gave me the next clue!): How could the question 'Where do I see myself' lead me to the answer?

Aha! The hallway mirror (which I accidentally (was it?) broke)! I looked at my reflection. I saw myself—at least the outside of me. And, in one of the pieces, my reflection was upside down and I remembered: This project will turn your world upside down.

So, I decided to paint it—my world, upside down. I had to figure out where I am in the world. And I heard in my head: A person's perspective on the world depends on where they've stood—where they were from and what they experienced. I see myself in the mirror, exactly where I am, exactly as I am.

The secret is that the world is my mirror!

The world is a reflection of myself.

The world is your mirror. The world reflects you.

You only experience yourself in this world.

Everyone and everything in this world is you.

When I found Grandpa at Frank's, he told me I had to have the experience of discovering the secret by myself—from my perceality. The process is unique to me. Only I could have done it! I discovered the right answer for me through my perception of reality.

The secret of life:

The world is a reflection of me. I am a reflection of the world.

Unconscious emotions lead to unconscious manifestations. I can raise the consciousness to the positive! I'm going to change the world by manifesting the good stuff myself which will impact others—whether they know it or not! If they know, they'll choose to manifest the good stuff too!

What one person cannot achieve alone, a number of people can accomplish together.

I asked Grandpa to write down what he said on our walk home from Frank's place. This is from him:

It's simple, yet it also appears complex. Once you discover the secret, it has far-reaching consequences, reshaping your perspective on everything in the world.

Actions have reactions. Small actions can have significant consequences. All individuals collectively shape the events on this planet through their thoughts and emotions. It's called the collective consciousness.

Today, most of humanity has lost touch with this knowledge. We address problems merely at the surface level, treating the symptoms instead of addressing the root cause. That's why your discovery of the secret is so crucial. With the insight it brings, we can restore balance to the world.

I feel like so much has focused on my project. I need to help restore balance to Grandpa's world.

CHAPTER 21 | Action → Reaction

Anticipate More

When she finished journaling and came down the stairs, Lisa found Grandpa, stoking a small fire in the fireplace. She settled onto the couch beside a purring Sera-cat, and watched as Grandpa stood and paused to reverently admire the photograph of Grandma on the mantle.

He gently lifted a red tulip from the small vase beside the photo and moved to where Lisa was seated. "Lisa, your discovery today... I'm so proud of you." He nodded toward Grandma's photo, "*We* are so proud of you. Permission to place this in your hair?" he asked.

With a nod from Lisa, Grandpa carefully tucked the flower behind her right ear. "Perfect," he said, his voice tinged with emotion.

Lisa whispered, "I feel this beautiful flower connecting me closer with Grandma."

Grandpa's eyes glistened, "The tulip represents to us perfect love—a love for your Grandma I only fully grasped after she was gone. It's also a symbol of rebirth, of new beginnings. And that's exactly what you've sparked today in your own life, your own world, using your unique energy and intuition." He smiled warmly. "The tulip embodies blossoming femininity as well, beautifully reminding us about the potential our world has with a new equilibrium of energies, a beacon of light in the universe. I want to acknowledge the new light in you—all of the light! *Namaste*, Lisa." With that, he bowed forward, hands clasped over his heart in a gesture of deep respect.

Lisa placed her hands over his and placed her forehead on his. "*Namaste*, Grandpa. I honor my connection with you. Thank you."

They stayed together and took a collective breath.

Lisa broke the quiet reverie after a few minutes, "Well, I've uncovered the secret. My project is complete. Time to relax." Lisa sank further back on the cushions.

Grandpa chuckled, "Now, do you really think that is so? Welcome to the Lifelong Wanderer's Club. Relaxation may be elusive. Good luck with that."

She sat up abruptly, "Okay, now what's up? What do you mean by that?"

"I mean you'll never be content sitting still now. You'll always be on the lookout for the next mystery, the next adventure, and thus forever embarking on new journeys."

"Uh—so, there will be another project?"

"What do you think?"

"How many projects are there?"

"That's for you to decide."

"But this project was about the secret of life. Once you uncover the secret, isn't there nothing left to explore?"

"On the contrary," Grandpa said, "once you've discovered the secret of life, that's when everything begins. THE secret becomes *A secret*, with many more to discover."

"But all that effort—"

"Close your eyes," Grandpa said. Lisa set her drink down and closed her eyes. "Now picture a roller coaster. A massive, towering roller coaster. Can you see it?"

Lisa nodded.

"Good. Imagine you and I getting into a cart together. We fasten our seat belts, and the cart starts moving. What happens next?"

"We start going up."

"Exactly, slowly but surely. You hear the *tick-tick-tick* as you glance around, going higher and higher. The view expands before your eyes. We're filled with anticipation, maybe even a little fear. And then, the ticking stops. We reach a standstill. We're at the highest point, where it feels like we can see the whole world. The view is breathtaking. Can you feel it? Can you see it?"

Lisa nodded.

"Excellent. That's the point, the moment when you've discovered the secret of life. Actually, it's when you remember it. You're at that very point now!"

Lisa kept her eyes closed. "But now we have to plunge down and ride the entire roller coaster?"

"Exactly," Grandpa said. "As I mentioned, once you've unraveled the secret of life, everything begins. Then the roller coaster ride begins. Or, as Alice in Wonderland put it, you jump down the rabbit hole."

Lisa opened her eyes. She gazed thoughtfully ahead. After a while, she smiled. "I see. This isn't the end, but the beginning. It won't become dull after this. Everything will just become more vibrant and thrilling. How amazing."

Grandpa put his arm around her and gave her a hug. "You got it—again."

Lisa scanned the living room. She noticed the dark blue book, *A Course in Miracles*, resting on the table where she'd left it.

This could very well be just a dream. And thinking of dreams…

"Grandpa! Your turn. Your dream! We didn't finish yesterday when that little boy and his mom showed up."

She hopped off the couch to retrieve Grandpa's laptop. They had a dream to realize and balance to restore for Grandpa!

Ω

Lisa returned, talking before she entered the room, "Okay, so your dream was—or is—to live in a warm climate, a tropical island. We had started to work out the money part of it to see what you can afford."

"All right, Miss Fix-It, exploring is one thing, but—"

"We've already calculated how much your farm could be sold for," she said, opening the laptop. "Now, let's find out which warm country you should move to."

Grandpa clenched his jaw and hesitated to speak. He lost his moment. What followed was an entire exercise in which Lisa bombarded him with questions. She searched websites, copied photos and images, and began creating a vision board.

Her spirited efforts quickly accumulated an enticing collection of pictures: idyllic tropical landscapes with azure skies, abundant sunshine, swaying palm trees, and pristine sandy beaches. He could almost feel the warmth penetrating his bones. If he ever decided to move, he wouldn't mind settling in such a place.

"Now, we need to see which countries offer the best of these things and decide which one you like the most," Lisa said matter-of-factly.

She grilled Grandpa like a seasoned planner: what should be the highest and lowest temperatures? Would occasional rain or storms bother him? Which languages could he speak? The questions seemed never-ending.

When the interrogation concluded, Lisa mentioned she needed some time to find countries that met all the criteria. "Grandpa, while you cook dinner, I'll search for your new home."

Once again, his heart skipped a beat at her words. It was one thing to see pretty pictures and another to think about a new home—or actually moving. It felt as if the dream he had released was now taking on a life of its own. That wasn't his original intention.

Nevertheless, Grandpa set out to prepare a celebratory supper. It was Lisa's day. She had tackled the Secret of Life Project—Wait! *The Girl Who Changed the World Project*—with fervor and now, accruing wisdom.

Maybe I've done my job too well.

The thought made him smile. It also made him nervous. He was accountable.

Ω

After dessert, Lisa retrieved the laptop again. "I've found the perfect place for you," she beamed, showing Grandpa the vision board she created with her findings. Grandpa had some knowledge of the island she had chosen and had to admit it looked appealing. Lisa presented everything she had discovered, including some houses that he could easily purchase if the farm sold for the expected amount.

"Should we ask Mom to put the farm on the market tomorrow?" Lisa asked after her presentation came to an end.

Grandpa fell silent.

"Lisa, you've put together something truly beautiful here," he began reluctantly, "but I never actually said I wanted to do this."

"But this is your lifelong dream, right? You told me yourself! We've done all this work. And now your dream can finally come true. Isn't that fantastic?"

Grandpa stared at his hands. "I also told you that when you're as old as me, you learn to accept things as they are and that my dreams revolve around you, your future. I don't want to leave you and your mother. I have no ambitions to fulfill my old dreams. Everything is fine the way it is. I have a good life here."

Lisa looked at him, genuinely shocked. "Grandpa, what's the point of having dreams if you don't pursue them? What are you afraid of? What's holding you back? Are you even conscious of it?" Once again, it seemed like she was saying things she hadn't consciously thought of, but they flowed naturally from within her, as if she were connected to something greater.

"Lisa, young people like you should certainly chase after your dreams. I've had my chances and moments, and I accept where I am now. I should have made different choices when I still had the ability—when I still could."

"Grandpa! I can't believe what you're saying. I don't think you truly mean it. It feels like you're just saying something to avoid change. But everything is constantly changing. Isn't that what the symbol in the painting at your front door represents? That's part of the secret, right? I completed my project, so why don't you want to complete yours?"

Grandpa let out a sigh. "Is it not true that your project was something you wanted to do for yourself? But my project is being imposed on me by you. Now, you want me to change just like you, but that's *your* desire, not *mine*."

"If you point to the other person as the cause of the situation, nothing will change," she echoed his earlier words. "So, maybe I shouldn't expect you to change. Instead, should I see myself as the cause and strive to change something within myself?"

Grandpa sighed again, this time with relief. "You've remembered that wisdom well. I'm glad."

Grandpa's stubborn stance was beginning to grate on Lisa. It ignited a fire within her that craved destruction. She stared at her hands. "But how does that wisdom apply to how you dealt with Dad?" She deliberately dropped this bombshell on the table.

Grandpa froze.

"You know," Lisa continued, her voice dripping with coolness as she kept her eyes fixed on her hands, "your son, the man who made a mistake that took someone's life? Wouldn't you say you can't blame Dad for that, because you should see yourself as the cause? So, in a way, it's actually your fault?" She locked eyes with Grandpa, defiantly awaiting his response.

Grandpa slammed his palm on the table and sprung up toppling his chair. "If only you knew how much I blame myself for that every single day!"

Lisa was outwardly composed as she watched Grandpa storm out of the room. Soon, she heard the resounding slam of the front door behind him.

Inside, she trembled, and the new fire within her raged.

THE GIRL WHO CHANGED THE WORLD PROJECT
JOURNAL-DAY 7-continued…

I'll admit that I'm writing this when I'm mad-at Grandpa and at myself. We just argued-about him selling the farm and moving. Unwilling! And, about not making up with Dad-unwilling! Argh…

I thought my project was complete, but of course changing the world happens every day. And there is more than one secret. So now, along with Grandpa, I am a member of the: Lifelong Wanderer's Club.

It means I'll always be on the lookout for what's next.

Once you've unraveled the secret of life, everything begins. Then the roller coaster ride begins. (Or, as Alice in Wonderland put it, you jump down the rabbit hole.)

I have to be accountable. Grandpa has to be (must be!) accountable too. For anyone who reads my journal (like Mom)-you need to be accountable too!

What's the point of having dreams if you don't pursue them? What are you afraid of? What's holding you back?

I confronted Grandpa about this because he's avoiding change-and that's impossible because the world is constantly changing. He has no ambition to follow his dream-and he is not dealing with the 'incident' with Dad. I had to change first-and that change was to point it out to him that he is choosing to be stuck! He got mad, said what happened to Dad was his fault.

He left and is still away.

I'm holding him accountable-for applying his own wisdom!

CHAPTER 22 | Catharsis

After restoring the kitchen to order, Lisa sat on the couch with Sera-cat and her journal. She'd lit another match to the fire—literally in the fireplace before her, but in reality within herself—and now, Grandpa. She knew he was somewhere nearby, processing. She felt safe, and even serene. It had been an emotional day of highs and lows. Grandpa's rollercoaster analogy was fitting. She made her way upstairs to prepare for sleep.

She settled into bed thinking of the meaning in the mural before her. She reached out for the tulip on her nightstand and rested it on her heart. She had neglected putting it in water, but the petals were unwilted.

Just as she was about to rise to place it in her drinking glass, she heard Grandpa return. A minute later, she heard him ascend the stairs and stop in the hallway. In a soft voice, he said, "I'm sorry about that, Lisa. We'll talk more about it tomorrow. I hope you sleep well. I love you. Good night."

Once Grandpa turned off the hallway light and left, Lisa found it difficult to fall asleep. She attempted to focus on pleasant thoughts, picturing her mom and dad and eventually she entered a light dream state.

Unexpectedly, the unwelcome image of the large, black, furry spider invaded her mind. She didn't want to visualize it, yet it persisted in every mental image she conjured. Irritation grew within her.

"Go away," she uttered aloud, addressing the arachnid intruder in her thoughts. "Go scare someone else. I hate you. Leave me alone!"

More spiders began to scuttle into Lisa's imagination. It felt like she was trapped between wakefulness and a nightmarish state, with no control over what was happening. The spiders multiplied and started crawling all over her body. Fear and desperation consumed her. Suddenly, she saw herself standing outside her own body, as if observing herself from a reflection.

"You know you don't have to fear them," her reflection calmly stated.

"But I do!" the real Lisa shouted. "Please, help me."

"I can't," her reflection said. "You can only help yourself. Be cautious."

In Lisa's mind's eye, she saw the large spider on her chest now. She froze, panicked. It was perched on her heart, causing an immediate sharp pain. Lisa bolted upright, screaming, and burst into tears. Her heart pounding, she leaped out of bed and rushed down the stairs. Grandpa was already on the bottom step. Lisa stopped halfway down the stairs, trance-like, sobbing and catching her breath.

Grandpa called to her, "Lisa! Wake up!"

"You're not being honest!" she yelled at him, her words erupting. "You say one thing, but you act differently! You possess profound wisdom, yet you don't apply it in your own life. You tell me not to fear spiders, that they can't harm me, but how can I believe you? How can I trust you when you're afraid of so many things yourself? You won't even pursue your own dream and follow your heart.

"You claim that everyone creates their own reality, that everyone is always right, but you've judged Dad, your own son, for making a mistake. You tell me I create my own life and can make my dreams come true, yet at the same time, you say your dreams don't matter. If that's how you're going to be, then I don't want you to be my grandpa anymore!"

Grandpa stood motionless, struck hard. Lisa's eyes held his hauntingly familiar fear.

"Don't you see, Grandpa? You've passed on your pain and your fear to Dad and me! I want you to stop doing that. Stop it **now**!" she cried out and stormed up the stairs to her room.

Grandpa remained on the stairs stunned, paralyzed, and wounded.

Ω

Later that night, Lisa experienced another vivid dream.

Her body floated through the darkness, surrounded by stars as if traversing the universe. When she glanced downward, she noticed stars emanating from her mouth, shooting out into the cosmos. The stars returned, circling her like an infinite loop, reentering her body through her navel. It felt as though she embodied the universe itself—each new star born from her, every old star dying within her. An eternal cycle.

She *was* the universe. She was *everything*.

Suddenly, an eye appeared on her leg. Through that eye, she could observe her own face by gazing upward. *That's funny*, Lisa thought in her dream, *I've never really been able to look at my face. I've never seen myself this way.*

A sense of tranquility enveloped her, and she noticed a gentle rocking motion, as if someone were cradling her. It felt immensely comforting, loving, warm, and safe. Lisa surrendered herself to it completely, feeling like a baby being cared for by her mom. Yet, when she tried to focus on her mother, she realized she was the one rocking herself. It felt magnificent, but the thought arose, *This is impossible, right?*

Lisa surveyed her surroundings and discovered that the stars had vanished, leaving only pitch darkness. In an instant, she was abruptly torn away from the blissful sensation and found herself facing an enormous white spider dangling from a web. She regarded the repulsive creature with fear and disgust, experiencing a sharp pain in her heart, as if the spider was about to seize her.

The spider was horrifying, yet something prevented Lisa from averting her gaze. It was a peculiar spider—it wasn't black, but white. In fact, it felt as though she had encountered this spider before, as if it were familiar.

Then, a realization struck her: *If I am the universe, if I am everything, then I am also this spider. Then I am also my own fear!*

As if understanding Lisa's thoughts, the spider began descending from its web to the ground. Once on the ground, it started stomping its feet, one by one. *BANG! BANG! BANG!* It seemed as though the spider was attempting to awaken her.

When Lisa opened her eyes, she still heard the sound of the spider stomping.

DAY 8

PROJECT NEXT

CHAPTER 23 | Liberating Pain

The rhythmic thuds persisted. Lisa glanced around, searching for any trace of the spider, but she found herself safe within her room, sunlight streaming through the curtains. The sound was originating from outside. She hurriedly got out of bed, approached the window, and pulled back the curtains. And there she saw Grandpa in the front yard, vigorously driving a wooden pole into the ground, almost manically.

She rushed downstairs and stepped outside, breathless as she called out, "What are you doing, Grandpa?" Her eyes fixed on him as she made her way toward him. Then she noticed Grandpa attaching a large sign he had painted onto the pole. In bold letters, it read, "FOR SALE."

Perplexed, Lisa gazed at Grandpa. He appeared weary, yet she detected a glimmer in his eyes that she had never seen before. He looked years younger, brimming with energy and fire. Setting down his tools, he approached her.

"The third time," Grandpa proclaimed, his voice resonating with enthusiasm and eyes filled with tears, as he enveloped her in a tight embrace.

Lisa was genuinely astonished. "What do you mean? What has happened to you?"

Grandpa released her from his embrace and began speaking with fervor.

"I've been struck by lightning for the third time! You struck me! Again! You opened my eyes," Grandpa exclaimed, a smile spreading across his face. "You held up a mirror to me, and for the first time in my life, I truly saw myself. I saw my authentic self, who I truly am. And I also saw who I had become, and I despised that image!

"You were absolutely right about everything you confronted me with last night. When you went back to bed, I experienced excruciating pain. You had touched the pain I had concealed so well. I returned to the living room, sat on the couch, and pondered what to do with it. And then my own words resurfaced: *If you resist it, it will intensify. If you welcome it, it will dissipate.* So, I invited the pain to the surface, to emerge from its hiding place, and tell me—to help me recall—why it had resurfaced. This might sound peculiar, but the pain actually began conversing with me! We had a dialogue."

Lisa displayed no surprise. She'd talked to a couple spiders after all. "What did it say, Grandpa? What did it tell you?"

Grandpa took a deep breath and relaxed slightly. Speaking with less fervor, he continued, "The pain informed me that it was much older than myself. It had existed within me from the moment I was born. Back then, it wasn't my pain. It belonged to my parents. It was a fusion of their pain, passed down to me."

"*That's how it works,* the pain explained, '*I am passed down from parents to their children, from grandparents to their grandchildren, traversing ancestral lines for generations.*'

"It revealed to me that it is as ancient as humanity itself, as old as the first humans on Earth. I asked it, '*If you weren't my pain before, when did you become my pain? And what exactly are you, to have always existed and caused such suffering in people?*' Then something peculiar occurred.

"The pain responded, '*What do you think?*' It posed a question to me!"

Lisa's demeanor remained undisturbed, as though this were the most natural conversation. "And then what happened, Grandpa?"

"Well, I wasn't particularly astonished by the pain asking me a question. It felt as though I were engaged in a regular conversation with someone.

"So, I replied to the pain, '*I believe you are what I've painted. You represent everything that eludes human perception, the invisible aspects of our existence. As we navigate the course of life, we remain uncertain— unaware of our destination, unsure if we'll succeed or stumble, uncertain when or how our lives will end. We don't know if we'll lose loved ones, experience hurt, or make mistakes along this journey. You embody our insecurity, our fear. We become so deeply attached to life and our loved ones that we fear losing everything. Consequently, we grow even more attached to them, intensifying our fears. And fear hurts. Losing loved ones hurts. But my parents couldn't love me unconditionally because they hadn't learned to love themselves. They were burdened by too much pain. Pain that had been passed down to them by their parents. They struggled through life to make a living, to gain status, to earn the respect of others. Deep down, all they yearned for was unconditional love, though they were unaware of this truth. And so, they couldn't fully love me. And that hurt. Thus, the pain within me—you—grew. I didn't want that. I found you annoying, pain, and so I hid you away.*'

"'*Nobody likes pain,*' the pain responded to me with sadness.

"And I said to the pain, '*That must be incredibly lonely. That must hurt.*'

"'*It's the first time someone has spoken so kindly to me,*' the pain confessed, seemingly on the verge of tears.

"'*Come here, come to me,*' I beckoned to the pain, opening my arms. Now, this may sound incredibly strange, but it genuinely felt as though someone—or something—entered my embrace. I could physically wrap my arms around him, her, or it. I embraced the pain. I embraced *my* pain.

"And then, I felt the pain closer and more intensely than ever before. I began weeping, truly weeping, like a baby. I felt a knot in my stomach, and that pain spread throughout my entire being. I noticed that the pain was weeping, too, so we cried together. Darkness consumed my mind, and I focused my attention on the area of my body where the pain was most acute. Suddenly, I relived all the pain of my life. However, it unfolded in reverse, as if I were rolling back the brushstroke of my existence, retracing it to the moment of my birth.

"I felt the anguish of being confined to this cold climate. I felt the pain of solitude, of losing Grandma, and enduring the subsequent loneliness. I felt the ache of missing your dad, of banishing my own son from my life, of withholding my love from him. And then, I felt the agony of my childhood, when my parents couldn't love me the way I longed for them to. I experienced the overwhelming guilt that consumed me when my sister passed away. I realized that I was perpetuating the same cycle with your dad as my parents had done with me, just as you pointed out. I was repeating their actions, passing on the same pain. I was following in the footsteps of countless ancestors who had lived through this pattern.

"When this realization dawned upon me, I could no longer weep. Instead, a smile emerged. I realized that I possessed the power to change everything. I am the architect of my own life! I desired to put an end to it all, to halt this cycle right here and now.

"The pain, whom I had cradled in my arms all this time, gradually lifted its gaze to meet mine. '*Do you now recognize me?*' it inquired.

"'*Yes, now I understand you. Now, I remember you once again. You are the absence of love for myself,*' I replied.

"The pain continued to stare at me, laughed, and said, '*Being pain isn't easy. People despise me and wish to rid themselves of me as swiftly as possible. They conceal me in the recesses where they don't have to face* me. *It hurts me, and I feel lonely. I grow when people are unhappy, when they fail to acknowledge me. And so, I inflict even more pain upon them. At their wit's end, they lock me away in a deep, dark dungeon, where I continue to haunt. There is only one moment of joy in the life of pain.'*

"'*And what moment is that?*' I asked.

"'*This very moment,*' the pain declared. '*The moment when my host or hostess recognizes me, remembers me, embraces me, speaks with me, accepts me for what I am, and then decides to forgive themselves and love themselves. That, my dear, is the most blissful moment. It signifies the instant when I know I have fulfilled my purpose and can dissolve into eternal love.'*

"And Lisa, I said to the pain, '*I can feel it. Thank you for accompanying me throughout my life. Thank you for reminding me of who you are and who I truly am. And please, always feel welcome within me, visit me whenever you wish. From now on, I will always welcome you with open arms, understanding that you are here to remind me to love myself.*'"

Lisa looked up at Grandpa, tears in her eyes. He took her hand and concluded, "And right then, the pain receded, dissolved, and vanished. I felt it within my body—I was liberated."

Lisa embraced him and whispered, "And now I am too."

THE GIRL WHO CHANGED THE WORLD PROJECT

JOURNAL–DAY 8

FOR SALE! The farm is for sale! I'm amazed by how he arrived at this decision! And so happy.

Grandpa talked to the pain. Sounds weird, huh? (But then, I talked to spiders in my dream last night. I'll write about that later.)

It was Grandpa's third lightning strike! Remember:

1)   My birth.

2)   Dad's incident.

3)   I held up a mirror and he saw himself.

He didn't like what he saw. So, he chose to confront his pain.

He told me:

- ▶   If you resist it, it will intensify. If you welcome it, it will dissipate.

- ► Pain exists within us from the moment we are born, passed along by parents, a long line of generations-to the first humans on Earth!
- ► Pain asked him what he thought, and he realized that his pain was painted (created) by: perceptions, uncertainty, loss of loved ones, mistakes, and becoming attached to others we love or even to our own ideas.
- ► Pain interferes with our ability to love ourselves. It intensifies our fears.
- ► We struggle to resolve pain by gaining status or respect of others when really what is needed is unconditional love.
- ► Struggling leads to hiding the truth-and hiding the pain.
- ► Nobody likes pain. Pain is lonely.

<u>TO DO</u>: Give pain a hug? (I'm not joking.)
- ► Embrace it and feel it-with the memories and the emotions (and it will hurt!).

- ▶ Do NOT conceal it-face it. Pain grows when you are unhappy and when it is not acknowledged. This causes even more pain.
- ▶ Release the pain-take a deep breath and let it go. This opens me to the power to change everything-to be the architect of my own life. Halt the cycle!

Pain - The absence of love for yourself.

<u>From Grandpa</u>: There is only one moment of joy in the life of pain and that is when we recognize it, remember it, embrace it, speak with it, accept it, and accept myself for who I am, and then decide to forgive. That, my dear, is the most blissful moment. It signifies the instant when I know I have fulfilled my purpose and can dissolve into eternal love.

Thank Pain. It reminds you to love yourself.
Be liberated.

CHAPTER 24 | Aftermath

A little while later, Lisa bounded down the stairs, freshly showered and dressed. The aroma of Grandpa's delectable breakfast wafted through the air. As she entered the dining room, she found him seated at the table, surrounded by a stack of mouthwatering pancakes.

His eyes gleamed with joy as he glanced at Lisa. "Hurry up, we need to get started. I could devour a whole pancake joint," Grandpa exclaimed, placing the first pancake on her plate.

Lisa settled into her chair and grabbed the syrup and peanut butter. "So, what happened next?" she asked, returning to Grandpa's story while he relished his second bite as if it were his first taste. "What made you decide to sell the house? And why did you mention that I changed your life again?"

"I'll tell you everything," Grandpa replied with a full mouth, taking a sip of coffee to wash down the pancake before continuing his story. "Once the pain had finally subsided, I felt free. I felt lighter, younger, as though I rediscovered my true self and what I truly desired in life. What the pain revealed to me was how my parents' anguish had been ingrained in me from the moment I was born. They had learned to conform to others' expectations, believing it would bring them love or what seemed like love, a job, financial security—a sense of safety.

Unknowingly, unintentionally, they raised me the same way. When I did 'good' things, I received rewards, and when I did 'bad' things, they grew angry, and I faced punishment."

"But isn't that normal?" Lisa interjected. "Mom does something similar with me. Don't all parents behave that way?"

"We all assume it's normal, I suppose, and it never crossed my mind until last night— but what I realized was that the underlying motive or emotion is the key. It's like manifesting, really. If the motive is, *If I adapt myself, I'll receive love and be safe*, then essentially, you're telling a child, *You're not good enough as you are, so conform to my desires, and then I'll love you*. That's how I was raised. And I recognized that's how we raised your father, too, Grandma and I. Particularly me, which is why that's been my approach throughout my life, always feeling like I had to earn someone else's love. I wanted Grandma to love me, so I did my best to engage in activities I knew she liked and avoid the things she despised."

"But that sounds kind of sweet, doesn't it?"

"Not necessarily. Not if it is to an extreme. Everyone perceives it as sweet, but it's actually causing immense harm to oneself. By prioritizing someone else's love, you place your own dreams and desires in second place. Last night, I discovered—or rather, remembered—that life isn't about seeking the love of others, no matter who they may be. It's about the love I have for myself. If love for myself overflows, then I have enough for others. But if a person—like me—feels unloved or even under-appreciated, it can lead to bad choices. And Lisa, I've made choices in my life that I'm not proud of, but I've also made truly terrible decisions. One in particular has always haunted me, and another resurfaced in my memory last night."

"What did you do, Grandpa?"

"I have thought a lot about whether to share this with you. Only a couple people know, like Theo for one. You are already aware that your grandpa is by no means perfect. And we both know you are wise beyond your years. It is with this knowledge—and my trust—that I am choosing to tell you." He paused to take a breath and let out a long exhale before beginning.

"The first truly awful thing I did was to your grandmother. We were together for about fifteen years, and our son—your dad—was only three at the time. Grandma was completely devoted to raising your dad, while I felt like I wasn't receiving the love from her that I craved and believed I needed. History repeating, so to speak, if you compare my thoughts about my parents.

"Then, at work, I met a woman who took a genuine interest in me. She listened to me, enjoyed my company, and made me feel loved and valued. It had been a long time since I had experienced such emotions. Of course, she was beautiful, and I fell head over heels for her—or so I thought. It felt incredible to receive the affection and warmth I believed I was missing.

"Eventually, Grandma discovered what was happening and she was furious with me. I can still recall the feeling when she yelled at me, as if it were yesterday. I felt guilty, remorseful. I had failed. I had done something objectively 'wrong,' causing immense grief and pain to the woman I genuinely loved.

"And as I confronted my pain last night, I realized that the feeling mirrored what I experienced when my parents were angry with me, especially after Mary's passing. It felt as though I no longer deserved to be loved."

Grandpa paused, gazing out the window, lost in thought.

Lisa uttered softly. "That must have hurt deeply."

"Yes, it did," Grandpa acknowledged, turning his attention back to Lisa. "It was my fault. I was consumed by guilt. And guilt is an incredibly potent pain, if left unaddressed. It permeates your entire being and renders you immobile.

"Grandma and I never discussed what transpired again. She wanted to continue our life together, and I did too because I truly loved her and wanted to make amends. But due to the overwhelming guilt, I never expressed my desires, needs, or dreams again. I molded myself to please her whenever possible, avoiding any further pain or anguish.

"And that's why we never relocated to that tropical country. Grandma didn't want to go, and I believed I had to compensate for my wrongdoing by wielding my desires to hers."

Lisa's brow furrowed and she reached for her words. "Grandpa, it is a lot to take in and honestly, I'm not sure how I feel about it, but I feel sorry for you. It makes me sad. Thank you, though. Thank you for sharing this with me, as if I were an adult."

"You're not an adult," Grandpa smiled, gazing at her affectionately. "You're an angel. Truly an angel."

A warm sensation enveloped Lisa. Grandpa had called her an *angel* before, but this time it felt deeper, truer. *Is this how it feels when someone loves you or is in love with you?* she pondered. *If so, I can understand why one would do anything for it, because it feels extraordinary.* She closed her eyes, immersing herself in that feeling entirely. *Could I cultivate this feeling within myself?* she wondered.

When Lisa reopened her eyes, Grandpa was still looking at her with adoration. Lisa fidgeted. "Not to break this spell, but you mentioned that what happened in your marriage was one of the two terrible things you've done in your life. Why did you call them terrible? In this case, it sounds more like something that happened, like you had no other choice, something explainable. From the way you told it, it makes sense. So why do you consider it terrible?"

"What a beautiful thing to say, my dear angel," Grandpa said. "You're absolutely right. I did what I felt was right for me at the time. I allowed myself to experience love and warmth again, knowing fully that I didn't want to hurt your grandma. But the ensuing guilt was so overwhelming that I never wanted to confront it again. Until last night. When I faced my pain, I was finally able to forgive myself for what I had done, but also for the perpetual burden of guilt I had carried. I realized that I didn't need to forgive myself for my actions because I couldn't have acted differently. I was who I was back then, and that is now a thing of the past."

"I guess that is completion. But what about the other 'terrible' thing?"

"That one, I really consider terrible," Grandpa insisted firmly. "Until last night, I didn't even realize how deeply wrong I was. Thanks to you, I now understand."

Grandpa closed his eyes and pressed on. "I refer to it as *The Incident* whenever I discuss what happened to your dad. I was so ashamed of it. Our only child caused an accident that took a man's life—a tragedy not only for that man's wife and children, but also for your mom and you, and many others. It was an accident, but your dad had been drinking. He shouldn't have gotten behind the wheel. It was his fault."

Lisa fell silent. She was aware of the story, but she had never heard it directly from Grandpa. She had always carried a sense of guilt and responsibility, knowing that *her* dad was the one responsible for this tragedy.

"And I felt guilty and responsible," Grandpa continued, his voice filled with regret. "Because it was my son who caused this tragedy."

Lisa's jaw dropped. *So Grandpa felt the same way! Could others feel this way too? Mom? Grandma?*

"When it happened that night, and the police called, I desperately hoped it wasn't true, that nobody had died. But when Grandma and I arrived at the hospital, it was painfully evident that it was wishful thinking. I saw the anguish in the eyes of the woman who had just lost her husband. It was true. And all I could think was *my son caused this. This is irreparable. This is unforgivable.*"

"Did you see Dad at the hospital? I know he was hurt in the crash." Lisa was treading on new territory.

"Just that night. We entered the room where he had been admitted with a few broken bones. I was furious, and I immediately went to his bedside, locked eyes with him, and demanded, 'Is this true?' I also snapped, 'You'll have to live with this for the rest of your life!' Enraged, I stormed out of the room, dragging Grandma with me, even though she wanted to stay. When we returned home, Grandma was devastated and wanted to talk to me. I was upset, too, but in a different way. It wasn't until last night that I discovered why.

"It felt as though I had done something wrong once again. I had failed to raise my son properly, to teach him right from wrong. And because of that, because of me, someone had lost his life—a tragedy of the highest magnitude for a family, leaving two young children without a father. At that moment, even though I didn't realize it then, it felt as though I didn't deserve my parents' love. Or Grandma's. I wasn't good enough. I didn't deserve to live. And unconsciously, I blamed your dad for it.

"I made the worst decision of my life. I distanced myself from my son when he needed me the most. I pushed him away and, in the process, pushed away your grandma. But most importantly, I pushed myself away.

"So, I made your dad's accident my own fault, and my reaction to him caused the subsequent misfortunes: his divorce from your mom and it impacted Grandma's passing. Grandma believed she had to stand by me, so she cut off contact with your dad after the accident. And that went against her true feelings. I witnessed her sinking into profound, helpless sorrow. When she fell terminally ill the following year, it was almost a release from her grief. I'm convinced she passed away from the weight of that sorrow, even though the doctors told us it was from the progression of the illness in her body for years. I, who claim to know so much about vibrations and energy, was only emitting negative frequencies of guilt, pain, and anger during that time. So, in one way or another, I'm also responsible for the premature loss of my wife, your grandma, even if I only triggered the progress of her illness."

———

Grandpa paused, tears glistening in his eyes.

"Are you okay?" Lisa asked, her concern evident.

"Yes, my dear. These tears are a sign that I'm feeling better than I have in a very long while," Grandpa replied. "I'm finally allowing myself to feel, and it's truly wonderful."

"But you mentioned feeling terribly guilty," Lisa noted.

"Incredibly guilty," Grandpa acknowledged. "And last night, I finally saw my pain for what it truly was. I felt it deeply. I cried for hours. But by truly experiencing it, embracing it, I found solace. My pain and I were finally able to forgive myself for everything I had carried guilt for—not for what I had done, because I realized there was no need for forgiveness in that regard. I couldn't have acted differently. I was who I was then. And now, that is all in the past."

Lisa cautiously chose her words. "You mentioned that I changed your life, that all of this happened because of me last night, but how?"

"You, my dear princess, are the most important person in my life," Grandpa declared.

Lisa looked taken aback. "Me?"

"Yes, you! I lost my wife, I lost my son, and now I understand that I also lost *myself*. You, my little angel, bring joy and happiness into my life. You make me forget my pain, and you make me genuinely happy. You're the only one close to me whom I haven't pushed away. And now I realize that I sought your approval, admiration, and love. No, not just sought—it was something I needed. So when you came down the stairs last night, almost entranced, and spoke the painful truth, you pierced straight into my heart, where it hurt the most.

"At that moment, it felt as though I had lost you too, and that pain was even more unbearable. It felt as though lightning had struck me once again, as though the ground vanished beneath my feet, and I sank into a quagmire of anguish and darkness."

"I'm truly sorry, Grandpa," Lisa uttered, her expression filled with sorrow.

———

"No, my dear, don't be sorry. Never apologize for being yourself or for speaking your truth—no, speaking your 'perceality,'" Grandpa corrected himself. "What you did yesterday was the best thing that ever happened to me. You changed my world! You made me feel the pain again, you reconnected me with my pain so that I could confront it, embrace it, and ultimately forgive myself. You genuinely changed me and my life.

"You see, all the things we've been doing for the project these past few days were based on logical thinking, analysis, reasoning—everything from the mind. That's how I approached it, at least. It was an old, masculine, or patriarchal way of addressing a problem or phenomenon.

"But you, my dear Lisa, effortlessly absorbed it all as if it required no effort at all. I now understand that it was all perfectly logical and natural to you, and you seamlessly blended it with your youthful, feminine intuition and sensitivity, a matriarchal approach. That's how *perceality* came into being, and through that, you changed the way this old man perceives life. I was trapped in my mind and had lost touch with my heart, my emotions. You opened my eyes and allowed me to rediscover them for myself, striking where it hurt the most."

"Wow. Wow ..."

"When the pain left me—and I have to say, it truly felt that way—I felt content and joyful. I sat on the couch and embraced myself, quite literally. I closed my eyes and envisioned myself as a young boy. I looked into that little boy's eyes, the *mini-me*, and I told him I loved him. I explained why I had kept him at arm's length all these years, and that little boy hugged me. It was just like the way you look at me, Lisa. He hugged me tightly. Then, I opened my eyes, approached the mirror, and peered deeply into my own eyes. I saw so much, but above all, I felt appreciation and love for that remarkable person staring back at me. So, over and over, I told my reflection, '*I love you.*' And with each repetition, I felt better.

"I returned to the couch, clutching a photo of Grandma and me in my hand, and I gazed at her. It was as though she came to life in that moment, and I began speaking to her. I shared everything that had transpired—my mistakes, and my feelings.

"And she responded, '*I know. I have always known. And I am so happy for you. Now, please follow your heart and make your dreams come true. I look forward to hearing your stories when we reunite where I already am. You still have years ahead of you. Make them the best years of your life.*'"

"Did you actually hear Grandma's voice?" Lisa asked with wonder.

Grandpa responded, his voice tender. "Not in the way I hear you now, but I heard her in my mind, in my body, and it felt so real and comforting. After she spoke those last words, I simply smiled, and I felt an incredible sense of peace. Then, I retrieved a photograph of my parents. I had tucked it away a long time ago, and it took some effort to find it. It's a photo of them together. I stared at it. I recalled their voices, their scents, and the things they used to say to me, to Mary—to us.

"That's when I started talking to them too. I shared my pain with them, explaining how their pain had become my own, and how their upbringing had perpetuated it. I opened up about Mary, the guilt I had carried for so long, and the feeling that they blamed me. I expressed how much I had yearned for their love and how deeply I had missed it. But I also acknowledged that they had done everything they knew how to do, raising me the only way they knew how. I forgave them completely for all the things that had caused my pain, and I embraced myself once again. I said to myself, '*I forgive you for everything that has happened, for the pain you've endured from your parents, and for the pain I've caused you.*'

"And then, something magical happened once more. '*Thank you,*' I heard my father say. And my mother said, '*Thank you for feeling our pain and helping us heal.*'

"'*We are so proud of you. We have always loved you,*' they both expressed.

"'*I love you,*' I told them, '*and I wish you could see your great-granddaughter. She's an absolute angel.*'"

Lisa allowed her tears to stream down her cheeks.

"'*We know. We know her,*' were their final words, and that was the end of it."

Lisa gasped. "Your father and mother know me? My great-grandparents?"

"That's what they said," Grandpa replied, pausing for a moment. "You know, at that moment I realized that through healing myself, I had also healed part of the pain of my parents, and their parents. It's not a one-way street, it works both ways. In the past lies the present, but by changing the present, the past also changed. Isn't that miraculous?"

"Wow," Lisa sighed, "I sure would have loved to know your mom and dad."

"Speaking of that, there's even more. There was one more person I hadn't spoken to, someone I also wanted to embrace."

"Dad!" Lisa exclaimed.

"Yes, so I decided to give him a call."

"In the middle of the night?"

"I *had* to. Call it selfish, but I needed to talk to him. When he answered, it was obvious I was crying. He was startled, thinking something was wrong with you. But I reassured him you were fine and explained what had transpired. I realized that cutting him out of my life was the biggest mistake I had ever made. I regretted not being there for him after the accident, offering only love instead of judgment. I expressed that I no longer needed to forgive him, and I hoped he could accept my apology and, perhaps one day, find it in his heart to forgive me."

"What did he say?"

"There was a long silence on his end, and then he abruptly hung up."

Lisa was disappointed.

"It's alright," Grandpa assured her. "You know, until yesterday, I was the one who had pushed him away for years. We had no contact. And just because I suddenly recognized all my mistakes doesn't mean he has to accept or forgive me. It may sound harsh, but I've come to realize that I don't need his forgiveness because I have already forgiven myself completely. Of course, I hope that one day he will be willing to reconnect, maybe even hug me. But that's up to him. It's his choice."

"Do you know what Dad did after the accident?"

"No, we had no contact after that."

"And have you never wondered why he didn't have to go to prison?"

"Of course, I've often wondered about that, but I didn't want to ask your mom or Theo or burden you with it. You now know that I tend to bury sensitive subjects, hiding them away. Well, at least that used to be my intention, but not anymore."

"Well, what would you have done, Grandpa, if you were in Dad's shoes?" Lisa looked straight into Grandpa's eyes. "What if you had the misfortune of causing that terrible accident due to your own fault?"

Grandpa sighed. "First and foremost, I would feel overwhelming guilt and remorse. But I would take responsibility for my actions and go to the widow and her family. I would express my deep sorrow, acknowledging that my actions were unforgivable and irreversible. I would assure them that I would do everything within my power to help them for the rest of my life."

"That's exactly what Dad did. He did what you—his father—would have done."

Grandpa caught his breath.

"He told me how difficult it was, but he did it. That woman was furious with him. She even struck him and kicked him out of her house. But eventually, she realized that Dad had done the right thing.

She recognized his bravery in reaching out to her, and she saw the value in his support, especially since she was left alone with two young children.

"So, Dad started visiting her more often, offering his assistance, and being there to talk. And over time, she forgave him. She even attended the trial and requested that he not be imprisoned. She believed it would only make things harder for her and for Dad. She wished for him to remain free so he could continue helping her and her children. That's why he didn't end up in jail."

Grandpa looked at Lisa. "Of course he did. How foolish of me. How did I not know? Have you met that woman and her children?"

"Yes, Dad took me to meet them a year ago. She's doing well. She smiles often, as do her kids. She shared with me that she made a conscious decision to create a beautiful and joyful future for herself and her children."

"That's wonderful. She moved on with her life when I could have done the same, but I convinced myself that I didn't deserve it and didn't know how. Now I know. And I hope your dad will still accept me as his father, but regardless, I will move forward with my life. It would certainly be more pleasant if he allows me to be a part of his life again, but it won't alter how I feel. Does that sound callous to you?"

"No, Grandpa," Lisa responded, "I understand you, and I know why you're saying this. I believe it's in everyone's best interest for you to move forward with your life."

"Which brings us to the matter of selling the farm."

"Yes, what else happened to lead you to the decision?"

"Well, after I called your dad and he hung up, I felt an incredible surge of life and joy. It's hard to believe that all of this unfolded in a single night, but it did.

"So, that exhilarating feeling lingered, and I found myself sitting on the couch, marveling at what had transpired. I suddenly noticed that the house looked different. It had been my home of many years, a place of comfort and safety. But at that moment, it no longer felt that way. It all appeared as mere objects and furniture, reminders of the past. Then I saw Grandma's picture again and remembered what she had said to me just an hour before, '*Will you finally follow your heart and make your dreams come true?*'

"It struck me that you had made a similar remark on the stairs a few hours earlier, as we sat together, looking at pictures of a tropical island I could escape to. It became clear to me what had been holding me back all these years. It was *me*! *I* had convinced myself that you and your mother needed me around, that I had become attached to familiar things, to a false sense of security. *I* had grown afraid of truly living, but most importantly, *I* didn't truly love myself.

"It was then that I realized that in order to love myself, I had to let go. I needed to release judgment, guilt, fear, and pain. Like I said, you held up a mirror to me last night. You showed me my fear of change, my fear of letting go of what I clung to, but also my craving for love from others and my struggle to forgive and fully accept reality. And as I sat on that couch, it all vanished.

"I was finally able to look back on my life and see the interconnectedness of every experience. It felt as if it had all been orchestrated. It finally made sense. So, I had my moment of realization."

Lisa knew he was referring to the painting with the ball and the beam—the path leading to right now, this present moment.

"And then I decided to sell the farm, to make my dream come true, and move to the tropical island we had been dreaming about yesterday. I don't know the exact details yet, but it feels like an adventure, and I'm as excited as a young boy!"

"I'm so happy for you, Grandpa! I'm genuinely proud. When Mom shows up today to pick me up, I bet she will say, 'This is a monumental decision, one that requires careful consideration.'"

Grandpa chuckled. "Trust me, young lady, I've lived long enough to recognize when something is the right decision. You can feel it because it resonates with your core. There's no need to hesitate or doubt such decisions. And this is one of those decisions."

"Don't you have any regrets?" Lisa inquired. "Don't you wish you had made this decision much earlier in your life when you were younger?"

"No, quite the contrary. I now understand that timing is inconsequential compared to the act of taking action. Even if you make a life-altering choice on the final day of your existence, all the puzzle pieces fall into place, and your life feels complete. For the first time, my life is truly complete. I am the ball on the beam. I can look back and see the trajectory of my life, how everything is interconnected. I am no longer afraid of falling off the beam, and I will live joyfully from this point forward until the ball disappears into the hole in the wall."

"And—all good things must come to an end." Lisa glanced at the clock. "Mom will be here in a few hours." She grasped Grandpa's hands.

"Ah, have I taught you nothing? With all endings …

"… come new beginnings."

THE GIRL WHO CHANGED THE WORLD PROJECT!
JOURNAL-DAY 8-continued...

Grandpa told me everything-about his pain, his reasons for not moving, for shunning my dad, and a lot more. He's lived his life to adapt in order to receive love, to be safe, and good enough-to be accepted. (I get that.)

It can be harmful if done to an extreme. He discovered that life isn't about seeking the love of others, no matter who they may be. It's about the love we have for ourselves!

If love for myself overflows, then I have enough for others.

If a person feels unloved or even under-appreciated, it can lead to bad choices. No one is perfect. Grandpa had an affair when Dad was really young. It makes me sad, and I don't know how I feel about it yet. I do understand Grandpa was missing what he needed at the time. I'm glad he and Grandma moved on.

Grandpa's guilt did not move on though. He decided to mold himself to Grandma's wishes and never expressed his dreams again. And that's why we never relocated to that tropical country. Grandma didn't want to go, and Grandpa compensated.

Pleasing others (to an extreme) can cause pain.

The other 'terrible' thing—The Incident: it was Dad driving under the influence, causing an accident, and the man who died had a wife and two children. Dad caused a lot of grief. Grandpa has carried a sense of guilt and responsibility, knowing that my dad was the one responsible for this tragedy. This is how I felt, too, knowing my dad did that! Maybe Grandma felt that way too. So much devastation.

They visited Dad in the hospital and Grandpa yelled at him and hasn't seen him since. Grandpa felt he had done something wrong once again: he failed to raise his son properly. And unconsciously, he blamed Dad.

Grandma was broken and Grandpa thinks losing her son like that may have accelerated her passing. Grandpa didn't know that Dad had reached out to the widow and helped her and her family. She testified on Dad's behalf, which was a big reason he didn't go to jail.

Grandpa called me an angel. I put the mirror in front of him and he is seeing the truth for the first time in a long while. He's finally allowing himself to feel and forgive himself for all of the guilt he carried. I am his angel who brings joy and happiness into his life—and helped him forget his pain. <u>That makes ME genuinely happy.</u>

Never apologize for being yourself or for speaking your truth. Your perceality!

I changed Grandpa's world! I changed my world!

Grandpa was able to speak with his parents last night while I was sleeping. He could 'hear' them say, "Thank you, we're proud of you, and have always loved you." And they said they know me—their great-granddaughter! Now, that's pretty cool (and a little weird)!

Big News: Grandpa called Dad and told him he loves him and apologized. We both hope Dad will now find it in his heart to forgive Grandpa.

I believe it's in everyone's best interest for you to move forward with your life.

As for the farm being on sale now: Grandpa realized he was holding himself back all these years. He had grown afraid of truly living, but most importantly, he didn't truly love himself. He realized that in order to love himself, he had to let go.

Like I said, I held up a mirror to him and showed him his fear of change, fear of letting go, his craving for love from others, and his struggle to forgive and fully accept reality—and it vanished.

It finally made sense. He has no regrets and says, "Timing is inconsequential compared to the act of taking action. Even if you make a life-altering choice on the final day of your existence, all the puzzle pieces fall into place, and your life feels complete."

With all endings ... come new beginnings.

CHAPTER 25 | Fresh Start/ New Beginnings

It probably looked like a scene out of a Norman Rockwell[12] painting—Grandpa and Lisa settled into the living room in their favorite spots on the couch, book and journal in contented hands, with Sera-cat happily purring between them. As Pablo Picasso once noted, "The purpose of art is washing the dust of daily life off our souls."

The doorbell rang and Grandpa grinned and called out, "The door is open!"

"Why didn't you come to me to sell the farm?" boomed a deep voice in the hallway, and Frank strode into the living room.

"Or maybe I know a guy," he winked at Lisa and stood to greet their guest. "It's a long story, Frank. News travels fast! Yes, the farm is up for sale."

"No, it's not," Frank declared, giving Grandpa a meaningful look.

"What do you mean?"

"I'm buying your farm," Frank announced, slapping Grandpa on the back, and letting out his familiar hearty laugh. "I was walking over to borrow a book my nephew, Jacob, asked about and saw that sign. Didn't have to think. I'm buying!"

"But you don't even know the asking price!"

"I know you're an honorable man, so I trust that you'll ask for a fair price. Besides, a neighbor's property only comes up for sale once in a lifetime. I want to buy it—and will give you whatever time and flexibility you need to move or find a new place."

"Well, actually, I'm planning to leave this month if that's alright with you," Grandpa grinned.

"I like to get things done quickly. But I've never seen anyone leave in such a hurry. What happened? Is the devil after you?"

"On the contrary. I've been inspired by an angel." He put his arm around Lisa.

"Well, I'm not entirely sure what you mean, but I agree that your granddaughter truly looks angelic. And even angels can be afraid of spiders," Frank teased, winking. "So, do we have a gentleman's deal?" Frank extended his hand toward Grandpa.

"Deal! And this angel here will be our witness. I'll ask my daughter-in-law, who is a real estate agent, to handle the paperwork. She happens to be on her way here to retrieve Lisa."

"Sounds like a plan. Now, I suggest you retrieve the paint you used for the '*FOR SALE*' sign and paint '*SOLD*' over it immediately!"

Ω

After seeing Frank off, Grandpa returned to the living room. "Well, well," he said to Lisa, "It looks like our next vacation together will be on a tropical island!"

They high-fived and stepped out of their hug when they heard a car door shut.

"Someone else interested in buying the farm?" Grandpa raised an eyebrow. "Too late!" He looked over Lisa's head toward the open door and stopped flat.

"It's never too late," a voice stated firmly.

Lisa recognized that voice instantly and swung around to run to him. "Dad!"

Dad embraced Lisa and then met the eyes of his father. He opened his other arm for Grandpa to join them, tears streaming down their faces.

"There's much to discuss," Grandpa whispered, and pulled back to view his son. "I've missed you."

They melted together, time of no essence.

"And I, you."

Lisa felt weightless, as if time had ceased to exist, leaving only this blissful moment.

Ω

For Lisa, this bliss carried her to heights of elation. She sat with her dad and her grandpa, observing a fluidity of conversation that was unexpected, a little unreal, and incredible to witness. They were together. Really together.

"That was wonderful," Lisa's dad, Matthew, remarked about the lunch Grandpa had prepared. "But what storm has blown through here? I mean, you contact me, you sell the farm, and now you're moving to a tropical paradise? It all sounds incredible, but what happened?"

Grandpa turned to Lisa. "Want to do the honors?"

"In a nutshell only," Lisa replied, locking eyes with her dad.

"That's a skill few adults can master," Grandpa commented. "I'm truly curious now."

The men leaned in.

"Okay," Lisa began, "Grandpa taught me that the world as we perceive it is not the whole picture. There's so much more happening beyond our limited senses. Additionally, each person is unique, shaped by their age, body, experiences, and beliefs. And where they stand—

their perspective—makes a difference too. Two people can't occupy the exact same position at the same time.

"So everyone has their own version of reality. I called it *perceality*," she paused, letting them take in the word. "Now, with each person having their own distinct truth, everyone can be right, and no one is truly wrong. The only time you can be wrong is when your view of life becomes distorted to the point where you can't pursue your own deepest desires anymore. That's when it becomes painful, and most people try to avoid that pain. But Grandpa didn't want to avoid it anymore.

"To me, it felt like Grandpa taught me all these beautiful lessons, yet he wasn't fully living by them. He told me not to fear spiders, but he himself was afraid to let go and chase his dreams. I know—big difference between spiders and dream chasing, but you get the point. So, when I confronted him about this, it hurt him deeply. He couldn't avoid that pain any longer. He faced it, confronted it, and ultimately embraced it. That's when he realized that true self-love leaves no room for pain. And that's why he called you."

Dad and Grandpa stared at Lisa, mouths agape, their eyes filled with wonder. Then, they glanced at each other. "That's *your* granddaughter," Dad said.

"That's *your* daughter, Matt," Grandpa said, proudly.

A moment of silence followed, and they heard steps on the porch. Lisa peeked through the window and spotted a familiar car parked in the driveway.

"Mom!" she shouted, dashing to the front door and opening it as her mom, Emily, was about to enter. Lisa nearly knocked her off her feet with a hug.

Mom was bewildered, not only by Lisa's greeting, but she saw Dad and Grandpa walking toward them on the porch. "Well, hello. What's going on? Why is your father here? Is something wrong?"

"No! Everything is right! And now, it is very right!" Lisa rushed. "I understand why you are overprotective, and then I get confused when you tell me to grow up. It's because you love me and care about me. You see life as something to worry about, something frightening. But that's not it! Grandpa taught me that in the past few days. And I'm okay with you continuing because I know it comes from a place of love. I don't care anymore about what other kids think. And Grandpa has something to share with you too."

Grandpa jumped in, "Yes. I'm leaving. I'm going to fulfill my dream by emigrating to a tropical island. My son is going house hunting with me. We could use your help with real estate advice."

Mom stammered, "Bu-bu-but why, how, and where are you going? What!?"

Grandpa, Dad and Lisa laughed, with Mom utterly confused.

"I don't know where I'll end up just yet, but I'm taking the first step by simply going. I am not too old, and it is not too late! If I follow my heart and pursue my dreams—what I truly desire—then life will unfold as it should. Lisa reminded me of that."

"Lisa? How?"

"She turned the world upside down. It started with her."

"I'm a girl who changed the world!"

This time, it's time. A new beginning …

The End …

Or Is It?

May you experience an increasingly beautiful world.

Your world.

Our world.

A LETTER TO THE PEOPLE
OF THE WORLD

Dear People of the World,

My wish for you is to see the most beautiful possible reflection of yourself, and everyone around you, always and everywhere. Society often insists we focus on our imperfections, yet I've come to embrace a profound truth: we are inherently flawless in our unique ways. Our capacity for kindness and love far exceeds our own understanding. Take a moment, or several, to envision the bounty that life offers you—to see yourself in a state of tranquility and harmony with existence.

You must be willing to see it—the opportunity and possibility. If you are not, I ask, "Is that working for you?" If you don't try, well, stay stuck. I love you. I love our world. Please don't stay stuck. I wish for your beliefs—your thoughts—to be focused on the possibilities of what you can cultivate and create. The world doesn't just happen to you—you can choose to happen to it.

What is your perceality—your perception of reality? Are moments of blame, complaint, sorrow, or anger frequent visitors in your life? Yes, life comes with its fair share of challenges, but remember, the world expands in generosity and opportunity as you grow in self-awareness and self-love. This isn't selfishness; it's preparing yourself to offer greater love, acceptance, and a spirit of generosity. This path, I firmly believe, leads to deeper fulfillment.

Embrace love, practice forgiveness, and progress forward. Place fear in its rightful context. Transform belief into your most potent force. The truest riches lie not outside, but within you. Elevate your heart and vision, infusing your being with life. As you ascend, your energy will draw and manifest abundance for you and your loved ones. Whether it's the immediate joy of a positive feeling or the patience in knowing the Universe is responding, always ask with gratitude, as if your desires are already fulfilled.

If everything was simple, I'm not sure it would matter as much to us. I'm not sure we would matter as much—to others or to ourselves. Trust me, it feels good to give it a go. The truth is that your thoughts alone have the power to influence the world. The reality is your actions have the power to change it.

Yes, you have that power. What would it feel like to own it? It is yours. You only have to be aware. Just practice being the YOU that you love. Practice is not a one-time shot. Practice during the ebbs and the flows, through the goods and the bads, and the ups and downs and all arounds, because life zig zags and curves and swoops.

Can you sense it? The thrill of this adventure? If not, pause and listen closely. Breathe deeply. Ask yourself: how can I view this in a more positive light? What perspective do I need to adopt? What shifts are necessary? Then, be willing. It will turn your life upside down—in a good way.

In the past lies the present—and the now holds what will become. What is to become of you? Yesterday is what was. Only the present moment, this perpetually evolving now, has the power to influence your immediate reality. Or perhaps, it is you who shapes it.

It only takes one. One to care. One to make a difference. I wish you and I both are one.

Love,
A Girl Who Changed the World
(No reason why it can't be you.)

Spread the word on social media about your encounters
with *The Girl Who Changed the World* by Machiel Hoek.

https://www.facebook.com/machiel.hoek

https://www.linkedin.com/in/machielhoek/

https://www.instagram.com/machielhoek/?hl=en

https://twitter.com/machielhoek

www.machielhoek.com

**To book Machiel Hoek for a book signing or speaking,
or to contact him, please visit www.machielhoek.com.**

ENDNOTES | The Girl Who Changed The World

1. Ancient wisdom refers to the knowledge and understanding of the world and human nature that was accumulated by human societies in the ancient past. This wisdom can encompass a wide range of subjects, including philosophy, religion, science, and art. It often reflects the beliefs and values of the society in which it was created and can offer insights into the human experience that are still relevant today. www.quora.com.

2. *A Course in Miracles*: This is the edition of A Course in Miracles that its two scribes, Drs. Helen Schucman and Bill Thetford, authorized for publication by the Foundation for Inner Peace in 1975. It is now available in translation in 27 languages and is widely used by students in thousands of Course study groups around the world. It makes a fundamental distinction between the real and the unreal, between knowledge and perception. Knowledge is truth, under one law, the law of love (or God). (ACIM, Preface.2:1-3)

3. *Conversations with God: An Uncommon Dialogue*, by Neale Donald Walsch

4. *The Alchemist: A Fable About Following Your Dream*, by Paulo Coelho

5. *The Secret,* by Rhonda Byrne

6. *Through the Looking Glass,* by Lewis Carroll

7. *Namaste*, pronounced "Nah-mah-stey," is usually spoken with a slight bow and with hands pressed together at the heart.

8. Ho'oponopono is a traditional Hawaiian practice of reconciliation and forgiveness. The Hawaiian word translates into English simply as correction, with the synonyms manage or supervise. Similar forgiveness practices are performed on islands throughout the South Pacific, including Hawaii, Samoa, Tahiti and New Zealand. – <u>Wikipedia</u>

9. "The belief in an external world independent of the perceiving subject is the basis of all natural science. Since, however, sense perception only gives information of this external world or of "physical reality" indirectly, we can only grasp the latter by speculative means. It follows from this that our notions of physical reality can never be final. We must always be ready to change these notions - that is to say, the axiomatic basis of physics - in order to do justice to perceived facts in the most perfect way." – Albert Einstein

10. Blackface – refers to the practice of wearing makeup to imitate the appearance of a Black person. The use of such makeup was associated with minstrel shows in the United States from the 1830s until the mid 20th century; it is now regarded as highly offensive. – *Oxford Language Dictionary*

11. *Mala* – According to traditional Buddhism, 108 represents the number of mortal desires of mankind which one must overcome to achieve Nirvana. Mala Beads are often used as a meditation tool. For this purpose, there are 108 beads so that a mantra can be recited 100 times as you move your fingers along the beads.

12. Norman Rockwell possessed a distinct ability to create works of art that evoke a strong emotional response. Many of the emotions drawn from the viewer are memories of formative events from their own lives, nostalgia toward a time long gone, or a feeling of Americans collectively united through war-time patriotism. – Norman Rockwell Museum, www. nrm.org

Author Bio

Machiel Hoek is a spiritual searcher determined to unravel *the secret of life*. Society's norms caused a detour in becoming an entrepreneur and CEO. In the throes of his professional career, an inner voice nudged him to radically alter his life's course. He knew, *if not now, then never*. Forsaking financial independence, 
Machiel stepped into his quest to unearth his mystery of life. Now, he offers an invitation for you to discover and unravel yours.

Machiel resides in The Netherlands.